**Also available from
Christina Dodd**

Forget What You Know
Welcome to Gothic (digital novella)
Point Last Seen
Right Motive (ebook novella)
Wrong Alibi

Cape Charade

Hard to Kill (ebook novella)
Dead Girl Running
Families and Other Enemies (ebook novella)
What Doesn't Kill Her
Hidden Truths (ebook novella)
Strangers She Knows

For additional books by Christina Dodd,
visit her website, christinadodd.com.

EVERY
SINGLE
SECRET

CHRISTINA DODD

EVERY SINGLE SECRET

CANARY STREET PRESS

**CANARY
STREET
PRESS™**

Recycling programs
for this product may
not exist in your area.

ISBN-13: 978-1-335-00850-3

Every Single Secret

Canary Street Press
22 Adelaide St. West, 41st Floor
Toronto, Ontario M5H 4E3, Canada
CanaryStPress.com

Printed in U.S.A.

For Shannon
With love

THE TIME BEFORE

1

Today
In the small California coastal town of Offbeat Bay

MR. BANDARA, Helen Lamb's first and dearest client, puttered in his kitchen, cleaning up their snack of coffee and biscotti. "I need a gardener to plant my spring flowers, the toilet is leaking, and I need an assassin to kill me."

She lifted her fingers off the keyboard and stared. "Excuse me?"

"My wife loved to do the planting and weeding, but it's never been a passion of mine, and—"

"Mr. Bandara...the part about the assassin?"

"Yes. Well." Mr. Bandara cleared his throat. "Remember a few weeks ago when I told you I was feeling lousy and you made an appointment for me with Dr. Devi? That woman is smart, which goes without saying, and interesting, which is rare enough to get my jaded old attention, and right away she ordered blood tests... There were a lot of tests." He put a comforting hand on Helen's shoulder. "I love you, honey, and I know you're fond of me."

Helen knew this was the time to say it. "I love you, too."

"Good. That's nice." He smiled. "You've filled a gap in my life, not to mention you've made it much easier." He pulled back his shoulders into his usual military posture. "Anyway. I hope this isn't too much of a shock, but I've got pancreatic cancer, and I'm not going to live much longer."

It *was* too much of a shock. Helen swallowed, and swallowed again. "I thought you said a tonic…"

"That was a little optimistic. I'm a typical case, no symptoms until stage four, then it's too late. We could try chemo or radiation, but as I told Dr. Devi, I'm seventy-two. I've had a good life. Why prolong it so I can be alive, lonely, and miserable? That radiation is tough on the body and not likely to do more than slightly delay the inevitable. Since I am facing a painful death very soon, what I'd like is someone to kill me while I'm in my garden enjoying the flowers somebody else has planted, or down at the beach listening to the waves, or I'm in my recliner, reading. A nice, quick, surprise death."

She had trouble getting a deep breath.

Mr. Bandara patted Helen's shoulder, went to the half bath off the kitchen, and jiggled the toilet handle. "Also, the dripping is annoying the hell out of me, so if you can find me a plumber right away, I'd appreciate it."

"I can replace the inner workings of a toilet," Helen said automatically. "I'll get the parts at the hardware store."

"You're handy. My Rebecca was like that. She could fix anything. It was all those years I was away with the Marines." He was chatting like everything was normal. Like he wanted her to feel normal. "I never learned, although I suppose I could, but thank heavens you came along with your fixer services so I didn't have to. You've been a godsend."

Helen Lamb owned The Fixer, a firm that specialized in

helping her clients connect with someone to do the jobs they needed done. Most of her work involved repairs: gardeners, plumbers, housekeepers, construction workers, handymen. But she prided herself on always matching her clients with the proper laborers, people who would fix, clean, plant, repair, and most of all listen.

For special clients, for an elevated fee, she also found travel agents, nannies, doctors, bankers, and now…an assassin?

No. She couldn't do it. She had the contact, although she hadn't touched base for years, but it wasn't ethical. It didn't bear thinking about. She would be killing a friend.

Helen stood. "I'll go get the parts right now." She sat down again. "What makes you think I know how to track down an assassin?"

The chair scraped the tile floor as Mr. Bandara seated himself at the table opposite Helen. "After I retired from the service, I became a schoolteacher here in town. Did you know that?"

"Yes. Or rather… I can tell." Red apple paintings and plaques decorated Mr. Bandara's home.

"I'd seen so much of death and those poor kids raised in a war zone holding rifles that I wanted to see what kind of difference I could make. Anyway, I taught fourth grade. For most children, that's the last real year of childhood before hormones set up shop and pressures develop. People stop asking what you want to do when you grow up and start asking what you want to do with your life. That kind of thing."

"I remember."

"Don't we all? I always tried to make it a good year for everyone, but for a few children, every year was a challenge. Every day. I got so I recognized the guarded look in a child's eyes… when life had taught them too much too soon." His basset hound face drooped. "Like those kids with the rifles."

"When I was in fourth grade, I was just a dopey kid."

"Good. Good!" Mr. Bandara took one of Helen's hands. "You have the eyes, but if I'm wrong—"

"I was fourteen when…" Helen brought herself to an abrupt halt. She couldn't tell Mr. Bandara what had happened that year. She had never told anyone the whole truth. Half her lifetime ago, and still she never would dare. Something almost like superstition stopped her; never dropping her guard had kept her safe. But also, a secret could only be kept by one. If she confided in Mr. Bandara, if they found him, he would suffer from a torture that would overshadow the agony the cancer caused him, and his assassin couldn't arrive soon enough.

Yet he'd looked in her eyes and he'd known, and how did she disguise her guarded soul from someone who cared enough to see?

She settled for, "My father got in trouble with some bad people. My mother died. I lost my sister."

Mr. Bandara shook his head. "It's tough at fourteen. Maybe more of a shock. No one should ever have to learn what you know."

"No, they shouldn't."

"What's your name?" Mr. Bandara surprised her with the insightful question.

For him, she didn't hesitate. "I'm Rowan Winterbourne."

"What a pretty name." He smiled. "I like Helen, too."

"My mother was Yvonne. My sister was Linden." Funny, this compulsion to share their names after so many years, almost as if it brought them back to her. But pain arrived, too, and a stunning reminder of loneliness, and she stood abruptly. "I can find an assassin for you."

"That's kind, and I'm grateful. Of course—" Mr. Bandara grinned at Helen "—this will be paid as part of your more expensive services."

Helen laughed unwillingly. "Yes. That's how I'll charge it,

and I do warn you, I'll have no haggling leverage on the assassin. The price will be what it will be."

"Let me know, and I'll make sure the entire amount is immediately deposited in your account." Mr. Bandara followed Helen to the back door and out to the driveway, where her car was parked. He waited until Helen was in the driver's seat, then leaned over and looked in the window.

Helen lowered it.

"I know you're upset about the assassin, but—"

"I'm not upset about the assassin. I'm upset because you're dying." Helen choked on the last word.

"Think about it—Rebecca and all my brothers and sisters had the good sense to predecease me. Because my daughter followed me into the military, she died in Afghanistan." Mr. Bandara leaned a hand on the door and took a supporting breath. "I have no descendants. That excellent estate attorney you found for me several years ago has set up my will exactly as I wish, with my estate going to a local charity for women and children in need. I'm at peace with the world and as ready as I can be." He straightened, closed his eyes and swayed. "The pain is already out of hand, and it's going to get worse. I don't want to die in a bed screaming for release." He opened his eyes and added sensibly, "Well...who does? Sooner is better than later. Don't dally."

Mr. Bandara had not allowed Helen to see the extent of his discomfort, but now he did—or maybe he had no choice.

Helen had thought she'd be killing a friend.

Not true; she would be helping him. Only one other person in Helen's life had suffered so much before death. That death had scoured the last of the Normal setting from Helen's soul.

Mr. Bandara had made the request. Helen would be doing her job...and she knew she couldn't allow another soul to die in agony. "I'll take care of it, Mr. Bandara. The garden, the toilet, and the assassin."

"Thank you. I knew I could depend on you… Rowan."

As she drove away, she drew comfort from the knowledge that good man knew her real name, and he would take it with him into the next world.

2

THE LIGHTHOUSE AT Point Offbeat faced into the teeth of the storm. Banshees howled around the tower, screaming unintelligible threats, the light circled and flashed through the clouds, and lightning blazed. During the two and a half years Helen had lived here, she'd only seen this kind of storm once before. She had gloried in it. The wildness, the waves, the glory was in absolute opposition to everything in her carefully orchestrated and carefully preserved life.

Tonight she thought hell had spat up the storm as a curse and a warning. She stood on the viewing platform, four stories off the ground and near the jutting edge of the cliff, facing into the slashing rain. At the base of the cliff, the Pacific Ocean roared and clawed, sending spray so high into the air she could taste salt before icy rain sluiced it away.

Or maybe she tasted her own tears.

Everything was black: sky, clouds, violence and nature's indifference. And white: the froth of the waves, the blinding flashes of lightning, the electrical discharges that danced through the air.

Standing out here, Helen was courting death. She deserved death. She had arranged to have a friend killed.

But like everything else, the lightning was indifferent to her defiance. It struck all around the lighthouse, slashed a tree in half, lit the skies with jagged flames and played in blinding sheets behind the clouds and up to the heavens, and left her untouched.

The gale blew her backward against the wall, forcing her toward safety. She took the hint. Even despair had its limits. She made her way around to the door, fought the wind to open it and utilized the wind to close and seal it. She hung up the yellow rain slicker on a hook, toed out of her boots, grabbed a towel off the stack she kept on a shelf and dried her shoulder-length hair. She trudged down the one flight of stairs, unlocked the door and was in her quarters, a snug one-bed apartment she had spent the first year remodeling. Below her were two more stories of roughly furnished living space, but except for the entry area, they were unused, a diversion. She showered, pulled on a loose off-white sweater and faded jeans, and stood over the heat vent until a thaw set in.

When she'd moved into the lighthouse, the place had been a wreck. The living areas on all three floors had been abandoned for years: moldering couches, filthy carpets, utilitarian lighting, damp insulation and faltering plaster. She had stripped the interior, doing most of the work herself while living in a tiny apartment in Offbeat Bay, the town eight miles south. When she had to, she used subcontractors for electricity, plumbing, the trades that required a license, but she had that all installed before she did any of the interior finish work. She wanted no one to know more about the floor plans than absolutely necessary.

During the remodel, she'd come upon a box of old cookbooks, speckled with damp and mold. She'd dried them out and found recipes marked by some long-ago cook, and found herself attempting from-scratch meals. They tasted better (when she didn't flub it), and she discovered she liked cooking. Tonight for the first time she was frying chicken. With mashed potatoes and gravy. And green beans with bacon.

She didn't do anything fancy with the chicken. She heated a little oil in the pan, placed the chicken skin-side down, let it brown and the fat render, then flipped it, covered it and lowered the flame.

What a day. For years and years, she had been moving away from her past, not forgetting—she could never forget—but learning to make trivial conversation about trivial things, to behave in a way that let her blend into the background.

Today Mr. Bandara had made it clear that, to the discerning observer, Helen remained a wounded soul, someone on the outside of mainstream society. Part of it was that traumatic year she was fourteen. Part of it was her time in foster care. Part of it was the payment she made to keep her past a secret, this acute and ongoing loneliness.

She valued loyalty. In her life, it was more rare than rubies, so on the way to the hardware store for Mr. Bandara's toilet parts, she had stopped on the shoulder of the road and emailed the one living person who knew her and all the truths about her: her father's girlfriend.

I need an assassin. Can you help?

She had provided a phone number for a burn phone. It had been ten years since she'd communicated with Kealoha, and who knew whether she was still alive, or free, or... Or.

People like her and Kealoha didn't usually survive for long, and when they did, they didn't take it for granted.

Yet within ten minutes, Kealoha had called, and the sound of her warm voice had immediately eased Helen's angst. "I'm so glad to hear from you. Sure, I can help you contact an assassin. I think he's still in the business. Let me text him." She didn't ask why Helen needed an assassin.

Helen didn't tell her.

Instead they discussed Kealoha's success as a studio musician after her move to a large east coast city. She didn't volunteer which one.

Helen didn't ask.

They discussed Helen's graduation eight years ago from technical school, and how she'd turned a degree in computer networking into a career that allowed her to work alone, to deal with clients both remotely and in person, and most of all, to move as she wished as often as she wished. Helen didn't volunteer exactly what she did or where she was currently located.

Kealoha didn't ask.

Kealoha broke off in the middle of a sentence. "I've made contact. He's officially retired, but he'll consider the job. He wants to know who and why. Once he knows the circumstances, if he thinks the cause is just and he'll survive, he'll provide the information for payment. When that's transferred into his account and he has the location, he'll handle the matter. Can I give him this number so the two of you can communicate?"

"Yes. Kealoha, thank you. If you need me, you know how to contact me."

"I barely remember. But yes, I know. Goodbye, dear. Take care."

The communication was over, a fond catching-up between two women who had walked through hell together. Yet each was aware the other could be taken at any time and tortured. They knew, they had seen, that it was better to know nothing than to have to fight not to give it up.

They hung up without making promises of another call.

The assassin made contact at once. Helen provided the information and transferred the fee. He assured her he'd fulfill Mr. Bandara's wishes to the letter. Helen returned to Mr. Bandara's home, toilet parts in hand, and let him know the deal had been made. If he wished to back out, all he had to do was not make the payment.

Mr. Bandara immediately transferred the funds into the assigned bank account.

Helen fixed the toilet.

Mr. Bandara embraced and thanked her as if the dripping toilet was the worst of his problems, but Helen recognized the thanks as what it was—gratitude and farewell.

Now, in the lighthouse, she stood for a moment and watched the slash of the light overhead as it circled and warned and cut through the storm, and on calm nights gave her the sense she was not alone.

She *was* alone. That was safest.

When she'd graduated from technical school with a degree in computer networking, she knew she wasn't going into that specific field. She wanted something unusual, something that didn't pin her down in one place. She created The Fixer, and when the time finally came that she no longer saw, heard, imagined a shadow at the edge of her vision, she determined to settle down. She chose the California coast and long-term leased the old lighthouse on Point Offbeat. She was close enough to the small town of Offbeat Bay for groceries and supplies and far enough that she couldn't see the nearest neighbor. More important, she had an unobstructed view of the land around her, and the one small rutted road that ran a mile off the main highway toward her lighthouse.

This place was, for her, a homecoming.

On a clear day, looking out to sea, she imagined she could see the shadows of the Channel Islands. With her binoculars, she had found the rocky spine of Raptor Island.

She stared at it more than was good for her. She loathed it more than was good for her.

The security sensor chimed, warning her someone or something had crossed onto her property. When she'd moved into the lighthouse, the first thing she did was install a state-of-the-art security system and enough alternates on her internet that she never lost contact. With the number of deer in the area, she got a lot of false warnings, so she sought a visual. She glanced out the window.

Headlights wove up the drive.

So…not a deer, which were the scourge of her meager raised box garden, or a low-flying hawk, but a someone who was not concerned with secrecy. She didn't invite people to the house, and when the occasional tourist showed up and asked for a tour, she brusquely refused. Although who would come out on a night like this? Maybe a delivery running late. She had an order of grocery staples coming from an online shop, scheduled for yesterday.

As she watched, the vehicle pulled into the spot marked for deliveries. The sensor light came on. The vehicle was a silver older-model Camry, crunched right front fender, California plates. So not a delivery.

The guy who stepped out wore a light raincoat designed for showers, not a California-coast, lightning-popping deluge. His hood was up, and he wore a baseball cap to keep it out of his eyes. He looked all the way up the lighthouse, right to the window where she stood, and observed her as she observed him.

She began to get an inkling of his identity. She turned off the flame, removed the chicken pieces from the oil, and set them on a plate beside the stove. Her fingers hovered over the collection of rings she had removed while cooking. If he was as dangerous as she thought he was, the rings were a good idea for many reasons. She donned them one by one. She pushed her feet into the dark pair of running shoes she kept close and moved toward the bank-vault-type door that guarded the spiral stairs. They descended to the ground floor inside what looked from the outside like a structural pillar. For Helen, it was all about security.

She could have let him in remotely, but if she had to let someone into her home, and that seldom happened, she always met them at the door and ushered them ahead of her up the other stairs.

He rang the doorbell.

Gloved hand. Impossible to identify him by his fingerprint on the sensor. Unlikely to be intentional but hard to tell.

She stopped on the landing and studied his face through the remote camera.

Deliberately he turned his head from one side to the other as if to make it easy for her to observe him.

Black hair, square chin with the hint of a black five-o'clock shadow, strong nose, shocking blue eyes set deep under an almost Neanderthal brow. As he rotated his head so the camera caught the other cheek, she saw the rippled scarring caused by an explosion? A fire? Sometime in the past.

Now she was almost certain she knew who he was.

Her camera recorded the image and loaded it into the database, and her computer began its run through the files of known possibilities starting with the most dangerous to her.

She was betting this guy would be unrecognizable. She also bet he was as dangerous outside the lighthouse as he was inside. At least in here, she knew the location of every one of her weapons, and she would not hesitate to neutralize him…and remove him from her property before leaving this place. Although—she sighed—for the first time in her adult life, leaving would be a wrench. Yet if they'd found her, she had no choice, and she made it a policy never to cry over what could not be changed.

By the time she stood in the small entry, her computer had assured her this man was not on her list of known dangers to her, and the program went to the next level of known dangers to society in general.

She shut the door to the spiral staircase; it locked automatically and in the shadow looked like part of the wall. The other, normal, straight-up stairway to a landing took off from the other side of the entry. She switched on the lights that led to the first landing, then a second set of stairs, and a third, all straight with a standard baluster. If this man was the assassin she'd hired, he'd found her when she should have been hidden.

Not good.

If he was an assassin sent to kill *her*...really not good.

So no shadows. No hiding places. Not for him.

She removed the small pistol from its resting place in the cupboard, checked that the safety was on, and tucked it in her waistband. She pulled her top over it—the loose weave did its job and disguised any telltale bulge—and opened the door.

3

HELEN SURVIVED LONG enough to say, "Come in."

She took her survival as a positive sign.

"Thank you." He stepped through the door, removed his hat and his coat. "Vile weather you have here."

Nice voice. Deep, calm, the kind that could convince a woman she was perfectly safe right before he put a bullet through her heart. Perhaps a faint accent. Scandinavian?

"Not always. Sometimes it's just windy." She indicated the rack on the wall beside the door. "Hang your coat there." She indicated the rack on the wall beside the door. As he did so, she noted his height against the markings on the wall. Six-three in his low-rise hiking boots, and probably one hundred ninety pounds.

He wore a damp button-up shirt and nice pair of jeans. Designer, she thought, and caution pinged in the watchful stillness of her brain. Why was he driving an older-model, crunched fender car if he could afford designer jeans?

She knew the answers: he'd bought them used, he cared about

clothes and not cars…or her database was wrong and he was indeed dangerous to her.

He appeared not to be carrying a firearm. She glanced at her watch. Her metal detector located a knife in his boot but no other weapons.

She went to the stairway, not her private spiral stair with steel doors, but the normal-looking stairway. She indicated he should proceed her.

He climbed and looked around as if interested. Not an unusual reaction; most people had never been in a lighthouse in their lives.

She knew what he could see. The entry was lit by two sconces. As they reached the next level, the motion sensors on the stairway turned on more lights, dim lights that barely illuminated the areas and furnishings. "With the storm, I'm using only the third floor," she told him. "I have a contract with the US Lighthouse Keepers to maintain the light, especially important in this kind of weather when a ship needs to give Point Offbeat wide berth."

"I believe most lighthouses are automated and unoccupied." Again that thoughtful, calm voice that could indicate a thoughtful, calm assassin for Mr. Bandara, or a thoughtful, calm assassin for Helen.

Although, she supposed, if he intended to kill her, she'd already be dead.

But so would he.

"They are automated—certainly this one is—but in the last few years, there's been a movement to return to an onsite keeper. Mechanisms break, especially a light facing into the teeth of a vicious storm." She was…not amused, really, at the vulnerability of the light, but resigned to the inevitability of failure. If life had been different, she would have joined the Coast Guard like her parents. As it was, she was also serious about her duty to maintain the light; she'd seen enough of death. She didn't want to be the cause of a single man lost at sea.

The assassin stopped at the second-story landing.

She leveled her hidden pistol at him.

He asked, "If the light went out, wouldn't an alarm go off somewhere?"

"It would, in town, but all too often, no one responds in time." She used her other hand to gesture up the stairs. "Or at all. Most people don't realize the loss of life and property that occurs at sea even today."

He nodded and looked around, again at a floor full of barely visible furniture. "You have a lot of space for one person."

"I've been remodeling." That was a lie. The first and second floor were filled with junk, cheap old things she'd gathered at garage and rummage sales and placed strategically to confuse, hinder and hurt anyone who broke in with intent to harm. "It goes slowly. It's a labor of love."

"You haven't asked my name."

"I thought any name you gave would be a lie."

"Yes. But we have to call each other something."

"Do we?"

"For instance, I'll call you Helen."

She froze. At the same time, her explosive heartbeat blew out the pipes. "Why would you call me that?"

"It's such a common name. It might be yours. At least, that's what they call you in town."

She revealed her pistol pointed at him. "I'm not the one you're here to kill."

"That's good, because I have no intention of killing you." Turning his back, he continued up the stairs. "I'm Joe Grantham." He reached the top and the trapdoor that led into the living room. He put his hand on the latch. "Very good. Intruders can't just slam the door open. They have to pop their heads up, one at a time, like groundhogs, and you can pick them off."

"That was my thought." She touched the keyboard inset into the wall. "It's open. Pop your head up."

He looked down at her. "You're not going to somehow blow it off?"

Even with the possibility of a bullet from her below him, or a booby trap above, he still sounded calm, and that annoyed her. If her heart had kicked into high gear, couldn't he have the decency to show a smidgeon of anxiety about his own possibly imminent death?

"I can't kill you. I need you to do your job. I have no further assassin connections."

He viewed her as if she were a curiosity, then lifted the trapdoor. Using his hands, he raised himself into her home. Of course nothing blew his head off…but yes, something could have if she had made that choice. She didn't feel the need to tell him that, and it would have been a waste of breath, since he'd figured it out himself.

Of necessity, he was in her home before her head had cleared the trapdoor, and she leaped straight up from the third step down and landed lightly on the floor.

"Very good!" His amazing blue eyes watched with approval. "As I expected, you're in extraordinary shape."

She didn't know if he deliberately chose his words to cause her worry, but he was doing a good job. She tucked her pistol into her waistband again and walked toward the stove. "Have you eaten?"

"I have not. I came here directly from LAX."

"You're welcome to share my dinner."

"Thank you."

She smiled in wide amusement. "You'd better wait to see how it comes out. I'm frying chicken for the first time. Apparently that can be a challenge." She turned on the burner, placed the frying pan over the flame, and when the oil was shimmering, placed the chicken in it once more.

"I'm happy to provide a critique. Popeye's is one of my favorites."

"How did you know the heights I aspired to?" She wasn't joking.

"I sensed you're a gourmet." He didn't seem to be joking, either. "May I take off my boots?"

"Please. The shoe rack is there by the door."

He sat on a chair at her round quartz stone kitchen table— the table she had chosen for its ability to deflect a bullet—and unlaced his boots. He placed the knife he'd taken out of the ankle holster on the side table. He placed the boots on the rack and tucked his socks inside. Which was his way, she guessed, of saying he had no more weapons on or around his feet. He'd had to strip off to completely reassure her, and even then she never underestimated what a man could do with his bare hands. Although—she eyed him—she wouldn't mind seeing him strip merely for the pleasure of watching. He was slender and fit, with good shoulders, long arms and big hands; maybe she was more right about that Neanderthal brow than she knew. He moved with a rhythm that suggested he would be good in bed.

She smiled at the merrily frying chicken.

"Yes, I am," he said.

She tensed. "What?" *Going to kill me?*

"Good in bed. Isn't that what you were thinking?"

4

"I'M THINKING YOU don't lack for confidence." Which wasn't a bad dodge, but if he turned out to be psychic, she'd have to get better at controlling her expression, and at repartee. She'd lived alone for years; she had little experience with either.

"Confidence and competence go together."

"You really know how to sell yourself." One thing she would never appreciate was a competent, bloodless lover.

"A man who maintains his competence while in the throes of passion is a rare find."

She glanced at him in surprise—was he truly psychic? Unfortunately she also noted that he might have been handsome if not for that wry, ragged masculinity. An air of weariness hung about him; he seemed like a man who'd seen all the viciousness the world had to offer and was not surprised by any of it.

"Do you have whiskey?" he asked.

She gestured at the cabinet over her small refrigerated wine cellar. "Help yourself."

He opened it, found the bottles and the glasses. "Ah. A good

Irish whiskey. You have the proper taste for a woman with Irish roots."

"I like tequila, too. And vodka. Grand Marnier. Sake. Canadian Club. And I enjoy the occasional Shiner Bock. I'm an American mutt." *Don't try to pin me down.*

"What would you like tonight, Helen?" He didn't sound as if he was asking about her choice of liquor.

"Two fingers of your Irish whiskey on ice, Joe." She intended to do no more than sip. Pistol in her waistband or not, she was in no position to be intoxicated.

He poured, for her and him, the exact same amount. He sipped, and sighed blissfully. He handed her that glass. "So you know it's not drugged."

"Thank you." She didn't deny her suspicions. In this day and age, every woman had them. "Can you peel the potatoes?"

"I can."

She pointed out the drawer with the peeler, indicated the russets in the sink and the pan, and left him to it.

He was efficient, as she suspected he would be, and soon the potatoes were simmering on the stove. As he set the table, she read her cookbook, used her meat thermometer, kept an eye on the clock, got the reasonably crisp chicken out, poured off some of the oil, and made the gravy. While it simmered, she chopped a piece of bacon into small pieces and got the green beans out of the freezer.

"I didn't figure you for a frozen vegetable person," he said.

"You're lucky. I recently graduated from instant mashed potatoes."

He winced.

She laughed. A foodie assassin. Who knew?

He searched her drawers until he found her brand-new masher, used it to pulverize the potatoes, frowned at her skim milk but used it without protest, and added enough butter to turn the russets a mellow gold. A wonder he looked fit if he ate like that.

Her gravy had thickened, her green beans and bacon lagged behind, but she judged that by the time she got everything on the table, the vegetables would be done. All in all, the timing of dinner had worked out pretty well, and she sat down, very relieved.

He went to her speaker, plugged in his phone and streamed mellow music, the kind of songs she thought might play in the background of an expensive restaurant. He sat down and took a thigh and a wing.

She tensed again.

He took a bite and chewed, swallowed and said, "Popeye's should be afraid. Very afraid."

She laughed and tried a bite. He was flattering her, of course, but the chicken was pretty darned good. So were the potatoes and gravy. "Next time, I'm going to pre-fry the bacon," she announced.

"You're a crispy bacon person?"

"I am."

"Me, too." He moved the limp bacon to the side, but he chowed down on the rest.

They ate and chatted about foods they liked and didn't like, places they'd visited, said things that could be said without exchanging much in the way of personal information. When they finished their meal, she produced a plate of Oreos, and they discussed the best way to eat them. Their opinions differed wildly. While she sipped her whiskey, he cleared the table and loaded the dishwasher.

"What exactly do you do?" he asked. "For a living?"

"I'm a person who procures services for my clients. I can find you someone to clean your house, weed your garden, repair your broken pipes. Whatever you need." Her voice thickened, and she repeated, "Whatever you need."

He glanced at her sharply, but asked only, "Where's your cellophane?"

"Left of the sink, bottom drawer."

As he covered the food, he asked, "How did you figure out you wanted such a job?"

" I wanted something unusual, something that didn't limit my travels."

"You're restless." He put all the dishes in the refrigerator, then picked up his whiskey, leaned against the counter and sipped.

He wasn't challenging her, exactly, but she bristled. "I'm un-attached, so why not?"

"Why not?" he echoed. "You have skills your classmates never imagined."

Her breath caught, as it had so many times tonight. "What do you mean?"

"You're the Point Offbeat Lighthouse keeper. That's an un-usual addition to a résumé." As she tried to decide if she should go back on full alert, he said, "You've moved a lot, and it didn't matter because you did most of your work online and on the phone."

"Yes." In the first five postgraduation years, she moved nine times, zigzagging across the US with no thought other than to be away…and alive. Moving was no hardship when you kept your possessions to a minimum and were willing to abandon all your personal belongings at the first shadow of trouble. Twice she even left her computer equipment behind, stripped of data and damaged beyond repair. She had everything backed up in various locations, online and in hand, and that was all she needed to continue her work. "I built an elite clientele composed of peo-ple who over time trusted me with their personal information."

"And you trust them."

"I'm not a very trusting sort."

He sipped his watered-down whiskey. "Yet you've lived here for nearly three years."

She was tired of ping-ponging between wary relaxation and the terror that she'd let her killer into her home. With a clink, she put her glass down unfinished. "Two and a half, and how do you know that?"

"I drove through town. The town named Offbeat Bay." He laughed at the name. "It is, too."

"Quiet in the winter, a few tourists in the summer. Never busy." She liked it that way.

"I thought I'd see the lighthouse from town, but nope. Not visible from Offbeat Bay. I stopped. I asked directions." His glance brooded and questioned. "People talk, especially about a young, attractive, reclusive lightkeeper. They speculate why she's here, why she keeps to herself. The clerk at MVP's Grocery has a crush on you and some imaginative stories of who your secret identity is. He's been watching too many Marvel movies. Or too many Hallmark movies, I'm not sure which."

"Elijah. He's a kid, and his name is Elijah." What Joe said made sense. He'd asked questions. People gossiped. She supposed that was the downside of a small town. "What does he think?"

"He wavered between you being a superhero and a princess in disguise."

She laughed. "No."

She reminded herself that Joe Grantham had not sneaked up on her. He hadn't caught her by surprise. He hadn't killed her. He performed domestic chores. Yes, he was a dodgy character, and he knew too much about her, but—he was an assassin. He'd be a fool not to investigate her, his employer. She might be a federal agent, or someone looking for revenge for a past killing.

Most important, in her view, the assassin was here with her, so she could relax. Mr. Bandara would live another day.

Guilt pinged Helen. She shouldn't want a delay. She had promised Mr. Bandara release. But she didn't want to say goodbye.

"There you go. The dishwasher is loaded." He offered her his hand.

She tightened her fingers on Joe's, and let him pull her to her feet and into his arms. She experienced the shock of warmth, of skin, of touching another person. For years, her only physical contact with another human being had been brief and impersonal, a handshake, an accidental touch in a grocery store checkout line as she handed over her cash—she only used cash—and accepted change.

He swung her into a slow dance to the music, the last thing she'd anticipated.

What kind of man did that? Danced when he could have grabbed or seduced or...

But dancing was very pleasant. She was right; he moved well, and more important, he led well. For someone who had never had the trust or the leisure to dance, it was a boon to have a man handle her with such confidence that she felt comfortable and graceful. His long limbs moved like a Latin dancer's, with an innate rhythm that made her think he... "Where did you learn to dance?" she asked.

"My mother runs a studio. As soon as I could walk, I was leading the little girls around the floor."

She squinted, trying to imagine him as a toddler, but while moving with him, breathing his scent, being warmed by his embrace...imagination was beyond her.

She had consumed an ounce of whiskey over the last two hours. She wasn't impaired. She was clearheaded, facing an attractive man who, like her, was forced by circumstances to live a solitary life. A lonely life. She was experienced in weighing risks and evaluating possible consequences. In this case, she thought the risk was worth taking. "I would like to have sex with you."

No answer. He considered her as if doing a little weighing and evaluating himself.

She wondered if he would refuse her, and beyond the possibility of embarrassment and hurt, she also knew relief. The invitation wasn't stupid if it didn't happen.

He smiled and pulled her tight against his body. "I'd like that very much."

5

JOE EMBRACED HELEN SLOWLY, giving her a chance to pull away, and for a moment she did wonder if she should save herself while she could. There were creatures, she knew, who liked to play with their prey before killing it.

"It's never too late," he said. "You can always change your mind."

With an exasperated sigh, she relaxed and resolved to be less transparent. "No. You're an attractive man who won't want involvement. That's a rare commodity."

He gave a bark of laughter. "You really know how to turn a compliment."

She didn't see what she'd said that was funny, but the amount of time she spent alone had moved her out of the mainstream of life, and she didn't understand nuances. Yet she knew how to make him forget her *faux pas*.

Pulling away, she walked into the bedroom, taking her time, sauntering with the sure awareness he watched that sensuous stroll she'd perfected so many years ago. Turning in the doorway, she reached under her sweater and unhooked her bra at the back.

He was on the move now, approaching like a lover stalking a wary nymph.

She finagled one strap off her shoulder, worked it down her arm and over her hand, then did the same with the other strap. As she walked around the bed, she leisurely pulled the bra out of her sleeve. Leaning down, she dropped it on the floor, while at the same time she removed the pistol from her waistband and tucked it under the mattress.

She turned back to see his attention fixed to her chest. Noted: with the right diversion, he was distractible.

He said, "I can see your nipples under, um…"

"It's the loose weave." She put her hands on the hem.

"Leave it on." His voice was hoarse, but he unbuttoned his shirt with steady fingers. He hung it neatly on the back of the chair, then unzipped his pants. Before he removed them, he took his wallet out of his pocket, found the condom packet and showed her.

She nodded. She kept a box in her nightstand. They'd been there ever since she'd moved in. Did condoms have an expiration date? She didn't know, and she didn't want to test it. Joe's condom, she would bet, was new enough to be effective.

She pulled her stretch jeans off in one smooth motion. Her white cotton boy short panties were nothing special. After all, she'd started the evening with no intentions of entertaining.

But his gaze dropped from her nipples to the place where her legs met her body, and he shoved his jeans and underwear off all at once, leaving him naked and splendid.

She'd intended to tease him, inch the panties down, but she found herself frozen in place, staring. Neanderthal. Caveman. All body parts sculpted and well-formed.

She really had to get out occasionally.

She walked around the end of the bed.

He met her. "Let me help you." He slid his hands under her sweater and around her waist, and again that shock of contact, of flesh against flesh, zinged through her nerves. She was alive with fear. A sensible fear—that he might yet kill her. And a different fear, the kind of fear that made her shudder with expectancy—that he would hurt her in the most intimate way possible, not because he was careless, but because of his size.

He pushed his hands inside her panties and slid them down her legs. Again, he seemed to know what she was thinking. "I promise we'll go slow. So slow." He urged her to sit on the bed.

Her panties puddled at her feet.

"I like slow, don't you?" His voice was smooth and rich and wicked, like hot fudge without ice cream, heated in the microwave and licked from her finger. When she didn't answer, he stopped. "Don't you?"

She had to think to remember the question. "Yes. I like slow."

He knelt before her, urged her knees apart, inserted himself between them. He locked eyes with her. "I like to kiss, deep and wet. Leisurely. Those kinds of kisses build anticipation. Mine. Yours. Do *you* like to kiss like that?"

Tension hummed between them.

She nodded. *Slowly*, because it seemed any sudden movement could trigger a languorous assault that would leave her desperate, clinging to thought, to sanity, to reality. When she'd started this, she had hoped for a moment's forgetfulness, and even more, she had hoped for pleasure.

Now she hoped she could cling to a sense of herself.

He leaned forward.

She parted her lips, ready for that kiss, deep and wet and slow. On the mouth.

But no. Joe Grantham might like to kiss mouth to mouth, but right now, that wasn't what he had in mind. Still looking into her face, he touched his lower lip with his tongue and leaned forward.

"This isn't...slow." Her voice seemed to have dropped an octave.

"This is preliminary." He slid one finger inside her. "So I can find out what you like." His finger curled in a gentle come-hither movement.

She took a hard breath.

"Yes...you do like that. You're watching me, big brown eyes anxious."

She truly had been alone too much if he could read her so well.

"You're not sure." His tone soothed her. "That's fair. You don't really know who I am, or whether I'll be rough or uninspiring or...find your sweet spot and never let up until you've come so much that tomorrow, when I'm not inside you, you think of me inside you, long for me inside you."

She thought she would never forget his sharp, knowing grin.

"Let's see which it is."

6

JOE WAS A man who kept his promises. He had been slow. He enjoyed kissing her…everywhere, wet and open, exploring. Behind her ear. The base of her spine. The soft, pale skin from her breast to her fingertips. He had surprised her, time and again. She never knew what part of her body he would delve into next. She was pliant, welcoming, yet he seemed to seek something…more.

What else could he want? What more was there?

When at last she couldn't hold back any longer, and she moaned, almost silent but still…no longer in total control, he paused, looked into her eyes, and murmured, "There." And, "Again."

He demanded, and he got what he wanted. Of course. She lost her last fragment of restraint, and after that, well… Joe Grantham seemed to be a man who always got his way. She didn't know exactly what she'd said or done. She only knew what she felt. She only knew that he granted her a time out of mind. He gave her, the always disciplined woman, a moment of forgetfulness.

When they were done, when she had returned to herself and

found he held her, body to body, her head on his shoulder, she wondered uncomfortably what she was supposed to do next. In her experience, when a man was done, he was done. He didn't hang around to hug her, and run his hand up and down her spine as if the touch of her gave him pleasure.

He must have felt her tense, for he chuckled. "A rapid decompression like that can cause the bends."

She didn't see the humor, and pressed her hand on his bare chest.

He loosened his arms and let her ease away, then rolled off the bed and stood. "Can I use your bathroom?"

She gestured him in that direction and watched him walk away, liking the view. He had a fine posterior, and she had been right about him. As he shut the door behind him, she smiled. For the first time in a very long time, she felt as if life had handed her a beautiful floral bouquet instead of a handful of stinkweed.

Her phone rang. She was still smiling when she looked at the number, then frowned as she read *Mr. Bandara*. She answered at once. "Mr. Bandara? What's wrong?"

A woman's voice spoke. "This is Mr. Bandara's neighbor. Remember me? Tory Tang?"

"I remember. I know." Rowan's hands got icy cold. "What's wrong?"

"I'm calling from his house. I saw you here today. I know you work for him. He always spoke so highly of you. I thought you should know—somebody visited this evening, a man about Mr. Bandara's age. I thought they were friends. I heard them in the backyard, arguing, laughing, playing cards, smoking cigars. The storm rolled in and the thunder was crashing. I figured they'd gone in." Her voice began to rise. "But when the worst of the storm was over, I looked out at Mr. Bandara's patio. The porch light was off, but the lights were on in the house. I could see him. He was still outside, but by himself. All the cards were scattered, and he was slumped in his chair."

Helen began to breathe too fast. Her heart felt blocked. Her vision swam with black dots. "Go on."

"I thought his friend had left and Mr. Bandara had had a stroke or something. I got an umbrella—it was still raining, you know—and I ran over. I was worried he'd died sitting there, but that wasn't it." Tory's voice got louder, more incredulous.

Helen clutched her phone so hard her knuckles hurt. "Tell me, please."

"I thought it was rain at first, all over his chest. I thought the wind had blown so hard. Thick rain. Red... He'd been shot through the chest!" Tory's voice shuddered. "I saw him! I saw Mr. Bandara *dead*."

"My God." *Impossible. Joe was with me.*

"I know. Who would do that? To that nice old man? His friend looked like a nice old man, too. They were playing cards. They were laughing. Mr. Bandara wouldn't fight over a card game." Tory's voice rose to a hysterical shriek. "Who was that man?"

An assassin. Joe isn't the assassin.

"Why would he do such a thing?"

For money. Because I hired him to. Joe isn't the assassin. Out of a dumbass desire to give Mr. Bandara a few more hours, I made a mistake. A potentially fatal mistake for me. She asked, "Did you call the police?"

"Yes. They just got here. I've need to go talk to them. I thought you ought to know." Tory's incredulity was breaking down. Her voice thickened with tears, but she managed, "I'm sorry for your loss."

Really, it's okay. Mr. Bandara has died, exactly as he wished: suddenly, unsuspectingly, happily. "Yes. Thank you." Helen's mouth was dry. Her lips could scarcely form the words. "I'm sorry for your loss, too."

"Everybody liked him. He was my fourth-grade teacher, you know?"

"He was a great guy."

The bathroom door rattled.

"Thank you for letting me know." Without saying goodbye, Helen hung up on Tory. She pulled her pistol from under the mattress.

Joe stepped out. He was just as long-limbed, moved just as rhythmically as before, and when she released the safety, he showed excellent reflexes by stopping short and balancing on one foot.

Helen understood betrayal, what people would do out of fear and what people would do for money, because they needed it or they wanted it.

Betrayal should never catch her off guard...yet this had. *"Who are you?"*

7

CAUTIOUSLY JOE PUT his foot down. "I told you. I'm Joe Grantham."

"What are you doing here?"

"That you didn't ask." He started toward her.

She held up her hand, the one without the pistol.

"It's a little late to be scared, isn't it? If I was going to kill you, I would have done it in the moment."

"You don't understand. I'm not scared." Livid. She was livid. "*I'm* trying to decide whether to kill *you*."

His answer was swift and brutal. "Then you'll be able to do nothing to help your sister."

Breathe. I have to breathe. And speak. "What do you mean?"

"I mean, *Helen*, when you were fourteen, your father made a deadly enemy who demanded every member of Coast Guard Lieutenant Lorenze Winterbourne's family should die."

Joe Grantham recited her past. Her carefully guarded, never-revealed-to-anyone-not-even-dear-Mr. Bandara past.

"Your mother did die. Your little sister Linden lived, but only because the assassin shot the wrong child *and* the teacher who tried to protect her."

The wrenching tragedy of those days, those weeks, stood in stark contrast to his calm tone.

"You and your father placed Linden in a location where she would be cared for and not noticed, an orphan among other orphans. Then you and Winterbourne vanished." Whoever Joe Grantham was, he knew everything, or at least enough.

Breathe. This is all my fault. I trusted the wrong man. So breathe. Listen. Breathe. Find out what he wants. Breathe.

"After months of being nowhere, your father went after Gregory Torval, cornered him, threatened him, and it must have been a good threat, one with teeth in it. He must have had the information to bring down Torval's entire crime organization, because Torval rescinded the obliviate order on the Winterbourne family. No one in his organization could kill any of the Winterbournes. Nor could he himself kill any of the Winterbournes. That had never happened before, and has never happened since." Joe had laid a winning hand on the table; every card was in place. "Do you mind if I put on my jeans? I'm getting chilly."

She nodded and gestured toward the crumpled pants Joe had so hurriedly removed on his way to the bed.

He used his hand to delve down a jean leg. Her finger tightened on the trigger, but he pulled out his underwear and stepped into them, yes, one leg at a time. "Once the obliviate order had been rescinded, your father disappeared again. Everyone knew it wasn't really safe for him to be seen. Everyone believed if Gregory Torval got the chance, canceled obliviate order or not, he would kill Winterbourne, and his family—it was believed only the elder daughter, whose name was *Rowan*, survived—would be found and eliminated."

"The man is a murderer, an arms dealer, and a crime lord. Who could possibly imagine he might lie, or even break his word?" Her sarcasm tasted bitter on her tongue. Or maybe it was her disappointment in herself.

You got it wrong, Rowan, and this time, you'll probably die.

Joe pulled the jeans on, then gestured to the dressing chair. "May I?"

She nodded.

In one of those slow, precise, well-coordinated movements that had enticed her into bed, he sat. He leaned forward placed his elbows on his thighs and looked her in the face. "Occasionally rumors surface on the LA streets that Lorenze Winterbourne has been seen again, rescuing an innocent or bringing down a drug operation or breaking up a human slavery ring. Any time a superhero steps in, that superhero always assumes your father's face." Joe tilted his head. "Personally, I believe he's dead."

The pistol shivered in her grasp. "Why would you think that?"

"What I have now is speculation, hearsay. At some point before Winterbourne blackmailed Torval into rescinding the obliviate order, one of Torval's men captured him. They took Winterbourne to Raptor Island, and on Torval's orders, he was horribly tortured."

"That's not speculation. On those same LA streets, that's well-known. His survival and escape are what made him a legend."

"Survival, yes. Escape?"

"Papa left the island alive. What else would you call it?"

"Escape, sure. But how? I'm an analyst. It's what I do. When this job came my way—"

Understanding dawned. "A job. Oh. Of course there's a job."

He widened those killer blue eyes in surprise. "Of course. Why else would I be here?"

"To fulfill Gregory Torval's greatest wish and kill my father's last surviving family member."

"But you're not your father's last surviving family member. Your seventeen-year-old sister is very much alive."

God. God, this was Helen's nightmare come true.

Joe kept his tone conversational. "Torval's torturer was—is—known for his love of breaking bones, specifically the leg bones. He likes to see people crawl in their attempts to escape. And the arm bones. He likes to watch people fight to free themselves."

The blood drained from Helen's head. Her ears buzzed, and her vision filled with black-and-red specks. The depth of Joe's knowledge terrified her, but it was the memories that made her ill. Papa's arm, the sharp white bits of bone poking through the skin. Papa's fingers, the joints so shattered they were almost jelly.

Joe continued, relentless. "If your father was so crushed, how did he escape from Raptor Island?"

Joe was so confident he knew the answer; Helen hated him.

"After your mother was murdered and your sister placed, Winterbourne went to ground and took you with him. It had to be that way. One three-year-old girl looks much the same as another, but you were fourteen. Your picture had been released across every social media network. You had a reward on your head. There was no place you could go, no measure you could take to change your appearance enough to avoid Torval's killers."

Helen remembered that, too, the shock of seeing online photos of her, taken that last day at school. Of her, falling down on the track. Of her, sharing the chocolate chip cookies she'd made with her friends. Of her, beaming as she was called out as the best software designer on her school's championship robotics team. Papa hadn't even come onshore and already Torval's people had marked her for extinction.

"Lorenze Winterbourne knew you had no chance without him, because he knew that world. Before Lorenze met your mother, he'd been a part of that world."

"Yes. Papa said Mom saved him from himself. He never forgave himself for bringing death on her." Helen wasn't really telling him. She was remembering her father's expression when he saw the photos Torval's people had posted on the internet. His wife's body, bruised and bloody, wracked by so many bullets she was almost shredded. Helen had only had a single glimpse before Lorenze shut it down, but she could never forget.

"Winterbourne trained you to survive. He trained you to think on your feet, to operate weaponry, to kill with your bare hands. Maybe you didn't want to, but you learned it all."

"I did want to learn. Even when I landed wrong. Even when I was bruised. I dreamed of revenge. I imagined what it would be like to kill the man who murdered my mother and destroyed my home. I still dream of…" She shut her mouth.

Too late. "You dream of home."

Joe understood so quickly. That analyst thing, she supposed, but she hated having him in her head and under her skin. The more clues she dropped about herself, the more he could manipulate her.

"During your months on the run, during your training, you learned a fierce loyalty to your father. Or rather—the man you called your father."

She should never have imagined she was safe. She should never have stayed here so long. She should never have schemed so vengefully. This man who called himself Joe Grantham even knew that Lorenze was her stepfather.

"Somewhere along the line, the two of you performed the rescue of a woman who had been treated badly by life. She'd been passed around among Gregory Torval's men, told she was no longer young enough or pretty enough, and literally dumped on the side of the road. Your father gathered her up because she knew things about Gregory Torval's operation that he needed to know. At some point, she became his lover."

Kealoha. He knew about Kealoha. Another survivor endangered by Helen's carelessness.

Joe continued, "Again, speculation, but I think they loved each other. She helped you, too, get through the ongoing trauma of being fourteen, then fifteen, in constant danger, without friends, trusting no one. Your father taught you to survive. She taught you how to live."

Joe Grantham implied there was something that needed to be done and he needed Helen's help. She wasn't dead yet, so she believed him. But if what she suspected was true, she wouldn't be alive for long.

"You are the one who went after your father. Somehow you got to Raptor Island, rescued him and got away. No one knows it was actually you."

She took a long breath. She could deny, but she recognized the futility of that. So she admitted, "You're right. It was me. And you're right, no one knows."

"Ah." Joe nodded. "I had wondered if that was the case. I'm glad to know what you can do. Or rather, what you could do when you were fifteen." He looked around. "You're even more fearsome today."

Joe Grantham had put his formidable logic to work and figured it all out, and Helen could either shoot him dead where he sat, dump his body off the cliffs, pick up her backpack and run—again—or admit she was cornered.

She wasn't capable of killing in cold blood. For her, that was the line between the beasts who had murdered her mother and that innocent child and her teacher, and people like her, who knew how to use violence and chose not to. "What do you want me to do?"

"In my wallet, there's a thumb drive with all the information you'll need." He tossed it to her, then watched as she opened the wallet and removed the thumb drive. "But in short, we must go to Raptor Island, retrieve a piece of electronics—"

"What kind of electronics?"

"An address book."

Rowan raised her eyebrows. "Address book?"

"—and bring it back to the woman who lost it."

"Out of the goodness of your heart, you're putting your life and mine at risk for an…electronic address book?"

"There's a reward."

"A reward? A large reward?"

"She is a very wealthy old woman."

That explained everything. He wasn't a federal agent or a man of noble heroics. "You're a mercenary."

"I have mercenary tendencies. Don't you?"

"I like to know the type of man I'm dealing with."

"You can't depend on type."

"I realize that now."

"I'm not going to hurt you," he assured her. "I need you."

"Got it." She did understand. She was safe until he had what he wanted. "To clarify—this is an electronic address book? Not an actual paper address book? Because lots of people still like paper, and if your client is old…"

"I…didn't even think that… *Paper?*" He seemed bumfuzzled at the thought.

"Yes. Maybe. You could ask her."

"No. There's no contacting her now. Not without putting her in danger."

Tie me to the tracks of the oncoming train, but by all means, protect the lady with the payout. "One last thing before you go."

"Go?"

"Leave my home." She corrected herself. "Leave this light-house. You threatened my sister. You can be satisfied that I'm not running. But you're not spending the night here." She desperately needed this next piece of information. "First tell me how you found me."

8

"I WENT TO visit *my* sister's grave. When she was three, she was murdered at her preschool...a case of mistaken identity." Joe placed his hand on his chest over his nonexistent heart. "You placed flowers on her tombstone."

Mila Weiss, the child who'd been killed in her sister's place. Lorenze Winterbourne would nod and tell Helen that conscience would do her in every time.

Yes, Papa, but you raised me to have a conscience.

Helen pointed out, "You said your name was Grantham."

"My mother remarried. Mila was my stepsister."

"Of course." Also, he could be lying about his name. After all, she was.

"After you visited my sister's grave, you went to the teacher's grave and placed flowers there. You cried."

"I only went once."

"Once was enough."

No good deed goes unpunished. Her father had taught her that, too. She cradled the thumb drive in her palm. Get the facts right from the horse's mouth. Or the horse's ass, in this case. Then compare it to his written plan. "We're going to land on the island. How?"

"We're going on a launch as one of Torval's guests. We're going to his birthday party."

"Happy birthday to him. How old is the uncircumcised prick?"

"How do you know he's uncircumcised?"

"He wears a tie because if he doesn't, his foreskin flips over his head."

Joe barked a laugh.

"Torval sees me, recognizes me, kills me, and what good does that do you?"

Joe got serious again. "A couple of things."

"Glad to know my death will profit you."

He waved that away.

What a great guy.

He said, "Torval is an old man bound by old rules. He made a vow to Lorenze Winterbourne to allow his family to live without harm."

"Right. I believe him. That's why I've been on the run for fourteen years."

"He can't break that vow in full view of his people—"

"My estate and will are in order." Cold comfort.

"—and all his people *will* be there. He'd take it badly if someone failed to show."

"As you said, he's an old man. What is he? Sixty? Old enough to be failing, old enough that the younger men will be watching him for signs of weakness, jostling each other for their chance to take him out and take over."

"The one that doesn't jostle is always the winner."

He was right, of course.

"Along with the invitation I received, I got a guarantee of hospitality to me and any companion I brought." His mouth quirked, but it didn't look like humor. "I was offered the use of a companion should I not wish to bring my own."

"What a swell guy."

"Who? Me or Torval?"

"Take your choice." God, she hated them both. The hate for Torval never went away. Like a coal in her chest, it burned blue and hot.

Yet Joe sat here, in her chair, wearing merely his pants. She knew what he looked like, smelled like, tasted like. Her body ached with that satisfying remembrance of good sex. Her hatred for him was new and immediate, harder to control. She wanted to fly at him, use her fighting skills, blind him, bruise him, rip his flesh. Because he'd betrayed her with words, with insinuations, with intimacy. She had fooled herself into thinking he was what she thought him to be—an assassin. Now he knew her better than any living creature, and she knew she was still, after all these years, a hopeful fool, easy to sucker and likely to die by her own desperate need for social contact. "I'm going as your companion?"

"Of course. What else are women for?" He didn't wait for an answer; probably a good thing. "It has to be you. You're the one person who can keep Torval distracted while I search. He won't hurt you—"

Rowan snorted.

"—But he's hunted you for years, and he'll never take his attention away from you. As you said, you made a fool of him."

Her smile was no more than a grimace. "Don't forget the part where I rendered his torturer unconscious with the tire iron he used to break my father's leg."

"Did you?" Joe laughed with real delight. "Good for you."

"I wanted to kill him." She remembered the way the cold metal met her hot skin, how good it felt to crack that horrible creature's skull, the way she wanted to continue to hit him again and again until he was nothing but a mass of shattered bone and leaking, coagulating blood…like her father. "Papa said no. He said…don't go down that path unless there's no other choice."

Joe nodded agreement.

"I tied that monster up so tightly that if God is fair, he never got the circulation back into his hands." Those long-fingered, beautifully manicured hands.

"Doug Moore is alive and well and plying his trade as commanded by Gregory Torval."

Doug Moore. She had never known his name. She wished she didn't now. "Papa was wrong. I should have killed Moore and saved all his victims their pain."

"Torval would have found someone else to teach his lessons. There are always creatures who are happy to give pain to another creature. Most in words. Some in deeds."

She knew that. But if she had known Doug Moore would live to torment more people, Lorenze would have had trouble stopping her.

"If it assuages your conscience," Joe said, "you took a Hollywood-handsome man and smashed in the side of his face. As a reminder of his failure, Torval won't allow him to have plastic surgery. Women and men used to worship Doug Moore, until he hurt them as he always did. Now all the enchanting fairy dust has fallen away, and he looks like the monster he is."

Joe Grantham knew a lot about Torval's operation. She supposed that made sense; this mercenary was putting his life on the line, and hers, to steal something from Gregory Torval. But all that familiarity made her intestines squirm with uneasiness, and in her head she heard Lorenze's voice say, *Listen to your instincts. They're always right.* Mercenaries killed for money, for treasure, for profit. If Joe was a mercenary, he had already reached the lowest level of humanity. Hadn't he?

Joe was wholly aware of the way she scrutinized him. "You are the perfect distraction. Word was that Lorenze took Moore down, and Lorenze escaped the island on his own."

"That escape created the legend of Lorenze Winterbourne."

"Precisely. No one suspects it might have been Lorenze's teenage daughter who arranged the escape, snuck onto the island and then whisked him away. No one except your stepfather, you, and the girlfriend."

Kealoha…but never would Helen breathe that name to anyone.

Joe continued, "If anyone ever found out—"

"Torval would be a laughingstock."

"He was already a laughingstock when your father vanished, then reappeared, still alive, with insider information that forced Torval to backtrack on his obliviation policy. He had to once again prove himself a leader to be feared; any man who challenged him died under his hand."

She didn't care. "They were not good men."

"No."

"In his business, retirement is rare and long life even more so."

"The casualty rate is exorbitant, but the profit is so high it's worth the risk."

Speaking of profit… "I have a business to run. How long will this take?"

"The gathering is scheduled for three days. So that, or less."

She nodded and made a mental note to email her clients about her impending absence.

Joe said, "No one except me knows that you're Torval's weakness. You're unendingly dangerous to him. If he could find you, he would watch you."

"To find my father."

"At least to find out if he's alive."

She smiled a half smile. "He lives."

Joe waited for her to say more.

She knew he probably had good luck with that tactic. Most people would babble to fill a silence. She was used to silence, and used to waiting. When, after a while, she sighed, leaned back on the pillow and closed her eyes, he spoke again.

"Once Torval knew everything about you, he would—not hurt you, because he promised, but your freedom would be sharply curtailed."

"I lost my freedom tonight. How much more loss can there be?"

"I won't let Torval kill you. When this is over, your life will be better."

"Don't make promises you can't keep."

"I did not promise."

"Fair enough. Now get out."

He finished dressing. "Be ready at ten a.m."

DAY ONE

9

WHEN JOE HAD driven away and she saw no sign of his return, no indication man or beast moved on her security camera, she brought out the computer she'd bought used. It was old, slow and cheap, but everything worked. She inserted the thumb drive Joe had left into the USB port and read through the information. He'd given her the meat of the matter without the emotional component—his sister's death.

Helen went to the USPS site and filled out the form to hold her mail for...she hesitated...five days. Torval's party was scheduled to last three days, but she didn't know what was going to happen. Disaster seemed possible and even likely, so padding the time was wise. Not that ever she got anything of interest, mostly catalogues around Christmas and Valentine's Day urging her to buy gifts for her loved ones, but mail delivery lent her the appearance of normalcy, at least in the eyes of her mail carrier. She kept a P.O. Box, too, to receive correspondence from her older clients, but whatever landed in there could stay until she picked it up on her return.

She rose and walked to the closet, and got out her backpack. She checked the contents, swapped out a few practical pieces of clothing for her few, very few, party items, and placed it by the door. She was done packing. Then she got the suitcase, rectangular lightweight pale yellow plastic on wheels, and opened it to check the contents. Everything was already there, packed perfectly. She shut it up again and stood, indecisive.

She couldn't sleep now. Maybe after she'd done a crossword puzzle or played ScramWord or... She erased the computer's drive again, went in with a fake identity, and opened her social media. She hadn't visited any of them in over a year. It was too dangerous, too addictive, and if one person had managed to figure out who she was—and he had—others could. She never wanted to point an arrow toward Irena—her sister's name was Irena now—but in this case, she could tell herself it was necessary. She needed to see that Linden was safe, unharmed, untouched, happy.

When the first video popped up of Irena Tremblay's seventeenth birthday party, Helen collapsed in relief on the keyboard, then turned up the sound and watched it over and over. Irena looked good. Glowing, surrounded by her extended family. Her parents were glowing, too, nice people who loved their daughter. Everyone at the table treated Irena like one of their own.

Helen supposed Irena *was* their own.

The video changed, and there was Irena talking seriously to the camera about her aspirations, what she'd done to make the world a better place, the literacy tutoring she'd done, the trip she hoped to make in the summer after she graduated from high school. Then another video of her stuffing envelopes with college and scholarship applications.

She had a bright future; Helen fought a tiny prickle of resentment. Irena would never know where she came from, never know what her father had sacrificed for her safety and what kind of life her sister had led. Which was good and right. Helen wanted that innocence for her but—still, she wished Irena could understand how valuable she was and always had been to her birth family.

With a sigh, Helen erased her browsing history and turned off the computer. She stepped out onto the spiral staircase's landing, and dropped the computer over the rail and all the way down three flights to the concrete floor below.

It shattered.

She smiled. That part was always satisfying.

While she was here, she took a moment to check the mechanism she had created, the one that would collapse the stairs under an intruder and plunge them to their death. It seemed a little stiff, so she lubed it and used it until she felt comfortable with its easy performance.

She went to bed, shed tears for Mr. Bandara, and slept. As had happened so often in her life, mourning had to wait; tomorrow she needed her wits about her.

10

HELEN OPENED HER front door and faced Joe, his hand raised to knock.

"Wow." His eyes widened in unflattering surprise. "You look great."

Of course she did. She stood five-nine in her bare feet and weighed one hundred thirty-two pounds. Every day she lifted weights and practiced self-defense. She wore clothes well, and for this occasion, she'd dressed to be invisible, Joe's companion, the woman men looked at, drooled over, and never saw. She wore a blue silk button-up blouse, knotted at the waist, white wide-leg viscose pants that clung to her thighs and butt, and white Tory Burch platform sandals with a low heel. She'd knotted a blue-and-white ombré scarf around her neck, hung a silver vintage duffel bag over her shoulder, and flung her black moto leather jacket over her back, hooked by one ringed finger. She smiled at his astonishment. "There." She gestured at the backpack and wheeled bag in the entry and stepped out onto the porch.

Like a well-trained dog, he gathered her luggage and brought it out on the walk.

She shut the door firmly behind her, and glanced at her phone. All the security measures snapped into action. "Come on," she said, and started toward his car.

He followed. "You can take a moment to bid farewell to your home."

"It's just a place." One she suspected she wouldn't live to see again, one that had been her first home since her fourteen-year-old world had been destroyed. If she felt wrenching sorrow, she didn't acknowledge it, for it would take the disintegration of Torval's empire before she could return. Could that happen? Of course, on the day justice ruled the earth and ruthless crime lords bowed to the law.

In the meantime, she wouldn't allow her sorrow to show. Emotion had betrayed her, and grief was weakness; she'd never show Joe weakness again. "Where do we meet the launch?"

"Down the coast." He put down her luggage and walked around her to open the car door.

She gave him a stern look. "Oh, don't even."

"My mother taught me to open any door for every female."

"Did she teach you to blackmail that female by suggesting their lack of cooperation would lead to her seventeen-year-old sister's death?"

"She'd be horrified."

Helen got into the passenger seat.

"Especially after the death of my sister." He shut the door behind her.

"I'll bet she'd be proud of you now," she said.

He wasn't in the car yet; he couldn't hear her. Yet he looked sharply at her, placed her bags in the trunk, got in and started the engine. The car looked ramshackle, but the engine purred a deep, powerful purr. If needed, this vehicle could move. She couldn't blame herself for not knowing that, only for dismissing the other hints that he was not what he seemed.

Just once during the forty-five minute ride did they speak.

"Who did you think I was?" Joe asked.

"An assassin. Talk about wishful thinking."

She waited for him to respond, and she could see him trying to form the questions: *Whose assassin?* And, *You think I'm worse than an assassin?*

Ultimately he decided he didn't want or perhaps deserve to know the answers, and returned his complete attention to the curves of the Pacific Coast Highway.

That was probably best; the vivid anger that had bolstered her through the discovery of his true identity had faded, and she feared if she spoke of Mr. Bandara, she would break down into tears. She didn't want Joe to know she'd lost a friend. If Joe could, he'd use her emotion to manipulate her, and he didn't need any more buttons to push. When Rowan thought of Mr. Bandara, she grieved. When she thought about her innocent, unknowing sister, she wanted to do as her father told her she mustn't: strike about her blindly, indiscriminately.

Joe's cool efficiency put Helen uncomfortably in mind of a man who studied his passions and learned to perform them well. Twenty-three miles down the twisting highway, Joe turned off on a narrow, badly paved road that cut back on itself, dropped off steeply and then settled into a series of potholes.

She had been here before…

The teenage girls sat in the van, two to a seat, staring out the dark tinted windows and speaking, if they had to, in monotones. They'd been chattering earlier until they heard the guards betting on which of them would get passed down to them, and that had shut down any pretense that this trip was a vacation. They were all fresh-faced and pretty— runaways, kids raised in rough homes—and all they knew was that they were headed to an island where they'd have nice clothes, regular meals, a roof over their heads and work that involved, as Kealoha said, ankles in the air.

Rowan sat in the middle of the van against the window, wondering if she was more frightened than the other girls. Regardless of all Kealoha's advice, she might end up as sexual prey for one of these guys. If she did, it didn't matter. She was here to accomplish one task, and a man's life depended on her.

Her father's life depended on her.

Back in the now, Helen concentrated on relaxing her jaw; she'd apparently been clenching it in her sleep, and her face muscles ached. She'd trained herself to be calm, to breathe, to accept the inevitable…when she was awake. At night, her subconscious scrubbed those instructions and rocketed off, imagining all the heinous possibilities of capture and painful death, and so her jaw hurt and she had a headache not even the darkest sunglasses could cure.

The road led to a metal gate manned by a burly guy who looked so much like an early James Bond villain that Helen waited for him to grin and show his solid gold teeth.

Instead he said, "Go on down, sir," and opened the gate with the reverence one might show to the crowned head of Franistan.

"Thank you, Dickie." Joe drove through, the road miraculously improved, and they parked in a lot with white lines painted on the pavement and restrooms for those in need.

Joe caught her looking at them. "The trip to Raptor Island is less than an hour, so wait if you can," he advised. "Unless you love chemical toilets."

She did not. "I can wait."

He glanced at the three cars already parked in the lot. "We're the last ones here, so the launch will leave as soon as we've boarded. Here's the setup."

"*Now* you want to tell me the setup?"

"I would have told you last night, but you threw me out."

"I'm sorry it didn't stick."

"Every time you turn around, I'll be there." He lifted his finger and held it right before her face. "Or so you'd better hope. If there comes a time when you're truly alone on Raptor Island, you won't be alive long."

She pushed his hand aside. "You told me Torval won't hurt me. Then you snorted." She pointed her finger just as he had. "He has a reputation for temper."

"Stick close." He caught her hand, held it and examined it. "You're fond of your collection of rings."

She knew what he was seeing. A dozen rings collected over the years. Expensive rings of platinum and diamond, or platinum and emerald. Antique rings of gold and enamel, or silver filigree. A series of narrow stacking rings. And one small, treasured high school graduation ring inscribed with initials that were not hers. "Fond. Yes."

"Because they provide protection for those delicate fingers when you punch?"

She laughed. "That, too."

"What else?"

She settled on telling him part of the truth. "When I purchased each ring, I knew it was undervalued and at the same time, the best I could afford."

"I think—" he tapped the platinum and emerald "—a few of these rings appraise at a large sum."

She tilted her head. "If at any time I'm unexpectedly forced to go on the run, I've still provided for myself."

"Very wise." He returned to business. "Everywhere in the Raptor Island house is monitored by camera and microphone. Nothing you say or do will be private."

"I'd like to be private in the bathroom."

"Understood, and I have my methods. But it's best to let them believe as much as possible that we're unaware of their surveillance. We don't want them to bring in new technology that I can't detect." As she climbed out and gathered her duffel bag, he opened the trunk, removed their luggage and put it beside the car. With a click, he locked the car, and he pocketed the keys.

She wanted to say something, inquire about the safety of the luggage, but she supposed in this instance, no one in their right mind would abscond with it. She did give the light yellow wheeled bag a worried glance, but she'd known when she bought it there was every likelihood it would be searched. She simply had to hope she'd done her camouflage well enough.

Taking her arm, he strolled with her toward the beach. "Wait. I forgot." He left her standing there while he hurried back to the car. He opened the door, put his head inside, dug around, got out, locked the door again and, with a frown, leaned down to examine the tire. He shook his head, straightened and came back to her. "Low tire pressure. I'll have to get that fixed."

They stepped out of the shadow of trees onto the hard-packed sand on the beach. A yacht bobbed in the water just beyond the surf; pulled onto the sand was a dinghy attended by three burly men who resembled the James Bond henchman at the gate. They wore coveralls and hip boots, and all had eyes the color of mean.

She remembered these guys from her teenage siege on the island, them or men like them, built by steroids into terrifying muscle machines. Her face ached; the reality of her situation came at her in waves, and she had clenched her jaw again.

Joe put his arm around her waist, pulled her around to face him, and said, "Melt into me."

She knew how to play this role. Long ago, her friend had taught her the basics of faking passion, and told her to play her part well. At the time, both Helen's life and her father's had depended on it.

Now she did as Joe demanded, and with a show of willingness pressed close against him, shoulder to groin. He bent her backward in a kiss, lips to lips, no tongues, no breath. It was still intimate enough to make her uncomfortable, so as he lifted his head, she smiled into his face and stroked her fingers through his hair. She hoped to make him equally uncomfortable.

Instead he said, "Good," as if she was a trained dog. "That's good. Keep up with those kinds of details. They'll have no doubt who owns you, and that'll save problems...most of them."

"Gosh." As she slid her hands down his shoulders and then stepped away, she fluttered her lashes. "Thanks ever so."

One corner of his mouth twitched in a grin. Taking her arm again, he made a show of helping her through the sand toward the dinghy.

The men spoke, one right after another. "Hello, Mr. Grantham."

"Greetings, Mr. Grantham."

"You're late. We expected you half an hour ago." This last was said with irritation by the only guy with a name on his coveralls. He was just Tyler. Tyler No Last Name.

"Is the tide turning?" Joe asked.

"Close."

"Then no problem. The tide won't wait, but you can. Everyone can wait...for me." His warm, quiet voice made him sound like the Joe of last night, but his words depicted another man, and to Helen's gaze he looked...different. Arrogant, uncaring, a superman who bounced bullets off his chest.

These men knew Joe, showed him a wary respect with a sprinkle of obsequiousness.

Helen wasn't sure what that could mean except that, yes, she had truly read Joe Grantham incorrectly and confirmed he was not the mild-mannered paid killer of her imagination. But what he was, she did not truly know.

Joe told them, "Our luggage is at the car. Bring it and put it in our room."

"I'll need the keys," Tyler said.

"No, you won't. The luggage is *at* the car, not *in* the car." Joe met Tyler's gaze. "The car is mine. I don't want it driven. I don't want it moved. I don't want it bugged or bombed. I don't want you to wash it or wax it or examine it. I want it left strictly alone. I'll hold you personally responsible... Tyler."

Tyler took a step away. "Right, Mr. Grantham." He put his hand to his earpiece listened, then said, "Yes, he's here. We're shoving off the beach right now." He winced at the answer. "Mr. Torval's been expecting you, Mr. Grantham. He was getting worried that you wouldn't come."

"Oh..." Joe dragged out the word, and his smile held an edge. "I wouldn't miss this for the world."

Tyler seemed to want to say...something more, something sharp and chiding. But Joe looked at him, and he said nothing.

Thug #3 rushed in to fill the silence. "Yes sir, Mr. Grantham, that's what I said, too, sir."

Tyler glared at his cohort, and when Thug #2 would have helped Helen into the dinghy, an unsmiling Joe stopped him with a grip on the arm. For a moment, Helen thought there would be words, but #2 stepped back with a grunt.

Joe himself picked her up, placed her in the dinghy, directed her to a seat and hopped in after her. He told the two men who stood in the surf, "You can push off now." He took Helen's scarf from around her throat and used it to tie back her hair. "It's going to be a rough trip through the surf," he told her, "and you don't want it in your eyes."

"Of course, Joe," she agreed, as if the proprietary move done without warning or permission didn't grind on her like wave-driven sand against the shore.

Tyler got in the boat. The other guys pushed it off, turned it to face into the surf and got it into deeper water. Tyler revved the powerful motor, and they headed toward the yacht.

Joe was right; the trip through the surf was rough—and exhilarating, and Helen laughed out loud.

Joe's arm tightened on her when she laughed, and he murmured in her ear, "You're so self-contained, but I guess you must love the sea or you wouldn't live where you live."

"It's primal. It's harsh. It's life incarnate and death to the un-wary. One thing I know—never turn your back on the ocean."

He didn't say anything more, but somehow she thought he'd added that to some internal database to be used as needed. But why bother? He had demanded; she had yielded. He needed nothing else.

She added—because why not?—"Never turn your back on *you*."

Of course, Joe took her insult with equanimity. "Shh. We don't want them—" he nodded at Torval's men "—to know that truth."

As they pulled up to the yacht, she viewed the rope ladder that hung off the deck, sighed, removed her sandals and stuck them in her duffel bag. While the dinghy motor idled and the waves rocked both the dinghy and the yacht, she gripped the ropes, put one bare foot after another on the metal rungs and climbed to the deck. A strange man helped her find her balance: the cap-tain of the vessel, she realized. She caught a glimpse of three men standing at the bow and four women in a cluster under an awning. Then Joe stood beside her and, as he'd done before, re-moved the captain's hand from her arm. "I'll take it from here." He sounded polite enough, but again his voice contained that proprietary note, and the captain took note of it.

All of the people on board took note of it.

With a hand on the back of her waist, he directed her toward the three men. "Rowan, this is Spencer Da Wit, Francisco Su-arez, and Wadell Davis." With a flourish in his voice, he said, "Gentlemen, this is Rowan Winterbourne."

11

ROWAN WINTERBOURNE.

She hadn't realized Joe would introduce her by her real name, nor had she realized that she'd feel as if she'd been struck by a lightning bolt from the clear blue sky. How many years had it been since she'd allowed herself to remember her own name? Now in the space of two days she'd betrayed that secret to a friend and had that secret betrayed by a man she should have shot while she had the chance.

While she sucked in a breath of cool sea air, trying to counteract the shock, Spencer and Wadell smiled vacantly, clearly uninterested in Joe Grantham's current woman.

Yet Francisco's heavy gray eyebrows rose to the place where his hairline would have been had he been twenty years younger, and he gave a dry cackle. "Well done, Joe. Well done." Taking Rowan's hand, he bowed over it. "I never dreamed I'd have the honor to meet you."

Joe's hand caressed her spine, up and down in a slow glide, not an apology for traumatizing her—he didn't care about that—but to keep her on her feet.

Yes. She should have shot him dead and tossed his body into the sea.

Wadell looked between Joe and Francisco. "Who is she?" he asked, as if she wasn't standing right there.

When Francisco would have explained, Joe said, "You'll find out soon enough."

Francisco nodded. "As you wish, Joe. You know I do as you wish whenever possible." He offered Joe his hand, and when Joe shook it, Francisco bowed over it, as he had Rowan's, but deeper and with more reverence.

The other two men shook hands with Joe in the same obsequious manner, and while Rowan watched with fascination, Joe accepted their tributes as his right.

There was so much more going on here than she understood.

A touch on her arm had her spinning around to face a gloriously tall and beautiful bathing suit model type. "I'm Savannah. We girls thought you'd rather spend the trip with us rather than listening to the men blather on about business."

"No, she wouldn't." Joe was definite in his refusal. "She'll stay with me."

"But Joe," Savannah protested, "she'll be bored."

"She wouldn't be bored no matter what we discussed. She's marvelously intelligent. But if I promise that we masculine brutes won't discuss business, could I entice you and the other ladies to let us join you?" Joe smiled with the kind of charm he'd showed Rowan last night.

Savannah fell for it. "Of course, we'd love to have the men join us! We'll try not to discuss silly women things and bore you, either." She was not insulted by Joe's insinuation that Rowan was the smartest of the women, and clearly didn't have a doubt that Joe would get his way.

Rowan felt as if she'd dropped into a 1960s television rerun

where women were subservient and none-too-bright or, if they
were intelligent, they took care to hide that from their men.
And again, she tried to understand Joe's place in Gregory Torval's world. Could any man here challenge Gregory Torval? Joe
Grantham, of course, but who else?

She slid a glance at Joe. Ohhh. Perhaps Joe had told her the
truth. Perhaps they were both here to grab a wealthy woman's
electronic address book and collect the reward. But in doing
so, Joe would be challenging Gregory Torval's control of the
area's criminal activities. Did Joe intend to start a war? Was she
cooperating with a man who maneuvered himself into place as
southwestern California's crime lord?

She tried to decide if she cared. After all, her hatred for Gregory Torval had ruled half her life. What did she care whether
the man who took him down moved into his position? As long
as someone took Torval down...

Before she could think through all the layers and possibilities,
she found herself under the tarp with Joe and the other men,
and Savannah, Kumara, Li and BeBée. The first three were so
interchangeable in height, grooming and manner Rowan had
trouble keeping them straight in her mind.

Not so with BeBée. "It's pronounced Bee-bay," she told
Rowan. "I picked it out myself. Before that I was Sally, and
who needs that?"

In one of her incarnations while living in East Texas, Rowan
had been a Sally, so she had a fondness for the name, but *BeBée*
definitely sounded exotic and perhaps erotic. Obviously, BeBée
was attached to none of these men, so who was she?

BeBée answered without being asked. "I'm Gregory Torval's
appointed hostess. His greeter. The woman who keeps him
happy." She winked. "If you want anything, ask me. I know
the routine."

"Thank you. I will."

Remarkably BeBée was not tall, thin, and Botox-perfect.

Rather, BeBée was petite, curvy, laughing, chattering, friendly, and the glue that held the gathering together.

Rowan examined her thoughtfully. Torval liked his women young, very young, and BeBée was probably Rowan's age. What did she have/do that kept her in Torval's good graces? Maybe her bouncy good humor, or the way she wore white shorts cut so high they showed off her butt cheeks, or her almost puppy-like enthusiasm for life. Rowan immediately liked BeBée, and that gave her pause. A spontaneous friendship seemed daring at a time when she should be utilizing all caution.

Yet the night before, she'd spent time examining Joe, thinking through his possible motivations, developing theories about his intentions, and look where that got her? In the end, she'd completely and humiliatingly misread him.

This time, with BeBée, she'd go with her gut.

"Look!" BeBée pointed. "There's Raptor Island. I'd better drive if I'm going to!" She dashed off toward the wheelhouse.

The cliffs grew taller on the horizon, no longer an Offbeat Bay blue shadow but unforgiving stone streaked in the creases with green trees and brown brush. Rowan could see the house, too, a mansion Torval had built to display his power over the region, three ascending layers of gray rock that rose from the cliff as if it had grown there, an untested and unassailable fortress.

Torval was a man who believed in putting his relatives through college, through law school, through medical school, through computer training. He paid their school debts and set them up in practice, with their own offices, and they paid him back with service. Rowan had done her research, and she knew that despite at least one serious "accident" involving a bullet wound, he never visited a hospital. No legal action had ever been successfully taken against him. His computer security was top-notch... for the most part. She smiled.

Joe broke off his conversation. "Are you amused, my love?"

"A passing thought," she answered.

Wadell studied her. "She doesn't say much, does she?"

"No, she doesn't," Rowan answered.

"Rowan believes in keeping her mouth shut and letting people believe she's a fool rather than, as so many others do, opening it and confirming their suspicions."

Wadell nodded; if he understood Joe's insinuation, he carefully didn't show it.

When they were about to enter Raptor Island harbor, BeBée returned, cheeks flushed with pleasure. "There's so much power in those motors, it's like riding a good, hard…motorcycle." She laughed at the men's expressions, then turned to Rowan. "Almost there. I remember the first time I arrived at Raptor Island. I was a teenager, in with a bunch of other girls."

Rowan did a double take. Did BeBée look familiar?

BeBée didn't seem to notice. "I was scared to death, but determined to take over the world." She leaned against the railing as they docked, and grinned at Rowan. "I've almost got it in my grip."

"Your grip on Torval looks pretty secure to me." Spencer laughed in a mean, meaningful way.

BeBée dimpled at him, yet Rowan thought she saw a flash of danger in her dark eyes.

The motors cut back. The yacht puttered across the last few feet of water. They docked, and for the first time in thirteen years, Rowan Winterbourne set foot on Raptor Island.

12

AS BEFORE, a lineup of jeeps waited to take the guests up the winding road to the fortress on the edge of the cliff. Joe steered Rowan toward the lead jeep, and she felt a resurgence of the nerves and the nausea that had assaulted her the first time. And, as before, she reviewed who would die if she failed to keep her head. That thought steadied her, and she thanked the young driver as he held the door.

Joe climbed in beside her and slid his arm around her shoulders. He leaned into her face. "Are you all right?"

"Yes."

"You looked a little wobbly for a moment."

"How annoying of you to notice."

As the door started to close, they heard a female shout, "Wait!" The door swung open again, and BeBée lavished a smile on the driver. "Walter, you're the best!" She piled in beside Joe and announced, "I want to ride with you."

Rowan leaned across him and smiled into BeBée's bright face.

"That would be great. I'd like to get to know you better." *To see if my gut and my head agree that you're worth investing with my trust.*

BeBée bounced on the seat. "Yay! That's the way I feel, too. Sometimes you just click, you know? Similar experiences, maybe."

Rowan immediately thought of that first trip to Raptor Island. But even if BeBée was on the same boat as Rowan, and did remember, she more likely meant that Rowan earned her existence as a professional consort. She settled back in the seat. "Yes. We're survivors."

BeBée waited until the driver had revved up the engine before leaning over Joe and saying in a low tone, "There are a couple of things I should warn you about. The first, the most important, is Torval's wife."

"He's still got a wife?" Rowan's voice rose.

BeBée gestured to her to quiet down. "Yes, he's still got a wife. The same wife he always had. The mother of his son."

More quietly, Rowan said, "I never thought she'd stick around."

"Are you kidding? Hanging around making other people miserable is her vocation. You'll recognize her—she always wears black. Nice black. Designer black. Unrelenting black, lots of hats and veils." BeBée widened her well-lashed eyes. "Mitzi loves her melodrama and her statement clothes."

It took Rowan a second. "Mitzi? Her name is *Mitzi*? Why not Kandy or one of the other cutesy names from a beach blanket movie?"

BeBée grasped Rowan's wrist. "All the jokes have been made, but don't let her hear you. She's one scary woman."

Rowan scooched back. "Got it. Thank you."

BeBée released her. "She wears the black to mourn her son. She says when the Torval finally grows some balls and kills Lorenze Winterbourne and his children, she'll wear color again. Don't be surprised when you notice how good she looks in black."

In Rowan's mind's eye, Mitzi had rapidly changed from a sweet elderly woman to a Greek fury draped in widow's weeds to a striking blonde in stylish designer clothes. "I can't wait to meet her." *Kidding.*

"She'll make an appearance. She likes to keep up her self-appointed task of tormenting Torval. She hasn't slept with him since he canceled the obliviate order on Winterbourne and his kids. That's why I've survived on the island." BeBée was straight-on serious. "I keep him off the top of her."

"If she won't sleep with him, why does she care one way or the other who he's with?"

"She's jealous as all hell. She works out, has had a nip and a tuck, and it's all to keep him panting after her."

"And he does?" This was soap-opera twisted.

"He does. She's got him by the short hairs. He wants her. She won't let him do it until he kills Winterbourne and his kids. She's totally pissed when she sees him touching me. He keeps his hand to himself when she's hovering because one way or another, she makes him miserable and because somewhere in her sweet little life, she became quite a poisoner…"

"It's a South American soap opera!"

"Yes, and I'm the star everyone cheers for. That keeps me going most days."

The jeep hit a pothole and tossed BeBée against her door and Rowan across Joe's lap.

"Damn it, Walt, watch where you're going!" BeBée shouted. Rubbing her shoulder, she leaned across Joe again. "The other thing to remember is—Torval has a temper. Most of the time, he lets it rip as a test to see what people are made of. Like the time I saw him rage at one of his men that he needed an anniversary present for Mitzi and he wanted Kevin to give him the gift he'd ordered for his daughter. Torval grabbed the packing box. Kevin wouldn't let it go. They wrestled. Torval shouted in Kevin's face that he would kill him. The guy wouldn't give it up. When the whole drama was over and Kevin still had the box, Torval told me, cool as a cucumber, that Kevin had good character. He promoted him to lead the night team security. He trusts him to do the right thing no matter what."

"Noted," Joe said.

Both Rowan and BeBée looked at him in surprise.

"Yes, I'm still here," he said.

BeBée shrugged in a way that rolled from her shoulders to her hips. "I figure you know all this."

Joe nodded. "It's good to have what I think I know confirmed."

"Yeah, well. Torval really does have a temper, and when he really loses it, he'll really kill you." BeBée wore a queasy expression that told Rowan she'd seen it happen. "That pistol he carries is small, but he's fast with it."

"How do you know which is which?" Rowan asked. "Which the genuine rage and which the testing?"

"He puts on a pretty good act with the testing temper. But when the rage takes him, his brown eyes turn cat-piss yellow." BeBée shivered. "Even if you're not the one he's mad at, you should get the hell away from him as fast as you can."

"Noted." Rowan said it this time, and glanced at Joe. She knew and he knew if Torval found out the truth of what they were doing, he'd kill them in cold blood, no temper needed. What he was going to do when he met Rowan, she hadn't a clue.

The house came into view, looking to Rowan less like a fortress and more like a prison, with a portico for the cars and a line of muscled men waiting to help with their arrival.

On this island, all the men seemed to be muscled.

"There he is. Gregory Torval. He's waiting on the porch to meet you." BeBée slid a sideways glance at Joe. "He doesn't trust you."

"He has good instincts," Joe answered.

Again Rowan wondered what Joe was doing, acting like the future godfather when all he wanted was an address book.

Or was he lying to her? To Rowan? And for what purpose?

"Yes," BeBée agreed with Joe. "Instincts have kept him alive through three assassination attempts. You can't say the same about the men who tried to bring him down."

"They're not alive?" Joe asked.

"Nobody in their organization is alive. Nobody in their family is alive. He's only canceled one obliviate order, and that was the important one. The one on Lorenze Winterbourne." BeBée leaned around Joe again and widened her eyes at Rowan. "Your father."

The shock of hearing her own name, of knowing that soon everyone on this island would know her real identity, made Rowan want to take the usual steps to vanish.

Instead, the jeep came to a stop by the broad front steps, and Rowan got her first glimpse at the man who had haunted her dreams, taken her family and hunted her footsteps.

Gregory Torval was a stocky man with shoulder-length shoe-polish-black hair slicked back from his forehead. His smooth, fair skin contrasted with his red lip stain. Or had the color had been tattooed on? His cheeks had sagged into jowls and his lids had sagged onto his lashes, and yet he towered over the scene with his sheer presence. No wonder he'd kept his dominance over an ever-expanding crime scene.

Walter opened the jeep door, and BeBée bounced out. "Daddy, did you miss me?" She flung her arms around Torval and smiled into his face.

He looked stern. "I told you not to go."

"But I wanted to drive the yacht."

"Steer. You wanted to steer—" Torval caught himself. "You are never supposed to go anywhere near the wheelhouse."

"I know, Daddy, but it's so much fun. Will you spank me later?"

Torval slapped her bottom. "I'd spank you now, but I have to greet my guests." He watched Joe and Rowan climb the steps. When they were close, he extended his hand. "Joe, I knew you couldn't stay away."

"I would never ignore an invitation to celebrate your birthday and view again how much you've achieved in such a relatively short time." Joe made a show of looking up at the house towering grimly above them. "It's an inspiration for me, especially as I plan my own long and successful operation. Under your tutelage, of course."

Torval grinned toothily. "Quite a proper sentiment." He turned to Spencer and shook his hand, then to Wadell, and to Francisco, and welcomed them one by one. Turning to Francisco's woman, he embraced her, kissed her cheek, said the appropriate words of welcome that put her in her place as a subordinate, and worked his way backward to Rowan. "I know all the lovely ladies who have accompanied my men except you, my dear. Introduce me, Joe."

Joe grinned as toothily as Torval had only a moment before. "Gregory Torval, I'd like you to meet the light of my life, Rowan Winterbourne."

In a flash, Torval's congenial face changed to pure wrath, and his brown eyes flashed yellow. Before Rowan could react, he pulled his pistol and pointed it between her eyes. "Die, bitch."

13

AS TORVAL FIRED, Joe slammed himself into Torval's body and with both hands knocked Torval's shooting arm up.

Standing so close, the blast deafened Rowan, immobile with shock. In her mind, Lorenze's knowledgeable words swirled. *If you heard the gunshot, you're still alive.*

The bullet struck the stone column of the portico. Granite shards blasted across the porch.

Women screamed. Men shouted.

Terror fogged Rowan's vision. *Dad, I don't want to die. Not here, not now. Not after coming so far.*

Lorenze's voice spoke in her mind. *Don't panic, Rowan. Run or stand. Whatever will serve you best.*

Joe gripped Torval's upraised arm. From two inches away, he stared into Torval's face, and his expression should have scared Torval. It should have. "Perhaps you didn't hear me." His voice was quiet, his tone forceful. "I said Rowan Winterbourne is the light of my life."

Rowan took her first breath. Her chest rose. Oxygen fed her starved, shocked lungs.

"You brought Winterbourne's daughter to my house? The whelp of the man who killed my son?" Torval was out of control, straining, shrieking, fighting. "Have you no respect?"

Rowan breathed again, almost normally now. She had to speak. She had to say what needed to be said, to discover whether or not she had even the slightest chance of leaving this place alive. "Gregory Torval, you rescinded the obliviate order on my family. In front of this company, do you dare change your mind?" Her words were a challenge. Her tone was a slap. No one who heard her could imagine how close she was to blacking out.

Torval switched his attention from Joe's hard-set face to hers. His grip on the pistol tightened.

Joe braced himself.

Without warning, Torval relaxed, and his eyes cleared. "You're right. What was I thinking? Just because your father killed my only son, my only progeny, why would I want to kill his daughter? Rowan Winterbourne, pardon my loss of temper. That was foolishness on my part. I never break my word. After all, we're not animals. If nothing else, we're governed by the rules of hospitality." Every word was dipped in poison.

"After that gracious speech, I feel so much more at home." Rowan proved she was fluent in that dipped-in-poison language.

All around them, guests and guards were getting to their feet, staggering, swaying.

Torval watched them, and Rowan suspected the two guards who had flung themselves on the floor for safety had just been demoted to maid service.

"Rowan, you didn't drop when I brought out the gun." Torval sounded mildly interested. "Why is that? It's safer."

"How safer?"

"You're less likely to be hit by a stray bullet."

"If I'm flat on my face, I'm more likely to be shot in the back."

She met his eyes without flinching. "If you're going to kill me, you'll be looking me in the eyes. And if I'm going to kill you… well, I have no idea if you'll be on your feet or kneeling and howling for mercy."

"Hmph." Starting at her head, Torval examined her all the way down to her toes. "I see your father in you."

"Stepfather, and thank you."

"Stepfather? Really?" Torval looked diverted. "Did I know that?"

"I have no idea," Rowan said, "and I don't know why you'd care."

"Information is always worth collecting. Sometimes it proves useful when you least expect it." Torval turned back to Joe, who was still clutching him tightly. "You can take my gun if it makes you feel better."

Joe removed it from Torval's hand. "Not because I don't trust you. Of course I trust you to keep your word. But because I surrendered my firearm before boarding the yacht, and having this makes me feel so much more secure." Joe stepped away from Torval and tucked the pistol in his belt.

One of Torval's guards moved forward.

Torval shook his head at him.

The guard halted, but watched Joe with narrowed eyes.

In an affable tone, Torval asked, "Tell me, my dear Rowan, how is your father?"

"Lorenze Winterbourne is well, as I'm sure you know."

"I've forgotten. Where does he live now?"

"Los Angeles. Surely you've heard about his exploits."

"I hear rumors, yes. Your father is famous in a superhero kind of way. If I didn't know better, I'd say he was merely a myth, this father of yours. Or rather, stepfather."

"Lorenze Winterbourne is no myth. He taught me everything I know of courage and loyalty."

"You do have courage when others do not." Torval smirked

at the recently prone Spencer, who stood brushing dust off the front of his shirt. "Come in. We've been waiting on lunch for you. Joe, you take BeBée." He waited to see Joe follow his order. Then, taking Rowan's arm, he led her toward the house. "Have we met before?"

"No." *Once.*

"Right. You do look familiar, though. Very familiar." Torval stopped and stared at her.

The hair rose on Rowan's arms. He was going to remember her from her arrival on the island. He was going to figure out she was the one who freed Lorenze Winterbourne. Joe would get his distraction then; while the men snickered about a fifteen-year-old girl outsmarting Torval and his men, she'd be bleeding to death on the floor, and nothing Joe did could change that.

"You're an attractive woman." Torval smiled at her the way a man smiles at a woman he likes. "Ambitious?"

"I have my ambitions." *Getting out of this alive.*

"I could do more for you than Joe Grantham."

She hadn't seen that coming. "No!"

"Take a moment to consider—"

"No!" Sleep with the man who had killed her mother? What could be more horrible?

"Daddy…" BeBée faced them, walked backward, spoke in a voice bubbling with such scandalized interest that she fixed Torval's attention on her. "Is Mitzi going to be at lunch?"

His gait developed a hitch. "No. I don't think so."

"But dinner? She'll make an appearance sometime this evening, won't she? Whatever will you do?"

Torval stopped and faced Joe and BeBée. "Make sure her sidearm is shooting blanks."

"This is going to be an exciting three days." BeBée left Joe and slid her arm through Rowan's. "You gentlemen go on. We girls need to freshen up before lunch. Meet you in the dining room!" She tugged Rowan toward a shut door in the hallway, pushed her through into a small room with a sink and toilet, shut the door behind them and locked it. Staring at Rowan, she said, "You're sort of sweaty-looking."

"Cold sweat." The delayed fear of those moments on the porch had swamped her, filled her veins with frustrated adrenalin and her mind with all the *what might have happened*s, and she was close to fainting or vomiting or… She went to the sink, gripped the edges with her hands, and breathed. In the mirror, she saw a terrified woman with large brown eyes and a clammy complexion.

BeBée took one of the rolled drying cloths, wet it with cold water and applied it to Rowan's forehead and cheeks. "You done good, honey," she crooned. "Torval might be a bastard, but he admires nerve, and you had it in spades. Now to convince him you're like your father, absolutely unafraid in every circumstance."

Rowan turned her head and stared at BeBée, who shone with admiration. "Were you here when he came? When my father came to blackmail Torval into rescinding the obliviate order?"

"I was. I will never forget it."

14

"I WAS YOUNG, you know." BeBée leaned against the wall and put her head back as if seeing the scene projected there. "Scared to death of this new world that was all men and guns and violence and—"

"Rape?" Now Rowan was sure BeBée had been part of the same shipment of girls she'd used to infiltrate the island.

"No. I saw another girl get off the boat and disappear, so I knew it was possible."

Me. That was me.

BeBée didn't hear Rowan's thoughts. Who would have suspected? "I kept to myself and watched, tried to figure out a strategy where I wasn't a victim. It was possible, I knew it, but I was so scared. Cowering, eating on the sly, watching everyone. Disguising myself. Binding my boobs tight, wearing the worst-fitting clothes I could scavenge."

Looking at BeBée now, Rowan couldn't imagine what kind of clothes could hide that figure.

"I hung around the kitchen staff, mingled with Mitzi's staff. I

did that for months, helped the maids, and I knew pretty soon I
had to either attach myself to one of the men…" BeBée's mouth
twisted. "Or jump off a cliff. Then your father arrived. I heard
he was coming. God, the news flew around the island like…
Everyone knew. Everyone positioned themselves to see him,
this man who had somehow negotiated safe passage for himself
when he was Torval's most hated enemy. Lorenze was…do you
remember what he looked like then?"

"Oh, yes." Even the memory shattered Rowan's heart.

"I've never seen a man, before or since, who had clearly been
broken so hard that his flesh was burned away and his spirit
shone through. He walked into Torval's throne room—"

"Throne room?"

"You'll see. Torval takes a lot of his staging from old Robin
Hood movies."

Rowan didn't bother to keep her contempt to herself. "I'm
sure he does."

"Your dad walked into the throne room, leaning on his cane,
head up, smiling at Torval in a way that said *Fuck you, asshole,
I'm going to win this one.* He had Torval by the gonads, and he
wasn't afraid of anything."

Rowan remembered Lorenze, tortured, maimed, yet so determined to free her from Torval's death sentence that he smiled as
he kissed her goodbye and left for Raptor Island. She had smiled
back, by God, until he was out of sight. Then the steel slid out
of her teenage spine, and she collapsed in fear, not for herself,
but for her father. Of all the lessons he'd taught her, that was
the most important. Sometimes your own life didn't matter as
much as love, justice…and revenge.

BeBée continued, "Torval sat on that stupid throne and
watched Lorenze make his way to the middle of the room.
He'd wanted everyone to view the ruin of a man, appreciate
what his torturer had done on his command. Right away you
could see he knew he'd made a mistake."

"That's not the only mistake he's made," Rowan said.

"It was the biggest. It casts the longest shadow. And he was too late to reverse course. Lorenze stopped in the middle of the room, not in front of Torval as Torval intended but in the middle of the room like he was a Shakespearean actor about to deliver a soliloquy." BeBée's face shone with pride in Lorenze's accomplishment. "In that soft, clear voice, he told Torval that he held evidence of Torval's operation, and unless he sent word within the hour that Torval had rescinded his scorched earth policy, unless it was made clear his daughter was to live a long and healthy life, it would be sent to the Feds."

"My dad had balls of platinum."

"He really did." Admiration infused BeBée's face. "Torval scoffed. The system was automated, Lorenze said. He started reeling off names and places. Torval stood and said, 'Come with me.' Lorenze refused. He wanted that policy removed in front of everyone. Torval lifted his pistol to shoot him. Lorenze smiled. He just…smiled." BeBée talked faster and faster. "Torval caved. In front of everybody, he caved, ordered the obliviate policy removed from all corners of the world. Lorenze said, 'You wasted time, and you don't have much left. Get me back to the mainland so I can stop the transmission.' He walked ever so slowly out of the room."

As Rowan pictured her father, shattered and so brave, tears filled her eyes.

"Afterward I thought the reason he wasn't afraid was that he'd already lost what mattered most, suffered all the pain, and all he had to do now was—fix the world for you."

Rowan's tears overflowed, and she leaned into the sink and sobbed, choking on her grief.

BeBée rubbed her back and made shushing sounds.

Then, as Lorenze had advised and as Rowan had trained herself to do, she swallowed her tears. When she had recovered enough composure to speak, she whispered, "Thank you. That means so much to me."

"It meant a lot to me, too. I figured out that I needed to stop cowering, to seize the day, and I set out to achieve Gregory Torval."

"Good choice."

"Are you being sarcastic?" BeBée's voice was neutral, but already Rowan knew her well enough to realize her feelings were involved.

"Not at all. If you must live in hell, better to reign." More than most, Rowan comprehended the *walk a mile in my shoes* sensibility. "That way, when it all craters, you've got a chance of getting out with the clothes on your back and a little more."

BeBée produced a slow, Grinch-like half smile. "I'd hoped you'd understand." She handed Rowan a fresh, cool, wet washcloth and gestured toward the tiered table loaded with toiletries. "Wash your face. There's foundation and blush, and either you have the best waterproof mascara in the history of the world or those are your real lashes."

"I paid for them and attached them myself, so they're mine."

"Awesome! Now I have to pee like a racehorse, and I bet you do, too." BeBée headed for the toilet, dropped her shorts, and proved she was right. "When you're fixed up, we'll get into the luncheon and see if the news of your arrival has found its way to Mitzi."

With awful irony, Rowan said, "Let the festivities begin."

15

AS SOON AS Rowan stepped through the door into the luncheon, she saw what BeBée meant about a throne room. This place had been built along the lines of a Hollywood-inspired medieval castle set. The walls were stone, and the floor was a dark textured hardwood. The arched ceiling rose fully twenty feet above their heads with massive walnut trusses stretching from side to side. Two long white-linen-covered tables stretched along the side walls with seating on one side only, facing into the room. At the back wall on a raised dais stood two chairs, one a black leather-upholstered chair that managed to look imposing and comfortable at the same time. Beside it was a similar chair, smaller and more delicate, but imposing nevertheless. Torval had seated his self-important rump on the throne chair. Joe stood on a lower step, speaking with him. Everyone else stood around, looking uncomfortable or furious or famished depending on their dispositions.

Not that anybody in the gathering of forty was complaining out loud; instead, a low buzz of conversation developed as the newcomers shared the story of what happened in the portico. Word spread that Rowan Winterbourne had arrived on Joe Grantham's arm, and those who didn't know the portent of that got a brief lesson in past events mixed with speculation about what could happen next.

"Uh-oh," BeBée muttered. "Daddy's in a mood. He won't let anybody eat until the assembly has gathered."

"The assembly?"

"Everybody who's expected. That's you and me. The kitchen staff will be holding the meal, and that makes Chef unhappy."

"You care what the chef and kitchen staff think?" Rowan asked.

"Who do you supposesupervises this household? Not Mitzi, my dear. She's too important. It's all me."

Rowan viewed BeBée with renewed respect. "Wow... You know you could make a fortune as a housekeeper for the rich and famous."

BeBée smiled, the picture of self-satisfaction. "I've got bigger plans than that."

"At last, here they are," Torval announced.

Joe saw Rowan and started toward her at once, hand outstretched. "Darling, I was getting worried."

"No need for that." She put her fingers in his and wished instead she could slap him for putting her into this situation. "We were freshening up."

He examined her face closely and lowered his voice. "Do you always freshen up in your own tears?"

Rowan looked around the great hall, imagined Lorenze standing in the middle of the floor leaning on his cane, upright and clear-minded, and she wanted to cry again. "As needed."

Torval sternly demanded an accounting. "BeBée, where have you been?"

"In the ladies' room. Rowan fell in love with all the toiletries you stock, and we started comparing makeup, and—" she shrugged using her signature voluptuous roll "—you know how it is when we girls start talking!"

Rowan couldn't believe the way BeBée used her sexuality to pacify Torval, manipulate the situation, make herself—and Rowan—into unknowing innocents. BeBée's actions were deliberate, brilliantly timed and admirable in a horrific 1950s housewife sort of way. Rowan wanted to object, yet BeBée was outmaneuvering everybody, especially Gregory Torval. How could Rowan have improved on BeBée's tactics?

She couldn't.

BeBée gestured toward the wings, where a uniformed staff member stood waiting, then mounted the dais and curled her hand into Torval's arm. "Come and eat, Daddy. You know how grumpy you are when you're hungry. You'll scare everybody!"

That was an understatement. As he stood, half of the assemblage took a step back.

Not Joe, of course. He seemed unfazed by any of this. In a low, intimate voice, he asked Rowan, "Do you feel up to lunch here in the great hall?"

"I'm fine."

"Because I can arrange for us to go to our rooms now so you can recline and nap. I know I kept you awake far too late last night."

Which he had, although not in the sexual way he insinuated. Once was no big deal, right? Yet Rowan noted the people around them edging closer to eavesdrop, and her smile felt more like a snarl. "I'd like to eat and get to know the other guests."

"Whatever you wish." He looked around, and the guests edged back again.

Rowan watched as the uniformed wait staff struggled to carry a heavy, elaborately carved wood table to the center of the room in front of the dais. With swift motions, they covered it with a white linen tablecloth. The two long tables on the sides were carried over to form a U shape, and the throne was carried to the center point of the head table. Chairs were moved into place along the long tables. The wait staff showed swift, meticulous precision as they placed chargers, utensils and glasses at every place.

Rowan felt as if she'd fallen into an episode of *Downton Abbey.*

BeBée escorted Torval to the throne at the head table, and as he lowered himself, she indicated the guests should find their name cards and seats. That operation happened with admirable efficiency, and when it was done, Joe was seated at Torval's right hand and Rowan beside him. BeBée sat on Torval's left hand and discreetly directed the staff who brought out plates each covered by one mammoth muffuletta sandwich and cup of gumbo. Pitchers of iced tea were placed in easy reach, and Torval filled his own glass. "One of my favorite meals," he proclaimed, by which Rowan knew during these three days, any gluten-free needs or aversions to meats were to be brushed aside and silently dealt with. Everyone would eat what Torval preferred.

Luckily for Rowan, the morning had given her an appetite, and a brief sojourn in New Orleans had given her a taste for Cajun. She listened to the conversations with one ear and polished off the gumbo and one quarter of the mighty muffuletta.

The talk between Torval and Joe and two of the men at this end of the table seemed to confirm Joe was in the running to be Torval's closest associate and successor. Joe knew far too much about the operations for someone who was merely a mercenary searching for an address book. That worried her; the more important Joe was perceived, the more likely he'd be taken out by someone who felt threatened by him, and in any way possible— and she along with him. Her role was as distraction, not casualty.

As Rowan contemplated that grim fact, the double doors to the great hall slammed open.

Silence descended like a blackout curtain.

A woman dressed in black with a mourning veil over her face stepped into a room of wide-eyed anticipation and wary breathlessness.

The woman paused to allow the effect to grip the hall. Her tactic worked well; Rowan's first, last and middle reaction was *uh-oh*. She leaned back far enough to see behind Joe and Torval's backs; BeBée gave her an anguished look and breathed a gusting sigh.

No doubt about it. This was Mitzi Torval.

16

GREGORY TORVAL CAME to his feet, and as if it had been staged, *everyone* came to their feet. As Rowan rose, she had a fleeting wish that she'd dressed more discreetly. Mitzi would not appreciate competition from any woman, and Rowan sat at the head table.

But too late for regrets.

Two women dressed in identical mourning flanked Mitzi, and as she swept forward, an effigy of outrage, they kept pace with her. She stopped in front of the head table, lifted her veil and stared at Torval in loathing.

She was, as BeBée had said, a striking woman, with pale skin that never saw the sun and contrasted particularly well with her black garb, wild black hair that looked as if she'd been tearing it in fury, and red, red lips. When she spoke, her deep, husky voice trembled with outrage. "Gregory, how dare you welcome into our house this spawn of the devil who killed our son?"

"Now, beloved." Torval used a patronizing tone that Rowan knew would instantly inflame Mitzi, since it irritated *her*. "We agreed that the vengeance we wreaked on Winterbourne's younger daughter and his wife was sufficient, and—"

"I didn't agree!"

"—and as I've just discovered, Rowan isn't even Winterbourne's blood. He's her stepfather."

Mitzi pulled a pistol out of the pocket hidden in her shirt and pointed it at Torval's face. "Her stepfather?" she shrieked. "What do I care whether or not they're blood kin? Rowan Winterbourne is tainted by her proximity to that vile beast, that murderer of children."

Rowan wanted to point out that that child of theirs had killed the Coastie father of two young children and wounded another officer so badly he'd been in the hospital for more than a month. But the weapon swung, and for the second time in less than two hours, Rowan found herself staring at the business end of a pistol.

Shit. This was getting old fast.

She couldn't tear her gaze away from the black hole, as if staring at it would stop the bullet, but as the seconds ticked on and nothing happened, she followed the firearm to the hand, up the arm, and looked into Mitzi's horrified eyes.

Mitzi stared into Rowan's face as if seeing something she had never imagined nor expected. Rowan had neither imagined or expected Mitzi, either, but who in the modern world would conceive of a woman who could play a scene of Shakespearean dimensions in such a theatrical setting?

As Rowan's gaze locked with Mitzi's, Rowan experienced an almost audible click, and she stared into a soul grieved, tormented, vindictive, a soul that delighted in her own madness and its ability to break the powerful man she loathed and loved. The woman lived in turmoil, lived to spread turmoil lusted for blood, and—

And suddenly, Mitzi's eyes sharpened. Her red lips parted, not to scream or curse, but in shock. Some unexpected tidal wave tumbled her into the deep, drowning her in horror. Whatever she saw, whatever it was, erased everything that Mitzi was and loved to be, leaving her mute.

Blessedly mute, Rowan thought. Or—dangerously mute?

Then some raw thrust of will shoved Mitzi back to the surface, back to this place, to the throne room filled with avid eyes. Rowan disappeared from her focus as if she'd never existed. Mitzi snapped the pistol back toward Torval and in a tone of loathing said, "You!"

He held up his hands. "Mitzi, no. It's not what you think."

Mitzi threw back her head and gave a wild burst of laughter.

Her gestures and emotions were so exaggerated, it was like watching a silent movie, but with sound, and at a volume that blasted the ears.

Mitzi waved her weapon around in a half circle, and as on the porch, a fair number of people (smart people) hit the deck. Pulling the pistol back, she again pointed it at Torval, then with a sob declared, "I sacrifice myself for my son!" and pointed the muzzle under her chin. As Torval shouted, "Mitzi, no!" she pulled the trigger.

The weapon clicked on a chamber empty of bullets. Mitzi gave a banshee wail and collapsed, caught only by her quick-moving attendants.

Definitely rehearsed, Rowan thought even as she broke a clammy sweat similar to the one she'd suffered when Torval fired in a rage.

Mitzi's attendants carried her out as she wept in despair and shrieked, "My baby! My only child! Your only son, Torval. How could you? How could you? Betrayal…" The last word wailed down that corridor and hung in the air.

Rowan didn't care to play Joe's games anymore. Not now, not here. She pushed her chair back, declared, "That's it for me! I'm heading for my room," and looked at BeBée. "If someone would show me where it is?"

BeBée gestured her toward the open doors.

As the other guests stared and whispered, Rowan walked around the edge of the great hall and into the corridor.

Before she'd gone ten steps, Joe caught up with her.

"You didn't fling yourself on me to protect me from *that* bullet," she observed acidly.

"When Mitzi made her entrance, Torval assured me the bullets in that gun had been removed."

"We believe him about this because...?"

"Because I had his own pistol pressed into his side during the whole event, and I knew *it* was loaded."

Rowan chuckled without amusement. "I suppose that was sufficient security."

An elderly, bald, formally dressed gentleman with ear tufts hurried toward them. "Mr. Grantham and Miss Winterbourne, I'm Szababos, Mr. Torval's butler. Your luggage awaits you. If you'll follow me, I'll show you the way." As he led them through the corridors and down several elevators, he pointed out the alcoves filled with sculptures and paintings, all subtly lit to highlight their best features. "Mr. Torval has impeccable taste in twentieth century and modern art, and has given me a free hand and a generous budget for the antiquities. Together we have collected quite an admirable display, if I do say so myself."

Rowan vaguely remembered the art from her previous fast flit through the mansion, but now she had time to slow down and enjoy the eccentricities of the pieces. She marveled how well she related to the sculptures Gregory Torval had picked out, and felt vaguely nauseated at connecting with anything he liked.

When they reached the next level, they found men—Rowan hesitated to call them bell staff when they carried pistols—waiting for them with a luggage cart stacked with their bags. She saw with a glance her yellow plastic bag had been searched; whoever had opened it had been unable to repack it correctly, and a wisp of yellow silk had been shut in the latch. She leveled her icy gaze on Szababos. "What happened to my gown?"

"Ah! It looks as if one of the latches must have come loose."
He told the lie glibly; obviously not the first time this had happened. "I'll have it taken down to the seamstress to be inspected,
and of course if there are any issues, it will be mended or re-
placed."

"*I'll* inspect it for issues. I don't need any more *issues* to occur."
She would definitely make the inspection, remove her gown
and hang it, do a repack, lock the bag and put it in the depths of
the closet where, she hoped, it would be out of sight and mind.

"As you wish." Szababos had the guts to sound huffy. "Here's
your suite." He ushered them into their rooms. "You have a
sitting room, bath and bedroom. The bedroom windows face
west, over the narrow part of the island and out to where the
horizon meets the Pacific Ocean." He seemed smug about the
view, as if he'd created it himself.

Rowan walked out on the balcony and gazed, not at the ocean,
but at the path below.

*Kealoha had drawn maps of the Torval estate. She had instructed
Rowan on where Lorenze Winterbourne would be held…and what was
being done to him. She had tested Rowan again and again on what she
should do in any instance, if Rowan failed to quickly get into disguise,
if she was grabbed by one of the men or, God forbid, someone recognized her, in her terror she might forget the script, the path, the need,
and condemn her father to death.*

*Rowan had willingly practiced, for she was terrified. When she
thought of the daunting task ahead, that of rescuing her father from
Gregory Torval's island citadel and from the gleeful, barbaric hands of
his torturer, she desperately wanted not to be chosen for this task.*

*But it had to be her. There was no one else. Mother dead. Sister
vanished. And her father—no, more than her father, her stepfather had
done everything to save her, train her, prepare her. She would bring him
back or die trying.*

Easy words.

Hard task.

She skulked along the path to Doug Moore's hut, dressed in her drab garb designed specifically to make her invisible, accompanied only by the ghosts of those who never returned. She passed through such ridiculously beautiful scenery, she could scarcely believe she trod in the footsteps of broken minds and vanquished souls...until, alone in the silent woods where not even a bird dared sing, she heard the first tortured scream.

A man's scream, high and almost unrecognizable.

But she knew.

Lorenze Winterbourne suffered.

Intolerable.

In a rage, Rowan picked up a tire iron and stalked toward the hut, and did what she had come to do.

And more...

Turning away, she caught Joe watching her.

He must have seen her remembered outrage, for he disappeared into the corridor. He returned almost at once and said, "We'll move across the hall."

"What? What?" Szababos's smile vanished. "But this is our best room. Mr. Torval himself instructed that you be placed here."

"I like the view the other direction better." Joe waved a hand at the bell staff. "We're moving across the hall to, um, to suite 425."

Everybody froze in place.

"This!" Szababos wrung his hands. "Our best room!"

"Move the bags!" Joe commanded.

The staff looked between the flummoxed butler and the hard-faced Joe. They backed the cart up.

Joe ushered Rowan across the hall and through the open door with the brass numbers 425.

The staff followed and placed the luggage on racks in the smaller suite.

"Thank you," Rowan said to them.

Szababos joined them. "Of course, while this suite is smaller, less grand, and was assigned to a different couple—" he obviously couldn't believe his well-ordered plans had been tinkered with "—you do have an eastern view across the Pacific Ocean to the California coast."

Rowan walked to the windows and gazed longingly at the misty blue land on the horizon. "Beautiful."

"If you need anything else, the phone will link you to all the usual departments a grand house will boast. Now we'll leave you—"

She turned to face Joe and Szababos.

"Here." Joe thrust a wad of money at the butler.

"Sir, Mr. Torval's butler has no need to accept tips," Szababos said haughtily.

"It's not for you. Divide it up among the bellboys. Pretty sure they'll take it." Joe shut the door in Szababos's astonished face, and dusted his fingertips. "There. That should place me in their minds."

"Yes. Overtipping is always a good idea. You're the *generous* guest." Rowan went to the king-sized bed and sank down on it. The almost sleepless night was catching up with her. Slowly she reclined on the pillows and closed her eyes. She heard him go into the bathroom and run water.

He placed a cool wet cloth on her forehead.

Rage, unexpected and uncontrollable, slashed through her. She slapped his hand away and threw the washcloth on the floor. "You ass. Don't try that solicitous crap when we're alone." She turned her back to him, tucked the pillow tightly under her chin, and curled her legs up.

Silence. Footsteps as he returned the cloth to the bathroom. A suitcase opening. The clicking of computer keys. Then, "I'm going out."

She rolled over to face him. "To search for the address book?"

"To scope out the territory." He pointed to a small electronic device on the bedside table. "My own casual search found microphones under the base of the lamp, in the floor heat vent, in the curtain fixture. It's safe to assume they're activated. That apparatus is creating a buzz in the line that allows them to hear us speak but not understand us. It's programmed to change the frequency of the buzz, cut in and out, and generally drive their electronics experts wild."

She wouldn't have thought that she could, but she smiled.

"In the meantime, if someone comes into the room and makes conversation, think before you speak."

Who would come in? Why would she speak to them?

Yet this house was run very much like a hotel, and there would be maids who might try to not-so-innocently chat with her. The other female guests, too, could try to advance their men's standing, and thus their own, by convincing her to say something incriminating. So— "Of course."

He put his hands on the mattress, leaned forward and looked into her eyes. "What did you see out the window? In the other room, what did you see?"

She turned back over. "The path to the torture compound."

Silence again. Then, "Torval put us there on purpose."

"Most of the rooms on that side would have that view. He doesn't realize I rescued my father. With what he thinks about women, I don't see why he would even suspect and—sexual equality be damned. In this world, females are weak, the prey. Each man is a king, and Torval is a god. He'd have been a laughingstock if it became known I freed Lorenze. Nothing brings down a crime boss faster than laughter." She was beginning to feel foolish about her outburst. She wasn't sorry. She was glad to set boundaries. But she'd lost control, and that was not the thing to do around Joe. "Thank you for insisting we change suites."

"You bet." The weight of his hands on the mattress lifted. "I spotted a microphone and camera as soon as we walked in that room."

Ah. She hadn't needed to thank Joe. He hadn't changed rooms because of her distress, but to thwart Torval.

"Go to sleep," he said. "I'll be back in time to change for dinner."

Another performance. Another round of pleasantries.

Another firearm in her face?

17

WHEN ROWAN WOKE UP, she had two hours of drool on her pillow and an hour to get ready for the cocktail party. Which normally would be no big deal, but she needed to shower, and while she knew how to apply makeup—Kealoha had taught her that—her self-imposed isolation had not required her to learn speed. On the other hand, she could never compete with BeBée's earthy sensuality or Savannah's graceful beauty.

When she came out of the bathroom wearing her variegated blue silk evening gown, she found Joe in the sitting room, sprawled in the lounge chair.

He leaned forward and clicked his blocking device, then nodded to her.

"Did you find anything?" She went to her jewelry bag and slid her rings on her fingers.

"I did." He looked grimly pleased. "Torval's computer mainframe is on this island."

"Why does that matter?" she asked with a touch of impatience.

"Is this woman's address book contained wholly on Torval's mainframe?"

"Possibly, and possibly I'll find it there. But knowledge is power, and if I don't find the address book, I can find information that can be used as leverage."

She might as well ask. He might not tell her, but…he might. "What are you doing, really? This seems to be so much more than a mercenary mission."

He watched her as she pulled her shoes out of the yellow bag. "Do you always discount the power of emotions so easily?"

"What do you mean?"

"I loved my sister. Money is important, but revenge is sweet."

His sister. Mila Weiss. The grave marker in the cemetery. Rowan had been so engrossed in her own fears and hates, she had forgotten Mila. He sounded calm when he spoke of her, but one night with Joe had taught her his calm hid…more than she wanted to remember.

He was right. Rowan was like all the rest of these people; she thought of no one but herself. But, really, who else was going to think of her? "Do you intend to shoot Torval down in flames?"

"A small conflagration is perhaps all I can manage."

"What are you up to?"

"I've set myself up as Gregory Torval's best, meanest, most likely successor."

"Ah." As she had suspected. When had a mercenary had the time to do that? Uneasy instinct stirred again. "He'll be concentrating on *you*. That's counter to your plan to have *me* distract him."

"Torval is a cold man. The only time he makes a mistake is when he loses that temper. My aim is to bury myself like a tick under his skin and see what kind of mistakes he can make when he's frantic with irritation."

"Do you think keeping his mainframe on this island gives him the illusion of safety?"

"That's exactly what I think."

"It's surely backed up—" she waved a hand "—somewhere."

"I have no doubt. But if utilized correctly, slashing the connection and doubling the time it takes to recover the data could be fatal to Torval's operation." When Joe smiled, he made her realize again how deadly this man might be; probably was.

"That all seems like a lot of extra work to steal an address book."

"That extra work is what makes it fun."

Was Joe really the kind of guy who poked a stick at a sleeping monster for the thrill of the pursuit? Had she once again misread this cool, soft-spoken man?

He stood. "Are you done in the bathroom? We don't want to be late tonight."

"Why not? You haven't cared before."

"Never establish a pattern. You know that."

"I do." She picked up her clutch. "Hurry then."

When Joe and Rowan walked early into the cocktail reception, only Torval and Szababos stood on the terrace. They appeared to be holding an intense conversation. At once, Szababos bowed himself out of the way, moving backward as if afraid to turn his back on Joe.

Joe watched and said to Torval, "I hope your butler wasn't too unnerved by our room change."

"I told him you were a wild card and he should expect the unexpected." Torval took Rowan's hand and looked searchingly into her eyes. "Are you comfortable? After this afternoon's traumatic events, that's what matters."

Considering he was the one who had been responsible for the afternoon's traumatic events *and* his earlier sexual offer, his avuncular tones made Rowan's stomach churn. "As long as Joe is close, I'm most comfortable, thank you." She tried to withdraw her hand.

Torval tightened his grip. "These are interesting rings." He stared at the collection of silver, gold, platinum and stones.

"Thank you."

He took her other hand and examined those rings, too. "I don't know of any other woman who could wear so many so well. Unique. I have seen one like this before." He touched the thin, worn silver band set with a miniscule blue stone. "It reminds me of someone I knew long ago."

She yanked at her hands. How dare he touch her mother's ring with his cruel, corpulent finger?

He released her. "It's such a beautiful day I decided to move the reception outside. Do you approve?"

Rowan looked around. The decorative paved terra-cotta terrace hung over the steep hillside, with handsome stone railings high enough to protect against a fall, and low enough to facilitate a shove. On either side of the terrace, two long tables of hot and cold appetizers awaited the guests. In the three corners, bartenders waited to pour drinks. A dozen tall round dining tables had been placed close against the house, but there was no seating. The message was clear: guests were to mingle.

The only odd note, and to Rowan's mind it was very odd, was the two pool tables holding center court. She supposed, as with the food choices at lunch, that Torval liked pool. Therefore, without care for anyone else's desires, pool would be played. "Very nice," she said politely.

Servers arrived carrying a table and all the accoutrements to set up a champagne fountain.

Joe confiscated a bottle, popped the cork, poured two flutes and offered one to Rowan and one to Torval. When Torval took it, he poured another glass for himself and lifted his flute in a toast. "Here's to Gregory Torval, the founder of California's most successful crime operation!"

"You are too kind." Torval patently didn't mean it.

Everyone sipped.

"We don't like to call it crime," Torval said. "Merely a redis-
tribution of wealth based on rules of fair play."

"Whose rules?" Joe asked.

"Mine, dear boy. All mine." Torval picked up a cue and gestured at the pool table. "Do you play?" Interestingly enough,
he looked at Rowan rather than Joe.

Probably because he figured he could crush a woman.

"I do. I'm good. Hustling is how I put myself through trade
school." Clear warning, she figured.

"Are you interested in a game of eight ball?" Torval signaled
toward the dim interior of the game room.

"Standard rules." She wanted no mistake about that. She
glanced at Joe. "Will you play?"

He warily eyed them both. "No, thanks. You two go at it,
and may the best man win."

Szababos appeared with two of Torval's bouncers; the men
pushed a rack of cues while Szababos paced majestically beside
them, a silver tray tucked under his arm.

"Pick your cue," Torval said.

She placed her glass on the tray Szababos offered, handled
the cues, and chose one of a good length that was weighted,
well-balanced and with a diameter that felt right in her hand.
She sighted down it, then rolled it on the table; it was always
a good idea to make sure the cue was straight, but in this case,
she was also making sure the table held no surprises. Not that
she didn't trust Torval…but she didn't trust Torval. She chalked
the tip, smaller and harder than the standard, and watched as
Torval racked the balls.

"You break." Torval wore a shit-eating grin, and that made
her want to crush him.

18

"OF COURSE. Please remember, I warned you." Rowan leaned into the table, lined up her shot and took the break shot. The nine and fifteen balls spun away and into two pockets. She called the next shot, and banked the eleven ball in the corner pocket. "Stripes are mine," she said.

Torval's eyebrows lifted.

She had to hand it to him: he did not call her lucky.

Three balls down. Some easy shots, of course. There were always easy shots. But some of the shots would require multiple banks, spins, kisses. She stood quietly and thought her way through her strategy.

"Worried?" Torval removed his jacket and rolled up his sleeves.

"No." She called the next two balls, and down they went. She had no way to complete another shot, so she called an absurd shot, placed two balls as obstructively as possible for him, and stepped back.

Torval called his first shot and sank the ball.

She glanced around. While she played, it was her gift to shut out distractions, and now she realized the other guests had arrived and stood around the table three deep, watching and murmuring. Cash and notes surreptitiously changed hands, and she wondered who was foolish enough to bet against Torval.

Torval, who called his second shot and sank the ball.

Joe had managed to obtain a bar stool, and he sat, sipping from not a champagne flute but a drinking glass of clear liquid. Water. Their eyes met, and he grinned as if he had the best seat in the house. Which he did; the only seat in the house.

Elbow cocked on his shoulder, BeBée leaned on him and shook her head at Rowan. "You live to make trouble, girl."

"I didn't start it." Rowan looked around. "What happened to my champagne?"

BeBée tapped on her watch, and Szababos appeared at Rowan's side with a fresh flute filled to the top.

All right. A new glass every time. Seemed a waste, but Rowan was merely a peasant in the palace. What did she know? "Thank you."

Torval called his shot and sank the third ball. As she suspected, he played well. But her artfully placed obstructions now gave him pause. Bristling with suspicion, he glared at her.

She lifted her glass to him. *Take that, asshole.*

On the landing strip below, a private plane revved its motor. Like everyone on the deck, she watched it ascend, buzz the house and fly toward the coast. When she looked back at Torval, he was scrutinizing her as if he could see her as she really was, stripped of this pretense as a mistress and prepared at all times to flee, to fight, to survive at all costs. The change from pissed-off game player to insightful villain signaled something… but what? She couldn't imagine.

Torval's attention returned to the table, and he called and flubbed the next shot.

Szababos was nowhere to be seen, so Joe took her glass. "We've played long enough, don't you think?" she said to Torval. "You have your guests to entertain."

"They are entertained." He shot a hard look around, and at once the betting and exchange of bills ceased. "You know you're supposed to let me win, right?"

"Do you wish that?" she asked.

"No." But his jaw clenched tightly.

She called each ball, sank each ball, and that cleared the stripes off the table. While she lined up the eight ball, she smiled at Torval. "I can still throw the game," she said, "if that's what you want."

"Did your father teach you to play?" It wasn't an answer, but he had made her decision for her.

"Eight ball in the corner pocket." She pointed with her cue, made sure Torval acknowledged the shot, and sank the ball.

She had more than won; she'd crushed Gregory Torval, and the applause was scattered, uncertain and fearful. Joe pushed off the stool as if getting to his feet to block another outburst of Torval's cinematic temper.

Yet Gregory Torval didn't move. He held his cue and stared at Rowan as if he couldn't believe what had just happened.

She looked into his stunned eyes, and gave an unnecessary explanation, one designed to enlighten and enrage. "My mother was born with an innate ability to visualize the shots in her head, and in some small part, so was I. With that gift, good pool is merely a matter of training and technique. So to sum up—my mother taught me to play pool, and I just competed against the man who murdered her. And I trounced him." With great precision, she placed the cue on the table. "As if that matters. She's still dead, and you're still the most worthless little prick in California."

In unison, the guests took a shocked breath and stepped away.

Rowan turned her back on Torval and walked away.

19

THE SILENT CROWD parted to let Rowan through.

Joe made to follow her.

BeBée put her hand on his shoulder. "I'll do it. She won't want you." The crowd parted for BeBée, too, and guests pointed the way Rowan had gone. It wasn't hard to figure out her location; the second ladies' room down the corridor was shut, and from inside, BeBée heard the sound of objects smacking into walls, fixtures and each other. A furious sobbing. And breaking glass. BeBée tapped on the door. "Rowan? Let me in. Rowan?"

Silence. A long moment. The lock clicked, the door opened a crack, and Rowan's swollen red eyes peered out. "What do you want?" She was hostile, angry.

"To help you break some more bottles."

Rowan considered that sullenly. Then, "Okay."

"You have to step back," BeBée warned, and pressed her hand to the door.

Rowan's eyes disappeared.

BeBée slipped through the smallest crack in the door any human being could manage.

The bathroom was a wreck. It looked as if Rowan had started by throwing the silver filigree containers of cotton swabs, soaps and lotions, and when that wasn't enough, she overturned the three-tiered glass-shelved cart. Individually wrapped rolls of toilet paper, glass shards, cotton balls and cosmetics lay scattered across the floor. Some galactic sense of humor had placed a sealed tampon on the closed toilet lid.

BeBée whistled. "I would have never expected you to do something like this."

"It was my first time."

"Not even Mitzi could have done it better," BeBée assured her.

"I simply cannot believe—" Rowan's voice began to waver "—that even for a second I forgot what Torval had done to my mother."

BeBée got serious in a hurry. "You didn't forget. You concentrated on beating the snot out of him in front of everybody. Everybody will remember your cool composure forever. You're now a legend."

"I don't care!" Rowan broke down in renewed weeping, and this time there was no fury, only sorrow.

BeBée found a sealed box of tissues—no glass that way—opened it and offered it to Rowan. Rowan took a dozen, bent her face into the wad and sobbed and choked and tried to muffle the noise while BeBée put her arm around Rowan's shoulders and hugged her. After a tough ten minutes, Rowan's grief began to ease, and BeBée said, "I guess it's true. You never stop missing your mother."

Rowan nodded, threw the tissues at the overturned trash can, and took another wad. In between smaller, hiccupping sobs, she asked, "What about your mother?"

"I didn't have a mother. I had a series of stepmothers. Some of them were okay. Some of them...wait a minute." BeBée picked up a sanitized drinking glass and flung it against the far wall. She dusted her fingers. "There. I enjoyed that. Two of my stepmothers liked to abuse children. One was an alcoholic who locked me in the car while she went into a bar. It was over one hundred degrees, and a passing policeman saved my life. One was a drug addict; when I was nine, she drove me to Mexico to sell me. Even my father saw the problem with that."

"Oh, dear friend." Rowan leaned her head on BeBée's shoulder. "We are a pair."

"Ain't it the truth?" Taking Rowan by the hand, BeBée led her to the sink and squirted facial cleanser into her palm. "Wash your face. Your beautiful self-applied lashes are matted, and that's not waterproof mascara you applied."

"No." Rowan looked in the mirror at her own red, blotchy face with its dark-rimmed bloodshot eyes. "No, not waterproof. I also didn't think I'd do anything tonight other than stand around and look pretty."

"That's your job after dinner."

Rowan moaned. "Do I have to go back?"

"After that magnificent rout—" BeBée gestured toward the patio "—are you going to turn tail and run?"

Rowan had to think about it.

"You can't leave Joe to do whatever the heck he's doing all by himself," BeBée warned.

"I'm not quite sure what he's doing but...yes, I'll go back. Let it be noted that I don't want to!"

"Atta girl." BeBée rubbed Rowan's neck. "We women have to stick together. You know, except when we stab each other in the back."

As BeBée intended, Rowan laughed, then turned on the cold water and started to work. Behind her, she heard someone tapping on the door. BeBée opened it a crack, and a furious whispering ensued. Rowan finished and, shook out a hand towel. and as she dried her face, she turned.

BeBée held the door open a crack, and at various heights, three female faces pressed against it. BeBée said, "It's Savannah, Kumara and Li. They want to help. Is that okay?"

"I guess." Rowan pressed the damp rag against her cheeks.

"Good, because nobody's better with cosmetics repair than Li." BeBée opened the door enough to allow the three women to ease inside, then shut and locked it behind them. "It's a makeup emergency."

The three women examined Rowan's face and tsked.

"I've got rose blossom refreshing spray." Savannah reached into her bag. "That'll ease the red and bring down the swelling."

"I've got aloe healing spray." Kumara whipped a small bottle out of her clutch. "It really works."

"Mine works better!" Savannah held hers up.

"Just because it's more expensive doesn't mean it's better!" Kumara glared.

Rowan couldn't believe it. *Makeup wars.*

"Don't tell me. You know I'm the cry expert," Savannah said.

Rowan blinked at BeBée.

"Savannah was a child actress," BeBée explained. "Tears on demand, that was her specialty." She turned to the others. "Tell you what. Savannah, you spray the left side of Rowan's face. Kumara, you spray the right side. We'll compare. It's science!"

Everyone's face lit up.

"Rowan, shut your eyes," Li instructed.

Rowan did, and got blasted by two different kinds of mist. When she opened her eyes, the four women were staring fixedly at her. No, not at her, at her skin.

"They're both good, but the aloe's a little ahead."

Savannah looked at her bottle in disgust. "I'll make a note."

"I know you will." Li picked up a medium-sized latched box that lay sideways on the floor and popped it open.

Rowan could see an array of small bottles with different names ranging from alabaster to dawn to sandalwood to espresso. Foundations, she realized. Li picked one out, held it up to Rowan's chin, shook her head, picked out another and tested it on Rowan's jawbone. She stepped back to let the others look, and at their murmur of agreement, she went to work. She never had to ask for anything; these women understood her unspoken commands and found what she needed among the chaos on the floor. She moisturized, sponged, brushed, smeared and painted, and less than ten minutes later, she stepped back. "What do you think?"

Rowan turned toward the mirror to look.

Li stopped her. "Not you."

"You're a master," Kumara breathed.

"You can make me up anytime," Savannah agreed.

"BeBée?" Li asked.

"Perfect, except the eyes are overdone. She's tall and thin and has that hunter look down to a T. Let's step it back a little." BeBée took a sponge and worked on the corners of Rowan's eyes and her lids, then lightly added color with a brush.

"That's good. But a hunter has to have a mouth to tear at its prey. Here." Taking up a box of pencils and a flat of bloodred stain, Li outlined and painted Rowan's lips.

The three women nodded.

"Savannah, what about her hair?" Li air-touched the strands around Rowan's face.

Savannah studied Rowan the way the other women studied Rowan—clinically, as if she were a mannequin—then pronounced, "Leave it. We don't want her to go back in with all signs of trauma erased. They don't have to know they made her cry, not this time, but we want those bastards to know what they've done, what they do."

BeBée and Li nodded.

Kumara looked doubtful.

"What do you think?" BeBée asked.

Rowan realized that for the first time, someone was actually talking *to* her, that *she* was finally invited to look in the mirror. When she did, it was the actual Cinderella moment. "Whoa." She was Rowan, but a Vaseline-on-the-lens Rowan, a dangerous-to-every-mate Rowan.

The Hunter Rowan.

How had these women seen who she was beneath her skin? How had they known why she'd returned to the West Coast close enough to see Raptor Island? How had they sensed what vengeance she plotted in the dark hours of the night?

She looked at them, the cluster of women so different from her, and experienced the bonding of sisterhood.

Li shook her finger at Rowan. "Girl, if you don't start wearing sunscreen every day all day, when you're eighty…you're going to look eighty."

Meekly, Rowan asked, "What brand should I use?"

A squabble broke out about serum sunscreen versus moisturizer sunscreen versus foundation sunscreen that continued through the door, down the corridor and back to the reception. There Rowan discovered that being part of that group meant that the attention that guests paid to her was diffused by the flutter of gowns and bestowing of smiles. The four women walked her over to Joe, who took her hand and pulled her close. "Thank you," he said to them.

They smiled seductively, as if being close to a man required seduction, and BeBée said, "You betcha. Now I've got to go find Szababos and tell him to send someone to clean that restroom. Rowan wrecked it! When she starts throwing things, you better duck."

"Advice I'll remember," he said.

"Where's Daddy?" BeBée craned her neck.

Savannah, who stood a good eight inches taller than BeBée, indicated a clump of men at the north end of the deck. "He's in the middle there."

"I'll check on him and his ego. I've never seen him lose at pool before." BeBée tapped Rowan on the arm. "You're supposed to let him win, you know."

"So I've been told," Rowan replied.

BeBée grinned, hurried over and elbowed her way into the center.

Savannah said, "Wadell is trying to get his attention. I'd better go help him. He's nothing without me, and how he hates that!"

As she glided off, in an undertone Kumara said, "Poor Savannah. She never gets laid."

Joe leaned in. "What?"

Li shook her head at Kumara.

"I probably shouldn't have said anything..." Clearly, Kumara relished the gossip. "But Wadell is married. He has a husband. With Gregory Torval being stuck in the twentieth century, Wadell can't bring a guy here, so Savannah fills in. But there's no security in that, not for her."

"Information that is good to know." Joe leaned back, his face smooth and without expression.

"Remember, Rowan," Li warned sternly, "sunscreen!" She dragged Kumara away, speaking in an angry whisper.

Joe kept his arm around Rowan. "BeBée wouldn't let me follow you. What happened?"

"I had a girlfriend initiation." She felt dazed, as if she'd fallen into a teen movie.

BeBée hurried back past them. "Forgot to pee while I was in the restroom!" she called, and headed into the corridor again.

Joe chuckled.

Rowan shut her eyes and sighed. Knowing BeBée was like being around a beguiling and far-too-honest five-year-old.

When she opened her eyes, Joe was staring fixedly at her face. "Do you like my makeup?" she asked.

"You always look great." If his tone was anything to go by, Joe couldn't have cared less.

That tone made her wonder if that was the case—that the one night had been enough for him, and now he didn't give a damn about her. Why would he? How could he? Had he ever? His only intention in visiting her lighthouse was to use her as a diversion, and he'd blackmailed her to get his way.

Yet with his arm around her and his solicitous air, it felt like caring.

What did she know about him? Just because they'd had sex...

He could be the kind of man who banged every knothole in the tree. *Face it, girl, most men will take sex if it's offered.* She had offered, he had taken, and it was only the memory of her slaughtered mother and her current emotional frailty that had sent her down this meandering road of useless reflection.

"What are you thinking?" he asked.

She smiled up into his face. She was here to act as if she adored him, and if he could pretend concern, she didn't have to pretend to believe him. "I was thinking...that you're a lying swindler mercenary who'll do anything to get ahead."

His hand tightened on her shoulder, not painfully, but to steer her out into the hallway and around a few corners into a place empty of any other guests. He looked around, and when he was satisfied, he got in her face. His smooth expression had been transformed. In a quiet voice vibrating with ferocity, he said, "Our time here would be much less fraught if you would let up with the constant low-level viperous hatred."

She took incredible pleasure in saying, "Not going to happen. It didn't mean anything to you, nothing but another fuck, but I don't give myself lightly." Why was she saying this, telling him the truth as if he'd give a damn? But she couldn't shut up. "If you'd refrained from taking what was offered, my level of loathing would be considerably lower, and your level of comfort would be—"

He grabbed her arms, pulled her against him.

His eyes were hot, angry...wanting. "I don't need *comfort*. I need *you*. We're here at the edge of the world, at the precipice of civilization, in danger so thick I can hear it buzzing in my ears, and am I smart enough to be thinking ahead, planning our moves? No. All I can imagine is how I would take you anytime, anywhere. Every moment, I'm watching you, waiting for you to offer it up again. Every moment, I plan how I'll fuck you next. Up against the wall. In front of the fireplace. From the back. Missionary style. In that chair." He gestured.

She glanced at the chair, a massive, carved medieval work of art. Then his compelling voice dragged her gaze back to him.

"I remember how you tasted, like ultimate female." He brought her up on her toes so they were pressed together from chest to groin. "And listen, woman, I intend to taste you again. For minutes, hours, until you come so often you're limp and barely moving. Slow…so slow… Then I'll slide my dick into you and bring you back to clawing, screaming life. When we were on your bed and you were under me, that was all-out full-throttle sex. Your scent, your heat, the way your cunt sucked at me, your screams… You couldn't hold back. I didn't hold back. I gave you everything, and I'm keeping everything you gave me. Make no mistake. Next time it won't be one time. We're going to have sex so often, forever after there won't be a moment that you forget me and what it's like when I'm inside you. You're going to long for me all the time, come to me wet and willing, and I'll fuck you again. It's never going to stop. Not for you. Not for me. We're going to be a hundred years old and still going at it like rabbits. Think about *that* while you're hating me." He put her back from his body. "You want me again? All you have to do is say *please*." He gradually loosened his grip, as if the process of letting her go took all his control, all his effort, and walked in the opposite direction of the party.

20

ROWAN STARED AFTER HIM, slack-jawed.

She heard a whimper behind her. She whipped around and found herself staring at BeBée in the doorway of a restroom, dabbing her damp, dewy face with a white towel.

BeBée stared back, wide-eyed. "Wow," she said. "My panties are drenched."

"I didn't know you even wore panties." Rowan's bitchy response lacked the appropriate emotion.

BeBée snickered.

Rowan didn't know why she felt obliged to stammer an explanation, but she couldn't seem to keep it back. "H-he wasn't like that when we had sex. What he said—he wasn't like that. He was good, I mean, you know—"

BeBée got an expression of indulgent wisdom on her cherubic face. "I know."

"—but sort of…underplayed. Nonaggressive. He acted like I was in charge."

"All that means is he was smart enough to get you to fuck him without alarming you at his intensity. If things were different, he would have slowly upped the ante. As it is, he's manipulating Torval and the other guys, juggling all those figurative balls in the air, he has a limited amount of time to do whatever the hell he's doing here…and you must have really pissed him off to get that—" BeBée jerked her thumb in the direction Joe had headed "—reaction. So now you know what you're up against. If you know what I mean." BeBée gave Rowan a figurative tip of the hat. "I suspect you'll be going after Joe, saying *please*—"

"No, I won't!" Did BeBée think she had no pride?

"Right…" BeBée imbued that single word with all the doubt in the world, and headed back toward the deck. Ten steps. Then she stopped, swiveled and pointed an admonishing finger at Rowan. "See you in the morning for the workout. Remember, in the gym, nine a.m. sharp!"

The last two days had been one stunner after another, but Rowan hadn't lost her mind. She hadn't signed up for a class. Sure, the consorts were required to keep in shape; it was part of the job. Rowan worked out six days a week, so no problem there, either. But a *class*? "I work out alone."

"Not here you don't. Required attendance. Mitzi is in charge."

"In charge?"

"She's the teacher." BeBée's smile was pained. "If you don't show up, well…speculation might start about you and Joe and what kind of lover he is, and someone might suggest that he kept you up all night doing the horizontal mambo—"

"You wouldn't!'

"Trust me, you don't want to face all those reactions at lunch. So…see you in the morning." BeBée twinkled her fingers at Rowan and sauntered away.

"I am truly tired of being blackmailed," Rowan announced to the empty corridor.

From down the hall and behind the drapes, one of Torval's armed guards materialized. "What?"

She stared at him, turned and walked in the opposite direction.

Had she doubted that Torval had ears everywhere? No more. At least the guard had been far enough away he hadn't heard Joe…she hoped, and tried to dispel the image of a group of Torval's avid bouncers listening in on Joe's sexual tirade.

She caught sight of herself in a gilt-framed mirror hanging behind a swirling blue glass art piece representing…wind? Somehow, Joe had managed to clear her disguise of consort and replace it with a woman of fire and passion. The men here noticed Rowan as if she was nothing but a sum of her body, her face, her clothes and cosmetics, but trailing pheromones with every step, they would pay her far too much attention, and all the wrong kind. She wasn't going back to that den of murderers and thieves looking like…this.

Where could she go?

BeBée was right. Rowan couldn't go back to the reception. She could go after Joe…

In her head, she heard his voice: *All you have to do is say please.*

No. She stopped. She wasn't that far gone. She should go back, mingle with the guests, have some pride, prove to Joe he couldn't manipulate her like that, with heat pouring off his body and lust igniting his every word and—

To hell with pride. She was too fevered to care about anything but sex…with Joe. Damn it. *Damn him.* She might hate him, but by God, he was right. She hadn't had a lot of experience, but that night was better than the best. It was a mating; she didn't dare yield again because the second time would convince him that she was willing to take his terms and—

She looked down at the massive chair that acquired such sexual connotations and laughed a little.

Yield? The first time she hadn't yielded. She had initiated. Now she had memories she couldn't erase, a bond she couldn't sever, and yes, drenched panties.

Where should she go? What should she do?

She should search the rooms of Torval's hotel/mansion and find the address book, of course. Once she did that, she could get off Raptor Island and back to her life…which would include another flight to an uncertain refuge.

Aware that cameras watched her every move, she wandered casually along, stopping at each painting, each sculpture, not critiquing, but liking them or not liking them.

Here and there maps were posted on the walls, providing directions to the public areas and, of course, stairwells and elevators.

As she walked farther and farther, away from the reception, she was running on her gut, her feelings. She entered every open room: a small dining room with still lifes of baskets filled with fruit and flowers, the gym where she would join a class at nine sharp, decorated with marble statues that looked both Greek and ancient, and were probably both. The library.

The library… As with everything in Torval's domain, it was the largest, the best, the most impressive. It was Disney's *Beauty and the Beast* on steroids: floor to twenty-foot ceiling walnut wood shelves packed with books of every description, a glassed-off and locked section of first editions, library ladders and warm secluded reading nooks. And paintings and statues of humans and fairies and elves and dragons reading in chairs, on couches, the forest, on mountaintops. The room was awesome and charming—and accentuated the desperation of the search for the lady's address book, if that address book was indeed paper.

One small item caught Rowan's attention. A silly bit of precious porcelain shaped like a dragon, dressed as a knight, prepared to take on all the shadows that threatened in the dark. She stared at it, and stared at it, and felt a pang of old loss and memory…and moved on.

Remembering that…would break her.

Overwhelmed, Rowan crept out of the library and into a tech room decorated with computers: the first Mac, a Commodore, an IBM PC. A room filled with arcade games and a massive LEGO sculpture created as a recreation of Raptor Island replete with tunnels, ridges, and beaches. She smiled as she traced the tiny figures until she stumbled upon a path that led to the cottage where her father had been tortured. A red stain seemed to seep across the threshold, and she wondered whose warped sense of humor had created this horror.

Almost running, she left the game room and realized her prayer to be released from her Joe-generated desire had been successfully and atrociously fulfilled. Painful memories populated her mind, and she turned back the way she had come... so she thought.

She realized she had gone wrong when she was passing closed doors—guest rooms, she supposed—and no one was anywhere in sight. The hallways were silent. Her fascination with the art had led her to that gruesome LEGO sculpture, and her horror at that discovery had led her deep into the house where she was very alone. For all that this house seemed more of a hotel than a home, in this area, no maps existed to guide her out. The decor here was dramatic: sooty blacks, bloodreds, gold leaf. The sconces flickered as if lit by candles. The art had been chosen with and lit by the same theatrical flair. The landscapes thrashed in the hands of wild nature. The statues writhed with torment. The portraits...

The portrait that caught her attention was just that—an oil portrait, large, beautifully framed, a dark-haired youth posed with one hand on a large dog's head, the other on a pile of leather-bound books. By its composition and style, Rowan at first thought the painting historical, eighteenth-century perhaps. The artist had worked hard to make the subject a person of interest, but the subject was nothing but a callow, sneering, privileged boy. Maybe that was what the artist intended, that the viewer recognize this adolescent as a caricature of arrogant young manhood.

Then Rowan saw what she had missed, that obvious clue: this teen wore a man's dark suit tailored to flatter, a crisp white shirt and a red tie with both ends dangling from beneath the collar. Looking closer into the background, she saw a desk with a monitor and keyboard and beyond that, a window where the ocean crashed against the rocks. Startled, she turned her gaze back to the boy's face and saw something she recognized. His eyes...

A door across the hall jerked open.

Rowan swung to face Mitzi Torval dressed in a floor-length black chiffon robe with drapey sleeves.

As Mitzi recognized her, her eyes kindled with rage. She lifted her arm. "You!" She pointed her skinny index finger at Rowan. "What are you doing here?"

"I got lost."

"Likely story." Mitzi advanced on her, that finger still stuck out.

Rowan noted the nail was long, red and filed to a point. It focused her attention; she barely noticed Mitzi's two cronies in the door watching her. That did not bode well, nor did the fact Rowan was forcibly reminded of every wicked witch the world of Hollywood had ever brought to life.

"You were looking at him!" The finger swerved away from Rowan's face and toward the portrait on the wall.

"Yes. I was."

"Do you know who that is?" Mitzi's voice rose.

Rowan had a pretty good idea. The boy's eyes matched Gregory Torval's. "Your son."

"My son." Mitzi tapped her chest with her finger. "My son. You dared look at him with your corrupted gaze, gloating over his death."

Rowan suspected the smart thing to do was disengage, but she couldn't stand to be unjustly accused. Possibly more important, she refused to turn her back on Lady Macbeth. "I did not."

"You stand there, Winterbourne's daughter, beside his likeness. Winterbourne, who killed him!"

Rowan's own temper flamed. She took a step toward Mitzi. "How dare you malign my father? Your son's death is *your* fault. Did you never teach your son not to point a weapon at an officer of the law?"

Mitzi's companions gasped.

Mitzi stared at Rowan, crumpled the front of her shirt in her fist, tilted her head back and looked from underneath her lowered lids as if seeing something she hated. Then— "My son…" Mitzi's despairing wail vibrated with melodrama. Turning, she collapsed into her sycophants' arms.

"Shove off. Go!" one of them hissed at Rowan.

Rowan looked up and down the corridor.

"That way!" The companion pointed left.

Rowan went even though she half expected she'd been sent to a cliff over the ocean.

21

ROWAN PASSED A WINDOW, looked outside at the well-lit grounds, and got her bearings. She found an elevator, descended to the right level, and walked down the corridor toward her room. Their room. Suite 425, the room she and Joe shared. Remembering what had happened this evening—her triumph over Gregory Torval, her loss of control in the restroom, the women who had come to her rescue, her reproach to Joe and his...his resounding response—she didn't know what she would do if Joe was inside. What would she say to a man who had declared his intentions so bluntly and explicitly? Her belly clenched. He had said she should say *please*, and damned if she would, but they shared the suite and, one supposed, a bed? What were the social mores of that?

The last couple of years in the lighthouse had been watchful, but relatively tranquil, and she realized now she'd lost her edge; those quick responses to crisis had slowed. Or perhaps after so many years of being alone, this abrupt plunge into a ambitious, half-crazed mass of humanity had shocked her emotionally.

Or she could stop lying to herself and admit Joe was beastly sexy, and his declaration had dragged her from cool, still watchfulness into a maelstrom of seething heated volcanic deep molten…oh, God. Her tour of the art and her meeting with Mitzi had…dried her panties, as it were, and yet she'd managed to put herself back in the mood with nothing but a memory of his face as he spelled out his intentions.

Maybe he wouldn't be in the suite. Hopefully.

Yet as soon as she set foot inside, Joe clicked on the microphone disrupter and stood. He'd been sitting across the room in a chair facing the door, and he hurriedly said, "I apologize for speaking to you the way I did."

"What?" She had been braced for a lot of things, but not that.

"No excuses. I understand the word *no*. I understand consent. I understand words have the power to intimidate. Let me assure you, I'm not going to rape you or pressure you."

"No, I didn't think that you—"

"No matter what I think or feel, a man doesn't speak to a woman the way I spoke to you. It's unforgiveable, especially in these circumstances where you're bravely facing the man who murdered your mother and hurt your father, and the danger here is so thick you could choke on it with every breath."

"That's true, but—"

"I would offer to ask for a different room, but that would send the wrong message to the men here, and you'd be…" his fists slowly closed "…required to defend yourself. I've electronically inspected this suite. They haven't yet placed a camera anywhere. Understand, I always did intend to share the bed with you, but I can and will sleep here in the sitting room and completely understand if that's what you prefer."

She waited a moment to see if he was going to talk over her again. When she was sure he was really through, she said, "Thank you for your thoughtful apology. Your words did startle me. You were very…outspoken." As she gave wing to her words, her tone became more forceful, her voice louder. "I'm not intimidated by you. I'm not threatened by you. I know you wouldn't force me. I at least know that well. If I thought that—" She focused on the couch. "Is that a sofa bed?"

"No."

She measured the couch with her gaze, then imagined Joe sleeping there. With his long arms and legs, he would be massively uncomfortable, and she took a moment to enjoy the mental picture of him wrestling with the throw and the pillows in his attempt to make himself comfortable.

Yet for her own safety as well as his, Joe needed to be alert and well-rested, so she looked through the door into the bedroom at the massive expanse of bed. "That's king-sized. I believe we can share it without intruding on each other's space."

"Yes. Thank you for trusting me that much." He looked down as if afraid to engage her in eye-to-eye contact, a man working to appear harmless.

She didn't know exactly what to say. Or think. Worse, she was embarrassed to realize she was not so much pacified as deflated by that excellent and apparently sincere apology. Feeling awkward—and why should she feel awkward?—she said, "I'll use the bathroom first." She gathered her nightclothes and went in, washed her face, an extended process that led to a mental note to ask Li, Kumara, BeBée and Savannah for recommendations on facial cleansers and mascara removers. She brushed her teeth, and when she came out, swaddled in her robe, she was armed with the practical question that had risen from the depths of her mind. "Joe, why do you think Torval's team hasn't placed a camera yet?"

He frowned. "I don't know."

"They've had the time and opportunity. You were sure they were going to use every tool at their disposal to spy on us. Why the restraint? Or is your electronic searcher thingy broken or out of date?"

His mouth quirked. "It's the newest 'searcher thingy' available, developed by a woman I know to be a genius with electronics. I trust it, and her, completely." He paced around the suite, looking specifically at the sites where he'd previously found microphones: under the base of the lamp, in the floor heat vent, in the curtain fixture. "The mikes are gone."

"Gone? Where?"

"They've been removed." He went back into the bedroom.

She followed and watched him rummage in his luggage.

He brought out a small device that fit in the palm of his hand and proceeded to scan the perimeter of the rooms. "I'm not detecting anything from outside the walls, or anything within the walls."

"Is something broken in Torval's main system? Or maybe… maybe the microphone disrupter made them think they needed to replace everything in here, and they'll do it in the morning?"

"Maybe. Sure. I don't know." He frowned at the device in his hand. "I don't like it when Torval's people behave contrary to expectation. It means we're missing a piece of the puzzle."

She could imagine a thousand possibilities: Torval intended to blow them up and wanted to save his electronics, Mitzi wanted to end their lives and wanted no one to know the killer, one of Joe's rivals planned a bloody coup and… "There are too many possibilities, and all of them violent."

"Perhaps you're right and the microphone disrupter has created problems I hadn't anticipated."

"That is the simplest explanation."

"Then probably the correct one, but…" He dragged a chair to the door and propped it under the door handle. "We won't sleep through a break-in with that in the way. I'll use the bathroom now."

She found the bed turned down and a chocolate on her pillow. Torval really did take his hotel-like services seriously. She debated about removing the robe, but marked that down as silly and threw it on the foot of the bed. As always, her nightwear could double as workout gear and/or an escape outfit: tight-fitting leggings and a snug long-sleeved top. Her running shoes and socks sat beside the bed, and her hoodie rested on the night table. She turned out the light, climbed into bed—staying close to her edge of the mattress—and waited.

Joe came out dressed in what looked like bike shorts and a loose-fitting training top…but he held his hoodie and shoes and socks, and he put them around the bed in the same position she had placed hers. She grinned wryly. They were both prepared to run at a moment's notice.

He left the bathroom door ajar, which gave them the faint glow of a nightlight, turned off his bedside lamp, and settled onto his side of the mattress, also close to the edge.

It was very quiet.

A long inhale, then she asked, "Why did you apologize?"

He made a snorting noise. "Huh? What?"

He'd been asleep. Just like that, asleep. In less than a minute, asleep, while she had been hanging onto the mattress by her toenails, working up the nerve to ask her question. Did he have *no* sensitivity to atmosphere? A little louder, she asked, "Why did you apologize?"

"Oh. That." He sighed as if wondering why they were having this discussion now. "If my father had heard me, he would have punched me in the face."

"Oh. Wow." She hadn't expected that.

"Yeah. He taught me to respect women. He said they were mostly better people than men and get a raw deal."

"True." Rowan wholeheartedly agreed.

"But better my father than my mother. She would make me *so* sorry." He was still kind of laughing, but he was serious, too.

"It sounds as if your parents are pretty great."

"Yes. God, yes. The best parents. They raised me right." His voice was fond and proud.

Somehow, that made her lose her temper. "What went wrong?" Joe didn't answer right away, and she pushed again. "You're a mercenary. You're consorting with thieves, smugglers and drug dealers. You're a blackmailer. Do your parents know?"

"No."

"You're so lucky to have good parents who are still...living." Her voice developed a hitch. "I hope they never find out the truth about their son. Will you ever do the right thing?"

"Sure," he said insolently. "After I've tried everything else."

"Bastard," she muttered. Turning her back, she tucked the covers tightly around her and stared into the darkness.

DAY TWO

22

STARING INTO THE darkness meant Rowan didn't get enough sleep. Not getting enough sleep meant she didn't get up in time, and finding the gym involved getting lost three times and arriving at 9:03. She found the class in full warm-up mode with Mitzi Torval, dressed in body-fitting gear, calling the shots.

BeBée stood at the back and gave Rowan that wide-eyed, *you're in trouble* look.

Rowan hastily shed her jacket, grabbed a resistance workout band, and joined them in squatting and stretching. They proceeded to side-to-side shuffles, then to fast footwork, then to... oh my God, something called the left-facing Cha-Cha Slide which involved everybody in the line turning, doing the romba slip (what the hell?), turning on command for the right-facing romba slip (what the *hell?*), and all of a sudden Mitzi screamed, "Left shuffle! Basketball jump! Right shuffle! Basketball jump! Grapevine!"

Rowan had no idea what was going on. She turned one way,

ran into the line of women headed her way, turned the other way, stumbled after the line of women moving away, missed the next turn, shouted, "What the hell?" and literally ran to keep up when everybody else was grapevining or shuffling or romba slipping or whatever madness had struck this roomful of women…in unison.

"Stop!" As Mitzi contemplated Rowan as if she was a black-and-yellow bag o' slime banana slug, the room fell still. "Everybody break for water."

At once the well-formed lines broke, and taut, spandex-clad bodies swarmed the table at the rear of the room where paper cups and a water cooler waited. Rowan ended up at the back of the line; since it was her first class, she had missed the initial rush. By the time she got to the water cooler and had her drink, the others had each taken a black marker, put their initials on their cup, placed it on the table and returned.

Swiftly she followed suit and ran to the line. But not fast enough; she missed the first steps.

BeBée slipped in line beside Rowan. "What happened last night?" she asked out of the corner of her mouth.

"Nothing."

"C'mon! You and Joe never came back to the party and, trust me, your absence was noted."

"And discussed, no doubt," Rowan said bitterly.

"As I heard it, when he dragged you out, everyone knew what he was going to say. And do. What happened?"

"I went back to the room. It was empty. I went to sleep." *If you're going to tell a lie, tell a big one.* "He arrived sometime in the night, climbed into bed, and when I woke up this morning, he was gone." Mostly true, except she'd watched him beneath her lashes as he'd dressed in a burnt-orange golf shirt and jeans, grabbed his handheld device that obscured their voices, and slipped from the room on some mission. To retrieve the address book, she supposed.

"So really, what happened?" BeBée clearly didn't believe any of Rowan's lies.

"I told you—"

"Ladies! If you're feeling so energetic that you need more exercise, we can start the class again!"

Since BeBée was red-faced and Rowan was sweating so much the back of her hair was wet from her neckline to her crown, they declined.

Rowan missed the second combination and ran into the line of women coming at her. "Sorry!"

Mitzi sharply clapped her hands.

Thirty women halted and stared at Rowan…except Kumara, who leaned down, rubbing her mashed foot.

Mitzi said, "Miss Winterbourne, have you ever done anything to improve yourself?"

"Not *this*."

BeBée rolled her eyes. That seemed to be her reaction to every one of Rowan's dumb answers.

Mitzi waited.

Previously, Rowan had remembered high school fondly as that time before when her most important issues were which color rubber band to use on her braces. Now, as she faced Mitzi, she was forcibly reminded of Mademoiselle Larson, who, during French class, had made fun of Rowan's execrable Western American accent. "This is *dancing*," Rowan stated.

"Are you opposed to dancing?" Mitzi asked haughtily.

"I've never taken a dance class."

The gasp that rose made Rowan think she'd committed a sin of biblical proportions, which was pretty gutsy considering they'd accepted Gregory Torval's invitation to party at his medieval den of infamy.

"I don't have time to teach you how to dance. Go work out by yourself." Mitzi flicked her fingers at Rowan and seemed to think she'd sent her into lonely exile.

Rowan turned toward the treadmills. "That's what I wanted to do anyway," she muttered. She warmed up with twenty minutes of hard running, did thirty box jumps, and by the time she moved to the weights, class was over and BeBée gestured her over to the group clustered around the water.

Rowan noted the dancers dabbed at their faces with towels. She was dripping with sweat. She didn't dab, she blotted.

"You have quite a workout," Savannah said. "How do you do it before breakfast?"

"I had room service." Rowan didn't understand the small, concerted inhalation of concern from the group. Were they critical of her possible food choices? She hastened to assure them. "Bowl of oatmeal, fruit plate, OJ and tea, plus a lot of water for hydration. That's my usual breakfast before workout. It gives me the fuel to get the work done. What do you eat?" She looked around for her paper cup.

"I have a cup of coffee with sweetener." Kumara dabbed more quickly.

"Me, too."

"I have tea with sweetener."

"This morning I was *starving*, so I had a piece of dry toast."

"When you don't eat and you work out, don't you feel faint?" Rowan wasn't having any luck.

"I can't eat whenever I'm hungry," Savannah explained. "I'm hungry all the time, and Wadell is very strict. He doesn't allow an extra ounce of weight."

Rowan gave a soft, incredulous moan.

As Mitzi wrapped herself in a gauzy black scarf, she watched Rowan with those dark, intense, critical eyes. "Did you *throw away* your cup? Do you have *no* concern for the environment?"

Rowan knew better than to feel defensive. *She did*, but Mitzi was so skilled at passive-aggressive. "I left it here on the table with my initials. I'm sure it's here...somewhere."

To her surprise, Savannah rescued her. "My fault. I'm sorry,

Mitzi! I'm sorry, Rowan! I grabbed the wrong cup and drank out of it, so I threw it away." She gestured toward the trash can.

Mitzi turned her back on them both. "You girls are so irresponsible," she muttered. Her sycophants followed as she stalked away.

"I define *irresponsible* as pointing a gun in someone else's face," Rowan muttered back. But she wasn't loud; the death of her son had driven Mitzi to teeter on the edge of a crumbling cliff of sanity. Rowan still had a day and a half at this party, and as before, as always, her goal was to survive.

Mitzi reached the door and swung back to face the assembled women.

The sycophants hastily cleared out of the way.

"This afternoon," Mitzi declared, "you have your free time to do whatever you wish. Make use of it, because tonight and tomorrow we spend honoring my husband for his accomplishments. Tonight we have a reception where his people—from the street, the boats, across the border, and of course from the great houses on the mainland—arrive to pay him homage. Tomorrow is the *actual* celebration." She smiled a kind and awful smile at BeBée.

Beside Rowan, BeBée flinched.

"BeBée and I have made sure it will be an occasion he'll never forget. Spread throughout the mansion and the grounds, there'll be baton twirlers, marching bands, dancing, a circus parade of animals, twenty-one-gun salutes—"

Great, a chance to be "accidentally" shot. Rowan interrupted. "Will there be barbecue?"

"What?" Mitzi barked.

"Barbecue. This sounds like a parade, and when I think of a parade, I think of hot dogs and turkey legs."

Again Mitzi viewed her as if she were a banana slug. Maybe an insane banana slug. "Of course there will be barbecue!" Whipping around, she trailed her wrap behind her as she stalked from the room.

"Hot dogs?" BeBée murmured in Rowan's ear. "Not even."

"Make it so," Rowan replied.

BeBée looked sideways at Rowan. "Sure. Why not?"

"Several setups. Lots of extra propane tanks. Wouldn't want to run out."

"Got it. Anything else you require?"

"A fan."

"A fan?" BeBée fluttered her fingers in front of her face.

"No." Rowan whirled her fingers in a circle. "Electric."

"Ah. Big fan? Little fan?"

"Little powerful fan." Rowan noted Li leaning in to listen.

Apparently so did BeBée, because in a typically BeBée perky tone, she asked, "Want to hike the island this afternoon?"

Rowan looked out the floor-to-ceiling windows at the vista that extended across cypress trees and cliffs, rocks and surprise riots of flowers, all the way to the horizon and on to the end of the universe. "Sure. I'll hike with you. The tread on these shoes should be good for a few trails."

"Daddy keeps supplies of new clothes and new shoes of all kinds in all sizes if you want to—"

"I'll wear these. They fit me." And she'd paid for them herself.

"You want to come, too, Li?" BeBée asked.

"Hike? After this?" Li looked horrified. "I'm going to relax by the pool."

"Raptor Island is one of the most beautiful places on the earth," BeBée told her.

"With a horizon pool begging to be enjoyed." Li took Savannah's arm and marched away.

Kumara shrugged at Rowan and BeBée and followed.

"Happy swimming!" Rowan called.

The three women looked back at Rowan as if she was speaking Martian.

BeBée laughed. "They might get in the pool and splash a little. But they won't ruin their hair by actually *swimming*."

Rowan was forcibly struck by how bad she was at being a consort. But then…so was BeBée. "Since there's a swimming pool, there must be life vests."

"Of course. Gregory Torval wouldn't want to break the law by failing to provide the required safety equipment."

The women looked at each other. They burst into laughter.

When they subsided, BeBée said, "I'll send a life vest to your room."

"Perfect. What time do you want to hike?"

BeBée glanced at the wall clock. "After lunch? One p.m. at the front door."

"I'll be there." As the other women headed out the doors, Rowan returned to the weights and finished her workout. If the moment came when she needed to save the world from Gregory Torval and his immoral crew of terrorists, and she wasn't quite strong enough, she would never forgive herself.

Never.

Also, she would be dead.

23

IN HER BROAD canvas hat, denim shirt and exercise bra, BeBée looked like a…like a hiker in the Sierras, the kind of person a man would pass on a trail in Yosemite and think, *She's well-built and I'd better hurry or she'll beat me to the top.* Of course he would hurry because it mattered to his ego. Meanwhile BeBée would dawdle along the trail, talking about wildflowers and the on-going threat to the bee population.

Rowan grinned, because while there were no men around, BeBée in fact was pointing out the wildflowers and discussing the horrifying diminishment of the local bee population.

"I'm glad you think it's funny, Rowan." BeBée said in a huff. "Do you know what's going to happen to California and the world production of fruit without bees to pollinate them?"

"I don't think it's funny, BeBée. I really don't." Rowan put her hand to her aching ribs and breathed. "But you have to know how very different you are than the BeBée you pretend to be in the mansion. Even I, who always suspected there was more to you than meets the eye…have the right to be surprised. Can we stop and rest?"

"The summit's up there." BeBée pointed with one of her hiking poles. "You can make it. There's a place to sit, and the view is unbelievable!"

With her gaze, Rowan traced the almost vertical trail, winding with hairpin turns. "It better be," she muttered. Leaning on her borrowed hiking poles, she kept climbing, but reserved the right to groan with every step.

When BeBée at last came to a halt in front of her, Rowan dragged herself up the last few feet…and the whole world unfolded before her. With their faults and their glistening forms, the rock cliffs spoke of the earth's fire meeting the ocean's freezing water, of being elevated and broken and shaped. How appropriate for the island. Raptor Island.

A little to the north, Rowan could see… She pointed. "That's my home. Or was. Point Offbeat Lighthouse."

"You live in a lighthouse? That's awesome."

"It really is."

They settled on the rocks and stared across the island and the Pacific Ocean toward the exotic east.

BeBée frowned. "But if we can see your lighthouse, you can see Raptor Island from there."

"I can."

"That's probably not good for your mental health."

"Probably not. But it doesn't matter. I probably can't stay there now anyway. Not forever. Not unless something changes, like my chances of survival."

"Right. Gregory Torval claimed he would honor his pledge not to kill you, but lying is the least of his sins."

"I'm not so easy to kill." Rowan thought of the defenses she had left in place in her home. "But after I clean out a few things, I won't hang around taunting death, either."

"We're survivors, you and me. We do what we have to do, and

we thrive." BeBée put her hand on Rowan's arm. "That other
BeBée is a part of me, sure. Funny, frivolous, sexual, taking the
burden of the household so Mitzi can spend her life being the
martyred mother of a murdered child. But who I really am…"
She propped her elbows up on her knees and stared at the horizon. "That's for me to know."

"I like all the BeBées I know."

"I like you, too," BeBée said simply. "I like being up here
with you."

"I love being on top of the world. It's good to have company
who likes it, too." Rowan got to the business at hand. "Do you
know, is there a way to the roof of the mansion? A stairway or
an elevator?"

"Sure, there's the freight elevator to keep the equipment running. But when I need to escape, I always take the stairs. North
corner, under the bell tower. The door is locked and requires an
actual metal key, but I can score you one."

"Thanks."

"You haven't even been here two days. You already want to
escape?"

"How long did it take you before you wanted to escape?"

"It came on me slowly. First there was so much to do—figure
out who to attach myself to, how to keep him, how to win."

"Win?"

"Stay alive."

"Oh. That." That was basic.

"One day I looked around, and it had been three years since
I'd arrived on the island, and I'd never been off. Not once. So
I asked Daddy if I could go on vacation. Like to San Diego or
Mexico. Nothing big, and I spoke some Spanish, so I thought
it would be fun to…do that." BeBée's soft mouth screwed up
tight. "He said no. No vacation for BeBée. Not then. Not ever.
You heard him. He doesn't even want me steering his yacht."

"He's afraid you're going to leave and not come back."

"One of Mitzi's lieutenants told me he had a mistress once he really liked, and she dumped him. I don't know, but he's got a real thing about not letting me escape, and now I...need time for myself. I need that time to get centered, find out who I am, become what I want to be."

BeBée's gaze dropped away from the horizon and onto the island, tracing the trails that led hither and yon, and her gaze traveled toward the torture compound Rowan remembered so well.

In an inspired leap of intuition, Rowan asked, "Do you want revenge?"

BeBée turned to her in surprise, then laughed. "You see a lot."

"I have my own revenge desires. Yours are different. You're right, this is one of the beautiful places of the earth. I've never seen such vistas. The beaches, the crashing of the waves, the call of the gulls, the drama packed on every inch of this island...and so much ugliness and pain hidden beneath the surface."

"So much pain... So many ghosts..." BeBée looked down at her hands, then sideways at Rowan. "One of the girls that came to Raptor with me was mouthy. No tact. Said what she thought about the men and the sex and the... Bonita said anything as long as it was funny. She made us laugh, all of us girls."

Rowan tried to remember if she'd met a Bonita. But when she came to the island, she was so focused on rescuing Lorenze, she had no clear memory of anyone of the other girls.

BeBée continued, "She was a friend to me, helped me set my goals, plan and really —she taught me to think. I loved her so much." She paused to wet her lips. "She laughed at the wrong man, and Torval let Moore have her the way you'd throw a mouse to a sharp-clawed cat. When she came back from his hut—"

"She came back?"

"Moore had instructions to train her, not to kill her." BeBée seemed to lose the thread of the story.

Rowan gave BeBée a moment, then prompted, "When she came back…"

BeBée heaved a sigh she didn't seem to notice. "She wasn't Bonita anymore. There wasn't a mark on her. She walked and she spoke and she smiled as a consort should, but all that warmth and bright spirit had been…vanquished. All that was left was that face and body and…emptiness. I cried over her. I begged the real Bonita to come back. She looked at me with those blank unblinking eyes and said, 'It hurts too much to be Bonita.'"

Rowan took BeBée's hand. Her fingers were clenched white.

BeBée said, "I was with her when she died of a fall from the cliffs."

"A fall?"

BeBée turned, and Rowan was shocked to see the cold stillness overlaid on that vivid face. "I pushed her."

"Oh." Rowan was less horrified than she should have been, she supposed.

"She didn't want to live like that."

"No…" But to see beneath BeBée's soft, sexual surface to the real steel beneath—that was a shock. "Moore has a lot to answer for."

"Someday, I don't know how, I will make him pay." It was a vow spoken in earnest.

Rowan had to ask. "And Torval? He gave Bonita to him."

"He did, didn't he?"

For the first time, Rowan realized that Gregory Torval gripped a live grenade primed to go off.

In a lightning change of mood that was as typical as it was startling, BeBée leaped to her feet. "Come on. The trip down'll take almost as long as the trip up, and we have to get showered and dressed for the reception and dinner. I'm wearing a classic Lanvin. A Marilyn-Monroe-style dress for curvy women like me. How about you?"

"I made my dress myself."

BeBée stopped in the trail and gave a wary glance back at Rowan. "That'll start rumors that Joe is underfunded."

"No, it won't. I had to learn how to sew silk for a project I was making. By the time that was over, making a dress was nothing. The women will be asking who the designer is."

"What will you say?"

Rowan smiled a Disney princess smile. "I'll tell them Joe has connections. That'll drive them into a frenzy."

BeBée cackled. "I can't wait to watch it."

24

BY THE TIME Rowan got back to her room, BeBée had dragged her up and down another mountain. She was sweaty, dirty, tired and hungry. And easily irritated, as she discovered when she opened the door to her room and found a casually dressed Joe lounging in a chair, reading a paperback novel.

He looked her up and down and started laughing.

She glared. "If you don't stop, I'm going to hit you with my shoe."

He glanced down again and made an exaggeratedly horrified face. "Where did you find mud on this island?"

"There are aquafers and springs. Who knew?" She toed her way out of her shoes.

"Not me. I'll replace the shoes." When she opened her mouth to refuse, he said, "It's not a gift or a bribe. You wouldn't be here if not for me, and I don't mean that you should lose from it."

She nodded grudgingly.

"Why are you carrying...?" He indicated the tank she held.

"Propane." She walked to the closet, maneuvered it into a

corner behind her suitcase, and shut the door. "On the way in, I picked it up from tomorrow's barbecue area. You never know when you might need a little propane."

"If I had a nickel for every time I said that…" He waved his hand toward the bathroom. "It's all yours."

"Good damned thing." She stalked toward the bathroom, dropping clumps of dirt as she walked. At the door, she turned. "What is the agenda for tonight?"

"This is our formal celebration of the wonderfulness that is Gregory Torval. We have a reception with light refreshments, go into the theater and watch a musical performance of *Les Misérables*."

"How apropos."

"After that, we'll enjoy a lavish dinner."

"We will?"

"We will."

"How long do I have to get ready?"

"As long as you wish."

"Give me a half hour."

When she came out, he had donned a white shirt and was knotting a red power tie around his neck. He looked her over from head to toe—and this time, he didn't laugh. "You clean up well."

"Ever the lavish compliments." The yellow silk draped and swirled, and when she walked she showed glimpses of long legs amid hidden panels of her signature blue-violet. "Shall we?"

He stripped off the red tie, went to the closet and came out carrying a plain, dark blue tie. He knotted it around his neck, shrugged into his black jacket and offered his arm. "Once more into the fray," he said.

As they neared the theater, she noted how alone they were. "We're early?"

"You were swift, so yes. Let's see what we can observe in the lobby."

What they observed was Gregory Torval gesturing as he conferred with Szababos in low tones. Seeing them, Torval slapped him on the shoulder, earning a pained look from Szababos, and sent him on his way. Torval came forward and shook hands with Joe. "Good to see you both. Rowan, BeBée's still napping after that hike you dragged her on. She's not as sturdy as you, you know!"

Rowan opened her mouth to point out it was BeBée who'd worn her out, when some remnant of wisdom stopped her. If BeBée wanted Torval to think she was a delicate flower, who was Rowan to destroy that myth?

Torval gestured one of the uniformed servers close. "The lady needs champagne."

The young woman nodded and scurried away to open a bottle.

"Do you like musical theater?" Torval asked Rowan.

"I have little experience with it except on PBS, but yes." She accepted the flute from the server with thanks. "It's one of my passions."

Torval smiled, as if her response made him particularly happy. "Me, too. I particularly enjoy *Come from Away*. It's such a testament to the human spirit of generosity and compassion."

She stared at him, wide-eyed. He liked a show that was a testament to the human spirit? Okay… "I'll make a point to see it."

"Come back when I bring the Broadway cast here. I know you'd enjoy it." Torval turned to Joe and started talking man talk, effectively shutting Rowan out.

Which was really a good thing, because Rowan didn't even understand why Torval would imagine she'd come back to Raptor Island unless she was served up on Mitzi's rotisserie.

She accepted her flute of champagne and arranged herself to appear supportive, relaxed and none-too-bright.

At the suggested time, guests surged into the lobby, and everyone noticed Joe had arrived early and was already deep in

conversation with Torval. Four women detached themselves
from their escorts and wove through the crowd to ease themselves between Rowan and Joe. Next they moved to detach Joe
from Torval, and Rowan watched in bemusement as they succeeded without either man realizing how they'd been manipulated. The people at this party were playing games that Rowan,
who had spent her life fleeing from society, couldn't begin to
comprehend.

Servers began circulating, offering canapés, hors d'oeuvres
and napkins.

Rowan accepted a bit of something with cold shrimp and
pesto, a bite of warm herbed goat cheese on top of puff pastry,
and a prosciutto-wrapped baby artichoke drizzled with something so garlicky and delicious that she grabbed the server back
as he tried to leave and picked up four more of the tasty treats. "I
hiked a long way today," she said to the startled young woman,
who nodded and sidled away.

BeBée sashayed in, dressed in sexy elegance so hot and pink
it scorched the retinas. One of the servers stopped to speak to
her, and BeBée listened intently. So did Rowan; she heard an
undertone of panic. BeBée put her hand on the server's shoulder and spoke in comforting tones.

When BeBée arrived at Rowan's side, all smiles and hugs,
Rowan murmured, "What's going on?"

"Lots of things. There are always lots of things. Rumors that
something big is going down, that Torval is about to be ousted,
and—" BeBée lowered her voice "—late at night, there have
been strange sightings in the hallways."

"Strange sightings? What? *Ghosts?*" Rowan was joking.

BeBée didn't laugh. "When the staff is hired—the kitchen
staff, housekeeping, on-site tech people—they're told only that
the wages are good and they have to sign a two-year contract. It's
a good contract, lots of wage hikes, benefits, bonuses. Then they
get here… Some of them thrive. Some of them move up in the

company. But mostly they're afraid, every minute of every day. They know the names of every person taken to Doug Moore for discipline. They know how random it seems. They know the names of the people who don't come back, and they know the horror of seeing their friends return, changed by the experience. They know they can't leave until their two years are up. Not for any reason. Not for family, not for friends, not for medical treatment. God forbid they try to escape." She looked around at the servers moving through the guests. "Yes. This house is haunted. This island is haunted. *I believe.*"

"Okay…" Rowan wanted to say something scathing, but BeBée had made her point. If there were such a thing as ghosts, this is the house they would prowl. "What kind of sightings?"

"A shadowy figure moving along the corridors, opening locked doors."

"Ghosts shouldn't have to walk along a corridor or open doors. They should be able to move through walls." That was logic as Rowan saw it.

BeBée snapped, "Do *you* know the ghost rules? I don't."

"No. I don't know the ghost rules, but then, I don't believe in ghosts. Have there been any acts of ghostly mischief?"

Savannah drifted over. "They move things."

Savannah believed this? "What kind of things?"

"The art."

That took Rowan aback. "Why would ghosts be interested in art?"

BeBée gestured impatiently. "Because the art is precious to Gregory Torval, and the ghosts want revenge."

Kumara had arrived to join the discussion. "I saw one of the ghosts."

Everyone turned to stare at her. Kumara continued, "Last night, I was late coming back to our room, and saw him. He was wearing—"

"A white sheet?" Sarcasm wasn't going to improve the conversation, but Rowan couldn't resist.

Kumara flicked a finger at Rowan's forehead. "No. He was wearing an orange golf shirt and jeans. I thought I could almost recognize him, but he was…fuzzy."

Li joined them. "Fuzzy?"

Rowan got a funny feeling in the pit of her stomach. "Fuzzy."

"He wasn't quite there." Kumara dropped her voice to a hush. "At the same time…as he walked, I could see the marks of his shoes on the carpet."

Rowan opened her mouth. And shut it. And thought, *I don't know anybody who last night wore an orange shirt and jeans and walked the halls and left marks of shoes on the carpet. At least…not officially.*

"Why do you look like that?" BeBée asked.

Rowan rearranged her face. "Like what?"

"Like you know something!"

"She's seen something, too!" Kumara said.

"No. No, really, I haven't seen anything even vaguely spooky." Rowan pointed her finger like a pistol. "Plenty of scary stuff, though."

Savannah pulled a disbelieving face. "Tell us the truth. You have seen a ghost!"

"I assure you I have not," Rowan said crisply. "If anybody has the right to be haunted, it is me, and never has my mother made an appearance in my life."

"Yeah, she's right," Li said.

"I forgot about that," Kumara agreed.

In the last two days, Rowan's story had spread in corners and whispers, and now everyone knew the details.

Man, how she *adored* being the object of curiosity. Someday she was going to make Joe pay. As the soft chimes that announced the coming performance soon, he stepped up, slid an arm around her back and smiled at the other women. "Darling, we should go find our seats before the theater fills up."

"Not to worry." BeBée grinned at Li, Kumara and Savannah as she announced to Joe, "You have reserved seats. Fifth row, center. Daddy specifically requested that you be seated to his right."

Joe nodded as if he wasn't surprised, and used that hand on Rowan's spine to move her toward the theater.

"Whatever you're doing, you're doing it right," Rowan murmured to him. "Those women have been outmaneuvered, and they are not happy."

An usher stepped up with a flashlight and led them down the dim aisle.

"Will they take it out on you?" Joe asked.

Rowan reflected. "Perhaps I'm naive, but I don't see how they can. I think the logical move for them would be to try and swap out their current partners for the new winner—that's you—and should they succeed, it's no skin off my teeth."

He winced and laughed. "When it comes to keeping my ego in check, you're the best. Thank you, I'll stick with the woman on my arm."

"Until this masquerade is over."

He gestured her into the aisle first.

She resisted. "It's you Torval wants at his right hand."

"Maybe. But you're here as a distraction, remember?"

"What if he gropes me?"

"When you punch him in the face, that will truly serve as a distraction."

"Quite correct." Rowan moved to the empty seat next to Gregory Torval. "It would almost be worth it."

25

IN FACT, even though BeBée sat on his other side, Torval groped nobody. Instead he watched the play with rapt attention, and after the final number before intermission, "One Day More," he was the first to leap to his feet and applaud.

The man enjoyed musical theater. No wonder Mitzi and BeBée had arranged to bring in the *Les Mis* cast to celebrate his birthday. There was probably some saying about this like, *A happy Torval was a less murderous Torval.* Or something equally cheery.

Intermission was the usual: women pushing their way up the aisles toward the ladies' room, men letting them go first because no guy wanted to admit to a demanding bladder. Rowan exited the ladies' room to find everyone congregated in the lobby, acquiring liquor and snacks, and voices rose in a pandemonium of gossip and speculation.

Joe was deep in conversation with Francisco, Wadell and two other well-dressed men who stood around him and listened as if every word he spoke was a pearl of wisdom.

A similar group of men surrounded Gregory Torval.

Her skin prickled as if lightning waited to strike nearby. It was almost as if—no, not almost, it was as if the two men were battling for social supremacy.

"Hey, girl." BeBée eased up beside Rowan.

Carrying bottles of spring water, Li, Savannah and Kumara found both of them.

In an uncanny imitation of the *Les Mis* pre-intermission finale, Kumara said solemnly, "One more day."

Nods all around.

"Then everything will be settled," Savannah said.

More nods.

"Maybe," BeBée said.

Reluctant nods.

"What's the schedule for tomorrow?" *How much more do I have to endure until I can leave?* Rowan meant. *Will a "fuzzy" ghost walk the halls tonight in Joe's clothes?*

"As a treat to them, tomorrow morning, all of Torval's street people are coming," BeBée said.

"Street people?" Li asked.

"You know—thugs, pushers and thieves." BeBée was matter-of-fact.

"Make sure your doors are locked," Kumara said.

"Sure. That might slow them down. We start the morning with a parade at the track. Required attendance. *On time.*" BeBée viewed Rowan severely.

"Late three minutes this morning," Rowan muttered.

"Then in the garden, a buffet and a huge drunken revel for Torval's street people, while the rest of us have what we hope is a civilized gathering in the great hall and on the deck with more food, more champagne and circus stuff, because Torval loves circuses."

"Circuses. All the animals are chained and trained. And the clowns…" Kumara hunched her shoulders.

"Clowns? I hate clowns." Li shivered.

"Don't we all," BeBée said. "The painted faces, the down-turned lips, the big eyes."

"They're so sad, and everybody picks on them, and we're supposed to laugh when they get beat up or run over or…" Li's eyes filled with tears.

"Clowns are only funny to people who've never been tormented or laughed at." Savannah hugged Li around the shoulders, and Li put her head on Savannah's chest.

Just for a moment; they separated quickly.

Rowan realized the damage that had been done to these women from an early age by the expectations of beauty and the sexual demands put on them. To them, the circus was a symbol of pain and servitude.

For Torval, having a circus perform for him was a sign of power. The sadness the circus deliberately portrayed could be mocked and laughed at, for he had no sadness. He delivered sadness. He was a shadow that passed over the land and left devastation behind.

Happy birthday to you, King Torval.

"We wind up with a big cake and candles. Led by one of the singers Torval has done favors for, we sing 'Happy Birthday,' Torval goes out on the deck and waves to the peasants below—"

"Like he's the king," Rowan said.

Savannah snorted, then glanced around to make sure no one heard her.

"And you all go home," BeBée finished.

Savannah's attention had been fixed on the door. "Scatter *now*," she said urgently. "Mitzi is on the scene."

Yes, a faintly smiling Mitzi had arrived in the lobby, dressed in a black silk designer gown with a full-length black silk wrap over her shoulders. Her glamorous black-clad sycophants walked behind and beside her; Mitzi's hand rested on the arm of a younger man.

BeBée, Savannah and Kumara slid away in different directions, leaving Rowan conspicuously alone. Yet after a single triumphant flick of a glance, Mitzi pretended not to notice her. Instead she wore her escort like a glittering accessory, taking him from group to group.

Rowan noted the way Torval reacted to Mitzi and her boy toy, glaring as if furious and insulted. And jealous?

The guests reacted to Boy Toy, too. He was never invited into a discussion, but he behaved like one of those men who imagined their opinion mattered, and when he broke into a conversation, the sharply dressed, athletic men and their glamorous consorts unobtrusively drew away from him. When he followed, they smiled and replied, but no one ever blinked; it was as if they feared what would happen with a single moment of lost attention.

Why? He seemed a supercilious ass, smirking with assumed superiority. He wore a blue pin-striped suit, a white shirt open at the throat and a gold chain with a large engraved pendant. He was barefoot.

Rowan covered her smirk with her hand. So not merely a supercilious ass, but one who did everything he could to stand out, unaware that he made himself ridiculous. His ash-brown thinning hair was cut at chin length, and he had a nervous tic, using first his right hand, then his left hand to toss his hair out of his face.

She glanced toward Joe. The crowd around him was deeper.

What was Mitzi doing with Boy Toy? Why did she observe his interactions and the guests' reactions with such a marked sneer? Whatever she was doing, whoever he was, Rowan knew enough about Mitzi to feel threatened, and she edged toward Joe.

Again Boy Toy flicked his hair back from his face.

Rowan saw his crumpled cheekbone, the way his skull caved in toward his ear—and she *knew*. She knew why the other guests avoided him, feared him. She knew who he was.

Doug Moore, the torturer.

As soon as her gaze sharpened on him, he turned his head and looked into her eyes.

Like everyone else, she froze and stared back.

His eyes were the same color as his hair, ash brown, and in them she saw a chilling intelligence unleavened by any human emotion. No compassion, no anger, no love, no resentment…it was like looking into an octopus's eyes, and she was nothing but prey, knowing one of those long, strong, slimy arms would lash out, grasp her, pull her close, crush her, hurt her, consume her.

If only she could melt out of sight.

But no. She owed everything to her father, including a reminder to this bully that as Lorenze Winterbourne escaped from Raptor Island, Doug Moore had been unconscious and bleeding in his own house of horrors.

Vividly she recalled the moment she had lifted the tire iron and slammed it across the side of Moore's head. Gruesome though it might be, she relished the memory of cracking bone and the sight of his sideways, broken puppet collapse against the wall.

Yes. She would not cower from this monster. Reaching up, she touched the side of her face that coincided with his crushed cheekbone—and she smiled.

She saw an emotion grow in those cold, colorless eyes.

It was anticipation.

Take that, asshole.

A swirl of movement blocked Rowan's view, and when the guests had dissipated, her visual connection was broken. The scene had changed. Mitzi and her sycophants were walking toward the theater. Torval watched his wife while the men around him continued to vie for his attention. Guests lined up to get their drinks before the final act began. The crowd around Joe had thickened.

Doug Moore was nowhere in sight.

BeBée wandered past, blew a kiss at Rowan and twinkled her fingers, then headed into the theater.

Rowan frowned at Joe. Should she remind him they needed to go in? Or was that a faux pas for a consort?

Then, oh God, then Doug Moore's voice, quiet, warm, gentle, spoke near Rowan's right shoulder.

26

"SOON, TORVAL WILL give me someone." Doug Moore's voice slid across the syllables like a snake tasting its prey. "Someone random, probably, or someone who displeased him somehow. That person will simply disappear from the party. No one will know where the unlucky bastard has gone, and no one will ask. Not if they're smart. I'll have him. Or her. It doesn't matter to *me* who it is—"

Please, God, I don't want to hear this. I don't want to be so afraid.

"Only that I get to practice my trade. I don't have nightmares about the screams and the smells and the sounds of bones breaking. I have nightmares if I go too long without hearing them. Torval likes to keep me happy. I'm the best in the business. If I'd had longer with Lorenze Winterbourne, I'd have known all about you and the woman."

Rowan took a fortifying breath and pivoted, a slight smile on her lips. "It's too bad for you my father managed to free himself, take you down and escape. You must still have nightmares about that."

Moore moved like lightning, grabbing Rowan's left wrist and leaning into her face. "He didn't free himself. He was securely locked to the table when I left him to investigate that noise. I was hit from behind." He shook her wrist and sprayed saliva as he spoke. "It was you. I know it was you, and I'll make you sorry."

She looked him right in the eyes. "That blow to the side of your head has addled your brain. It was Lorenze Winterbourne."

Moore squeezed her wrist and began the slow motion that would wrench it behind her back and dislocate her shoulder. "Confess," he murmured in his most comforting, kind tone. "Confess and I'll release you. Confess and the pain will stop..."

Rowan had the fighting talents, she could have freed herself, but Joe stood across the ballroom, and his advice echoed in her mind—*Don't let them know about your defense skills.*

Yet it was so hard to stand here and take it. She had suffered before, but pain was always new, always sharp, never expected, wanted, or easily borne. She could hold out until Joe got to her...couldn't she?

She realized the pin-striping on Doug Moore's dark blue suit was actually that: a series of sewing pins lined up in a row, and every third one dripped with blood.

God. God! Had she scoffed at ghosts in this house? Of course the dead haunted the halls. They wanted justice as surely as did Rowan's mother and Joe's baby sister.

Rescue came from an unexpected source.

"Get your hands off her!"

Through the maze of bruised skin and grinding bones, she recognized the voice.

Doug Moore turned with a snarl to the speaker, and when he saw Gregory Torval standing there, he froze in astonishment.

"Let her go." Torval's voice was harsh with anger and command.

Moore dropped Rowan's wrist and backed away.

Before Rowan could do more than cradle her arm in her

hand, Joe was beside her. He put his arm around her, pulled her tight against his body. "Get your mad dog under control, Torval, or I'll kill him."

Torval snapped his fingers at Doug Moore. "What are you doing here? You know better than to leave your hut in the woods and come to a party."

Moore put one insolent hand on his hip. "Mitzi brought me."

"Mitzi is not in charge here. I am. Get out!" Torval pointed to the door, and as Moore strolled away, Torval shouted, "Put on shoes, you freak!" Turning back to Rowan, he asked, "Is it broken? Did that cocksucker break any bones?" He hailed his hovering butler. "Szababos, get my doctor immediately!"

Before he'd finished speaking, Szababos was on his cell.

"No bones broken," she whispered, "but I feel faint." It was pain, of course, but more than that, it was the horror of listening to Doug Moore take such evil delight in what he would do, time and again, to some poor innocent soul: destroy a life, change a personality, crush and maim and torture.

"Do you want to return to our room?" Joe asked her.

"No. No! Don't go." Torval spun like a whirlwind. "Szababos, get ice. Ice for her wrist! An ice bag."

"Yes, sir." Szababos snapped his fingers at one of the servers. "Rick, it's worth your life to hurry."

The obsequious server dodged curious guests as he scurried toward the kitchen.

"Tell my doctor to bring a pain reliever," Torval yelled.

Immediately Szababos was back on the phone again, issuing instructions.

Rowan's hurt was easing, and now she became worried about the number of eyes watching them, weighing them, watching Gregory Torval, who seemed frantic to keep them. The crowd around them was growing; people were coming back out of the theater, lured by the promise of even greater entertainment in the lobby.

"Don't leave tonight of all nights!" Torval demanded.

"What's special about tonight?" Rowan didn't understand. "Besides the fact it's your birthday celebration?"

"You're here. You're here and you… We're like family, aren't we? You and… Joe are like family to me. My…heirs."

Rowan glanced at Joe. Had this been decided between them?

No, because Joe watched Torval as if puzzled, as if he expected a trick.

She could detect no sign that Torval was acting. He seemed floundering, trying to say something meaningful without saying too much, without revealing himself to the onlookers.

Then, like the evil fairy who shows up uninvited at the party, Mitzi appeared out of the theater entrance and stalked toward them, her sycophants rushing to catch up. Shaking her finger in Torval's face, Mitzi said, "You've forgotten what you owe your son."

"I know what I owe my son." Torval took a long, steadying breath. "But he's dead. It's not possible to change that."

Mitzi interrupted with a wild burst of laughter. "Do you think I don't know the reason you don't kill this stepdaughter of Lorenze Winterbourne? The stepdaughter of the man who murdered our son? *My* son." Mitzi stood, vibrating with outrage, and she gestured violently toward Rowan. "She's the daughter of that whore Yvonne—and she's your daughter!"

27

A BUCKET OF ice water slammed into Rowan's face.

No, not ice water.

Ice acid, blowing off Mitzi Torval in a rush of words that froze and burned.

"That's why Yvonne left you," Mitzi shrieked, "because she was pregnant. She didn't want your daughter to know you. To know her father, to be involved in the violence, to know such men, such beasts as stand in this room and stay in this house. I should have been so smart. I should have left you. If I had, our son would be alive today."

The silence in the theater lobby deafened Rowan. The staring eyes blinded her. Even Joe was staring, staring so hard she felt the weight of his shock.

She could focus on nothing clearly, nothing except a dark oval frame that, as she concentrated, tightened around Torval's face. Gregory Torval, who didn't look surprised by Mitzi's accusation, not horrified, not scornful. He wore none of the emotions

Rowan wanted him to wear. Instead he stared worriedly between his wife and… Rowan.

Between his wife and his daughter. In a patient, patronizing tone that fooled no one, he said, "Now, Mitzi, why would you think that about Rowan Winterbourne?"

"I never understood why you buckled under Lorenze Winterbourne's blackmail, why you gave up on your pursuit of every single member of his family. It's because she's not his daughter! She's yours!"

"That's not strictly true," Torval said.

Not true at all! Rowan had no breath, couldn't form words.

Mitzi saw her lips move and thrust that demented, enraged face into Rowan's. "Not true? Every time you look in the mirror, you stupid girl, you look at Gregory Torval. Don't you? Don't you?"

"No!" The word burst from the depths of Rowan's horror.

"Yes! The shape of the face, the color of the eyes, those lashes. You've got your whore mother's mouth—oh yes, I knew Yvonne well. I knew how hard Gregory chased her. How hard he begged her. He offered her everything. I didn't understand why, but now I do." Mitzi ranted like the madwoman she was. "The little whore slept with him to give him a baby—"

Rowan stepped forward so decisively Mitzi took a step back. "Don't call. My mother. A whore. Again."

"Gregory was married to *me*." Mitzi pounded her chest. "He had a son with *me*. Your mother, the little whore—"

Rowan moved with the speed of light, throwing a left-handed punch toward Mitzi's nose.

Mitzi moved as swiftly, catching her fist.

With her open right hand and using all her strength, Rowan slapped Mitzi's cheek and ear. The impact of the blow and the metal in Rowan's rings were enough to make Mitzi stumble sideways. Before she righted herself, Rowan said, "Don't call my mother a whore again." Turning on her heel, she walked out of the lobby, away from the swelling rise of shocked and eager conversation, and the rapidly rising scream of pain and outrage from Mitzi Torval.

As Rowan passed two of Torval's bouncers, one made a gesture to challenge her. The thug next to him said clearly, "Catfight." Neither stopped her.

Rowan started toward the room she shared with Joe, changed her mind and walked toward the pool, changed her mind and went to the gym. It was empty, of course, and that was good because she couldn't breathe, couldn't speak, didn't want to feel. What could she do to shut out her thoughts? How to handle this horrific surge of upended emotions?

Work out, sure. Work out so hard she couldn't hear herself think. She glanced at the bruises Doug Moore's cruel grip had put on her left wrist. Going to the weight rack, she picked up a twenty-five-pound weight, did a right-armed overhead press, and found herself staring into the full-length mirror at her own face. Torval's eyes? Lashes? The shape of his face?

No. No. It couldn't be true. As soon as Joe had introduced her, Torval tried to kill her. He hadn't been faking; he'd shot even as Joe shoved his arm up.

With a thud, she dropped the weight onto the mat. Leaning into the mirror, she put her fingers on her cheeks, opened her eyes wide, tried to pull her face long and change the general look of that person she saw every day of her other life. That person she didn't know…at all.

28

ROWAN WINTERBOURNE HAD *always known Lorenze Winter-bourne was not her genetic father. That hadn't mattered until she turned thirteen and her adolescent propensity for drama bloomed when an even more dramatic friend convinced her it was her right and duty to know who had sired her. Maybe her father was a spy. Maybe he was a super-hero. Maybe he was a billionaire. Maybe he'd been searching for her.*

Maybe she was a secret baby.

Ohhhh. Cooool.

The anticipation of such romance and adventure made Rowan's heart beat with all the heat generated by surging hormones. She came in from the playground and told her mother that she deserved to know, that she wanted to find her real father and establish a bond with him.

Her mother, who remarkably had once been thirteen herself, weighed her words carefully. "Your real father is Lorenze Winterbourne, the man who raised you, fed you, stayed up nights when you were sick, helped you with your reading, pushed you in the swing, let you drive his car in the stadium parking lot—" Seeing the expression on Rowan's face, she said, "Yes, I know about that."

"But my real father—"

"Your genetic father was a horrible mistake on my part."

Hurt, Rowan asked, "Was I a horrible mistake on your part?"

"I didn't mean to get pregnant, if that's what you mean, but you turned out to be the best thing in my life." Mom smoothed Rowan's bangs off her forehead.

Rowan thrilled to hear that. Then her pleasure soured. "Are you sure my sister's not the best thing in your life?"

Mom put ice in two glasses, split a rarely allowed can of Coke between them, and thus ensured Rowan followed her to the kitchen table and sat down. She pushed the glass toward Rowan. "Are you jealous of your sister, sweetheart?"

"No. Not really." Sometimes when Linden got all the cooing attention.

"Because she adores you so much, that would be a shame. Rowie…" Mom imitated Linden's loving nickname for Rowan.

Rowan was horrified. "Please, Mom, I beg you. Never tell anyone she calls me that."

"I won't, but it is blindingly cute. In preschool, when she sings, Rowie, Rowie, Rowie your boat—"

"Mother!"

Mom laughed so hard at the memory that Rowan finally joined her.

"Okay, it's cute. But Mom, do you want me to have my head flushed down the toilet at school? Do. Not. Tell. Anyone." Rowan glared.

"I won't. I promise I won't." Mom wiped a few happy tears off her cheeks. "You two are perfect together. You're so patient with her. You teach her so much. It shines between you, the way you love each other, and it makes my heart sing."

"She's my sister." Rowan thought that said it all.

"Honey, think about your friends. Sisters don't always get along. Sometimes, they hate each other. Sometimes, it's a gap that never heals."

"Yeah. I guess. But Linden's sweet. She's always so…" Rowan found herself smiling, too. "She's a nice kid."

"So are you. It runs in the family." Now Mom invited Rowan to laugh along with her. "But Linden's different. She's my baby girl who came along when I was married and secure. You came along when I was anything but. You're asking about your biological father... Haven't you ever wondered why you don't have grandparents?"

"I thought they were dead."

Mom spread her hands out, palms up. "I don't know. Neither does your father. Lorenze, I mean. We were both kids who deliberately don't quite remember our parents, and what we do remember isn't good. Drunk mothers, stepfathers with fists, lying to the cops about their drugs, times when we were hungry, times when we were cold."

Rowan felt her eyes popping out of her head. Her mother, her unflappable, boring, suburban mom, had had such a rough start in life? And Rowan never suspected?

The answer came at once. Rowan had never asked. She never thought anything at all about her mother's early life, or her father's. It hadn't been important, not as important as her own travails as she negotiated sixth grade under the guidance of the meanest teacher in the world.

While Rowan had her revelations, Mom was talking. "The last I heard, and I was about thirteen, my mother went to prison for... I don't know what for. It didn't make any difference in my life. I was already in foster care. I met your father there. Lorenze, I mean. We were both angry at the world. He ran away into the city. He emailed, said he started his own clan, that things were good. He told me to come, and eventually one of the foster fathers scared me enough I took the plunge." She paused and looked out the window as if she needed to see the sunshine outside. "Unfortunately, Lorenze wasn't quite as successful as I'd hoped. He ran afoul of a local thug, got beat up big-time, framed, and landed a three-year term in the state prison. I lived a miserable existence foraging in garbage cans, stealing food from convenience stores, stealing wallets."

Rowan tried to comprehend what she was hearing. "Not you. Not stealing."

"Definitely stealing. Getting caught, getting beaten, getting arrested... I've got a record. It was expunged after I served time, but as a lesson to myself, I hung on to the proof. Don't believe me? I'll show you sometime." Mom smiled at Rowan's choking denial. "All that was still better than that last foster care home."

Rowan wanted to ask what the foster father had done, but she was afraid to; she didn't want to know. Not for sure.

Mom touched the small silver ring she always wore on her right ring finger. "I stole this."

Rowan shook her head.

"Oh, yes. Because I wanted it. I was angry. I thought the world owed me. When I was released, I couldn't return the ring. It came from a temporary stall in the Saturday market, and I had no one to return it to. I kept it. I wear to remember what I was, that I didn't hurt the world, but that I hurt someone, took their work and their income on a whim." Mom's voice trembled, and her eyes filled with remorseful tears.

Rowan had come home wanting drama. She had it, but it wasn't about her. Instead, she was hurting for her mom, wishing she could save her, wanting to cover her ears and cower away from the revelations. All she knew to do was reach out and put her hands over her mom's, and cling to them in what she hoped was comfort.

Mom turned her hands over to clasp Rowan's. "This is your ring. I always meant for you to have it, to wear if you like, or not. Value-wise, it's not worth much. The stone is turquoise and it's cracked, and the silver is worn. But you know what it means now." She slipped it off and onto Rowan's ring finger. It didn't fit, so she moved it to Rowan's little finger.

"I've got giant hands." Rowan knew she was being inane, but she didn't know the right thing to say, and her friends teased her about her hands.

"You're going to be taller than me, I'll bet." Mom held Rowan's hand and looked at the ring. "It looks good on you."

"Thank you, Mom. I love you. I won't ever take it off. I'll use it to remember you by."

"To remember this story by, too." Mom took a breath as if preparing to plunge into deep water. "While I was out there on the streets, I met the man who...impregnated me."

"My real—"

"No!" For the first time, Mom's voice grew sharp. "He was—he is—a liar and a thief, murderer, gangster, and a man who likes pretty young women."

"He was...older?"

"Yes. A handsome older man. He charmed me, offered me food, a place to stay, all at no price. So I, of course, slept with him and..." Mom looked down at her hands, entwined on the table, as if she was ashamed. "That was the price. I simply didn't see it at the time. Don't ever let anyone convince you that you owe them sex for any reason."

Mute with disbelief and horror, Rowan nodded.

"When I realized I was expecting a baby, that was the wakeup call. I took a hard look at him, and a hard look at myself. Did I want a baby? I was seventeen. No, of course I didn't. How about an abortion?"

"You thought about an abortion?" Rowan's voice ended on such a high note even she winced.

"Of course. An abortion would have made my life so much simpler. Think, Rowan!" Mom leaned forward, her eyes hot and anxious. "For the first time in your life, walk in someone else's shoes."

Rowan understood what Mom meant, but...she was almost not born? And what did she mean, 'For the first time in your life'? Rowan wasn't completely selfish...was she?

"The other alternative was to completely change my life. Which I did." Mom sighed as if, even now, the effort made her weary. "I took money—I figured that man owed me—got far away from him. He killed without a qualm. If he'd taken offense because I left him, I'd be dead today. And you, my darling daughter, would never have seen the light of day."

Rowan didn't want to know, but the question blurted out of her. "Do I remind you of him?"

"No! No, honey. I don't worry about you hurting anyone, or stealing, or... You're not a criminal mastermind. You proved that in kindergarten when I asked why you'd used my perfume before you went to bed and you told me the smell made you invisible to dragons." Mom put her head in her hand and giggled at the memory.

"It was logical. You always smelled so good, and you weren't afraid of the dragons in the dark, so I thought you were invisible to them." Rowan watched her mother laugh some more. "It's not really funny, you know."

"I'm not laughing at you. I'm laughing with you."

"Parents always say that when they're laughing at you." Rowan crossed her arms over her chest. "I'm not laughing."

"I know. I'm sorry." Mom controlled herself. "It's the memory of your sweet little face, turned up to me so earnestly, telling me that tale, and Rowan…you smelled like you'd fallen into a bouquet of carnations with grapefruit zest thrown in. You used half the bottle!"

"Oh." Rowan relaxed a little. "I guess I spilled it on me."

"I'll never forget. You were so cute. That's when I bought you the dragon-knight to protect you."

"It worked, too." Rowan treasured that small, precious piece of porcelain. The dragon's face in the knight's helmet made her laugh, and somehow the dragons were never as fearful.

She didn't know then that the cruel-man-dragons were so much worse.

"I'm glad." Mom stroked Rowan's cheek. "I never want you to be afraid or ashamed. I want you to have all the good things. I merely happen to think the good things are loving parents, a stable home, food to eat and shared laughter."

"Me, too," Rowan mumbled. That's not what she'd thought at the beginning of the conversation, but she was coming around to her mother's point of view.

"Anyway." Her mom sat back in her chair. "After I left him, your biological father, I talked to social services. I started over. I gave birth and finished high school. Then I went to community college, and while I was there, I looked around for something I wanted to do. I decided on the Coast Guard. I liked that job. I liked making a difference. It taught me a lot about being aware, thinking ahead, not imagining what might be but seeing what is."

"You quit the Coast Guard when Linden was born."

"Right. Dad said you were at the age when you needed me even more than the baby did." Mom sighed a tiny sigh. "He was right. I'm glad I was home for you today."

"I thought you quit for the baby," Rowan mumbled.

"Babies are very resilient. Young women are more complicated."

"Oh." Remembering Linden's constant happy babble, remembering her own brooding outbursts… Rowan supposed that was true. "What happened with Dad? I sort of remember that before I started kindergarten, he didn't live with us."

"Right. When Lorenze got out of prison—he got out early for good behavior—he came to find me, and there I was with you. I told him no, I'd come a long way, I had a baby, and I wasn't hanging out with a criminal."

Self-righteous as only an almost-teen could be, Rowan snipped, "If he'd served his time, he wasn't a criminal."

"Right, but I wasn't being unreasonable. He didn't want to leave the streets. Prison had taught him a lot of stuff, honed his skills: fighting, surviving, computer hacking for fun and profit. He knew he could be successful in that world, and he wanted to stay. But he wanted me, too. So after some sulking and begging—his—he made his choice." Mom gestured around their small kitchen. "And here we are."

"What about… Didn't the…didn't the other guy—" Rowan didn't really want to call him her father again "—when he found out you were pregnant, didn't he want to marry you?"

"I didn't tell him I was pregnant. And he was already married."

29

ROWAN SAT BACK *hard against the chair, her hand over her mouth.*

Mom put her fingers to her forehead as if it ached. "That's everything you need to know about the man who impregnated me, don't you agree? That he was older, that he was married, and that he didn't even bother to inconvenience himself by making sure I was safe from disease and pregnancy."

Rowan nodded.

Mom reached across the table and hugged her. "Remember my story, darling. When a guy sees how beautiful you are and tries to take you to bed without a condom, right away you know to walk away and never look back."

Rowan nodded again, but at the same time, she had to say, "I'm not beautiful like you. No one's going to want me."

"You look like me. You're getting tall like me. You'll be even more beautiful than me, and everyone will want you."

Rowan didn't know if she believed that; her mom was the prettiest woman in town. But a sudden horrifying thought occurred. "Do I look like him? Like...?"

"When I look at you, I never see him in your face."

★ ★ ★

Mom spoke convincingly enough that Rowan had never worried about it since. But now, as she dissected the words and her mother's intent, she realized Mom had merely denied seeing a resemblance…because she didn't want to, and because she didn't want Rowan to fear she resembled a monster.

Closing her eyes to cut off the view of her own face, she leaned her forehead against the cool mirror.

God. She needed off this island now.

Opening her eyes, she looked at the small silver ring nestled among the others. Her mother's ring. That small, cheap, treasured ring.

"I'll use it to remember you by."

Rowan had said that to her mother, and neither one had realized how prophetic it would be. The loss of her mother lived with her every day. The memories of her mom's strength kept Rowan moving forward even as she cried at night, even as she fled from one place to another, even as she imagined a day without fear or isolation. Tears clung to Rowan's lashes, but they didn't fall. Her mother wouldn't want her to cry over this. Him.

After all, in reality, knowing her sperm donor's name had changed nothing.

She saw a movement behind her in the mirror. She gave a scream, raised her fists and twirled to face… BeBée.

BeBée lifted her hands to show Rowan she held no weapon, and she had no intention of fighting. "I came to check on you. You okay? I asked where you went, and the dumb guy at the door said you went to the pool, but you weren't there. I wanted to check on surveillance, but I thought I'd try this first, and… Are you okay?"

Rowan lowered her fists. "I want out of here."

"You can't leave before the party. You know you can't. Daddy would have a fit."

"Don't call him that!" Rowan snapped hard and fierce.

BeBée flinched. "You're right. That was thoughtless of me. Gregory won't let you go. Especially not now… I suspect after you arrived, he got a sample of your DNA—"

"How?" The answer bobbed immediately into her mind. "My champagne glass. But why? He doesn't seem like a man who thinks deeply, especially about women. In fact, on day one, after he tried to shoot me, he came on to me."

"Ew."

"Yes."

They both shuddered.

Rowan continued, "Why would he even think to check my DNA?" Oh, God. Her mother's ring.

But BeBée didn't know about the ring, and she had a different explanation, one that fit the timeline. "*Mitzi*. Mitzi figured it out. Don't you remember at lunch when she acted her little scene with the gun and pointed it at everyone? I remember her expression when she saw you. Really *saw* your face. I didn't understand then—I was too busy hoping I didn't get shot—but now I think that for one moment, she forgot her lines in her own little drama. After that, it was a matter of doing the math. How old were you? How long ago did Gregory f—" BeBée caught herself before she finished the sentence, and made a quick change. "How long ago was Gregory involved with your mother? I would bet Mitzi said something to him—"

"If she did, that was stupid. When their son had been killed and he had no other progeny, why would she tell him he had a child with another woman?"

"She's not stupid, but she is not quite…mentally stable."

Rowan snorted softly. "A polite way of saying it."

"I suspect she realized pretty quickly that she'd blundered. If she had goaded him into losing his temper…well, that's when he's scary, and you don't want to be anywhere close. She could have got him to kill you and Joe. Instead, she made him wonder if what she said was the truth…"

"Why wonder when you've put out an order to have me killed like he killed my mother?"

"In his right mind, Gregory's has the usual parental instincts."

Parental… "I feel ill." Rowan put her hand to her churning gut.

"He knew there was a chance Mitzi was lying, working him up to get revenge for her son's death." BeBée nodded solemnly. "I know when he received the results, don't you?"

Rowan thought back on the way Torval reacted when Doug Moore had hurt her, and his upset at the thought she would leave, and nodded. "Yes. Today. This afternoon. Yes. This is awful." An understatement.

"If it makes you feel better, after you slapped Mitzi, her cheek was bleeding, and she's going to have a bruise."

"I wish I'd landed the punch. She'd still be unconscious."

"I wish you had, too." BeBée linked arms with Rowan, turned her and walked toward the door. "What are you *really* doing here, Rowan?"

"Why do you want to know?"

BeBée stopped. "All of a sudden, you don't trust me?"

Do I? Rowan remembered the care BeBée showed for her staff. She thought back on the time they'd spent alone exploring the island, how she'd smiled to hear to BeBée carry on about the bees, the horror she'd felt when BeBée shared the story about her tortured friend Bonita and the pity that made BeBée shove her off the cliff.

When Rowan had stupidly trusted Joe, let him into her life, into her bed, and discovered he wanted to bring her here and use her for his own purposes, she had doubted herself and her instincts. How could she not? Sure, she'd been played, but she'd been a willing accomplice.

Yet…yet Joe had motives other than mercenary, more than monetary. He'd been plain about that. His three-year-old sister had died at Torval's command. His motives were not so straight-forward as she in her first rage would have liked them to be.

And about BeBée… Rowan had always known any woman who could handle Gregory Torval was intelligent and resourceful. In the air up on that cliff, BeBée had been clear: she would get revenge for Bonita and liberty for herself. She had showed Rowan her determination and shared bits of her joyful soul straining to be free.

"I trust you. Sometimes I don't trust myself. Sometimes I want to relax and never again hear a soft footstep behind me or wonder why a stranger looks at me twice."

BeBée hugged Rowan's shoulders again. "Yes on the soft footstep, but honey, I can tell you why a stranger looks at you twice. You're pretty even when you're sweaty and covered with mud."

"You have a way with compliments." Rowan started walking again, and BeBée's arm fell away. "I'm here because Joe wants me here."

"Sure. What's he here for? Really, what's he here for? He's doing a good job of undermining Gregory's authority, but I can't quite figure out why. He doesn't seem to be digging in for a fight, more upsetting the balance."

Why not tell her? What difference did it make? "He's a mercenary. He's looking for an address book. The elderly lady who had it stolen is offering a substantial reward for its return. I'm along as Lorenze Winterbourne's daughter, and as a distraction."

"Best of show, that's you."

"Maybe Joe does want to take over from Torval, and maybe he simply intends find the address book and get out while Torval's having a fit about me. Do you think Joe knew about Torval being my—" Rowan couldn't say it.

"After you slapped Mitzi and rushed out of the room, I caught a glimpse of Joe's expression. He's either the world's best actor, or he didn't know, and right then, I don't know why he would have been acting." BeBée crinkled her little nose. "An address book. Where have you looked?"

"*I* haven't looked anywhere. *I'm* not getting the reward."

Glancing around the library didn't count. "Joe has managed to find a chink in Torval's software, and he's systematically searching the computer files. No luck so far."

"Computer? Files?" BeBée rolled her eyes. "An elderly woman's address book is probably going to be...an address book. You know, like paper with a fancy leather cover."

"I thought that, too. I guess he might just be looking for the location. That makes more sense." If Rowan got the address book for Joe, she'd be out of here and on the road, running as far and as fast as she could away from Raptor Island and Gregory Torval. And...from Joe Grantham.

"Come on." BeBée steered Rowan along. "I bet I know where it is. We'll find it."

30

BEBÉE DIMPLED AT the guard who stood in front of the door of Torval's office. "My friend is looking for a book, and I'm sure I've seen it in Da—Gregory's office." When he didn't move, she put her hand on his arm. "Diego, didn't you hear what happened in the dining room? Do you know who my friend is?"

Diego's dark eyes shifted toward Rowan, then hastily away as if afraid merely looking at her would get him in trouble. With a stiff nod, he moved aside.

If ever Rowan needed proof that the infamous scene has spread, this was it.

"Come on." BeBée opened the studded door, gestured Rowan inside, then shut the door behind them. "Now. Do you have any clue what we're looking for?"

"Obviously not."

"A wealthy old lady, right? It's an address book? Whose address do you suppose is in it that she's so worried about revealing?"

"Joe called it an address book, but he also said… Damn. I wasn't paying attention. He said her guests filled it in and signed it."

"So a *guest* book."

Rowan nodded. "That would make it thicker, right?"

"I'm betting on a leather binding, but who knows?"

While BeBée talked, Rowan perused the shelves. Occasionally she pulled out a book, glanced through the pages, and put it back. "Interesting selection of books."

BeBée nodded. "Da—Gregory has some great first editions."

"And some old paperbacks with cracked spines. Why? He doesn't strike me as a reader."

BeBée's mouth twitched into a smile. "You shouldn't generalize. He reads a lot, mostly history and political strategy. That's how he's kept himself on top all this time. He's the only person I know who's actually read Machiavelli's *The Prince*."

"You're saying he's not a stupid man."

"It will take a brilliant man to bring him down."

Something about the way BeBée spoke nudged Rowan to ask, "Is Torval really the only person you know who's read *The Prince*?"

BeBée smiled a bright and charming smile. "You are smart. Yes, I've read it."

Rowan looked around at the shelves. "You've read a lot of the books in this room."

"It's good to understand how your man's mind works, and sometimes a book like that helps a girl make plans for her future."

"Yes, I can see how that would work." *If you plan to take over the world.*

BeBée didn't turn from her perusal of the shelves, and her voice was neutral when she asked, "Did you never wonder who your biological father was?"

"My mom didn't tell me his name."

BeBée sharply turned on her. "You didn't ask?"

"My mother said Lorenze was my father, and after she described the man who impregnated her, I didn't want to know *him*." Rowan rubbed her chest over her breastbone. Her heart and lungs hurt as if she'd landed on a different planet. Or maybe this world had simply changed to one so inhospitable she was breathing the wrong sort of air. "Lorenze Winterbourne taught me that honor is a bedrock, the place where you anchor your boat and the storms might batter at you, but you'll know where you are and who you are, and you can bravely face whatever life throws at you."

"You did everything to save Lorenze Winterbourne, and you did save him. Gregory might try to twist that story around, to make you more his, but as long as Lorenze Winterbourne lives…"

Rowan stared steadily into BeBée's eyes. "He does."

"…then Gregory Torval exists in fear and doubt. He might be as smart as your mother and as brave as your father, but he cannot inspire loyalty. His son is dead. On a regular basis, his wife tries to poison him. He is going to reach for you, try to grasp and hold you." BeBée's dark eyes were clear and sure; she understood human nature, and she knew Gregory Torval. "All he has for the future is his hope of you."

"Does he *not* understand who I am, where my loyalties lie?"

"No." BeBée returned to her search of the shelves.

"That the man who's responsible for my mother's death can never be my true father?"

"No."

"That the monster who ordered Doug Moore to torture my stepfather engenders nothing in me but a taste for revenge?"

"He doesn't understand human nature at all. If he did, he would be afraid of—" BeBée paused, and pulled out a yellowing, satin-bound guest book with wildflowers embroidered on the front and back. "Look. Here's the book." She extended it to Rowan. "You can take it, get the reward yourself, and screw Gregory Torval and Joe Grantham at the same time."

"I don't want to screw them. I want out. I want to get away from here before—" Before Moore disappeared with a guest and

Rowan was forced to think about the shrieks and the agony, bones breaking and blood feeding the hungry flies. Before Rowan had to make the decision to take the bait and go to the rescue. She loved no one here as she had loved Lorenze Winterbourne, the father who had been there for her, but he'd demonstrated to her all this bothersome sense of right and wrong, and she didn't know if she could ignore the screams that would play in her imagination. "I need to get off this island."

"You can't. Not until Gregory lets you go. I understand. I'd help you if I could. But I only have so much power, and there's always some younger woman tapping on his bedroom door."

"You don't have to help me. I always help myself." Rowan opened the book to the first page. In strong, clear penmanship, she read, "'This book is the beloved possession of Frances Sattimore.'"

"Hey, now you know who it is!" BeBée sounded impressed.

"I suppose."

"You don't know Frances Sattimore? She was a Hollywood designer way back when, beautiful woman. She quit when she married that prince guy, what's his name? Stephane. He smacked her around. Right in the middle of a party, she hit him with a full trash can that knocked him silly and spilled all his secret perversions for everyone to see. They divorced, of course, but he was humiliated."

"I vaguely remember, I guess..." Rowan really had never had time to worry about the lives of the rich and famous. She'd been too busy staying alive.

"That's why Gregory stole Mrs. Sattimore's guest book. It's clearly something she treasures, and Gregory and Stephane are friends."

"What a pal." Rowan injected sarcasm into the phrase.

"Stephane paid for the service, pretty sure. Gregory doesn't do anything for free." The door opened, and BeBée gave a gasp and a giggle. "Hi, Daddy."

Gregory Torval stood in the doorway, his expression changing from anger to bemusement to frustration. "What are you doing in my office?"

"Looking for a book. Show him, Rowan."

Rowan held up the book.

"Rowan needs it," BeBée said.

Torval smiled as if he knew better. In a cajoling tone, he asked, "Wouldn't Rowan rather have a pretty trinket? A precious gem to wear on her finger?"

Rowan wanted to slap him for his smug assumption that she was silly and frivolous and could be bought with jewelry.

BeBée swiftly stepped in. "No, Daddy. You know what she's like. She wants to collect the reward, use it to make herself important...like you." When Torval still hesitated, she laughed. "Besides, what do you care if she takes the book? You did your favor for Stephane. You don't owe him anything, and he isn't even grateful."

"He isn't?" Torval frowned.

"When was the last time he came to pay homage? It's your birthday. Where is he?" BeBée had made her point, and now seemed to lose interest. She picked up an old magazine and started to leaf through it.

"Listen." Torval earnestly considered Rowan. "I need to say..." He took a step toward her.

She clutched the guest book to her chest and retreated.

"You don't have to act like I'm a pervert." His voice rose. "I'm not going to attack you. I have familial feelings, you know."

"We're not family." Rowan's voice was glacial.

"I'm your father."

"Lorenze Winterbourne is my father." She found herself repeating Yvonne's lecture almost word for word. "He is the man who cared for me when I had the flu and I threw up all over his shoes. When I was in middle school, he helped me with those stupid word problems and my dyslexia exercises. He taught me to drive."

A flush rose in Torval's face, a face marred by possessiveness, cruelty and years of uninterrupted rule.

In a flat tone, Rowan said, "He saved me when you would have killed me."

31

TORVAL HUFFED. "For God's sake, you can't hold that against me. I didn't know you were my daughter!"

"You seem to think that makes a difference. That killing a fourteen-year-old girl is okay as long as you're not her parent."

"Well…"

"Yeah. Well." Rowan knew he didn't understand even now the pure evil of his intention. "You had sex with my mother, yet you still viciously murdered her."

He flushed again. His voice rose. "I didn't know she'd had my kid! The bitch never told me."

Rowan stopped her retreat and started back toward him. *"Don't call my mother a bitch."*

Torval clearly remembered that she'd slapped his wife for calling Yvonne a whore.

Yet he was Gregory Torval; he always got his way, and he could call any woman whatever he wished…except Mitzi. He treated Mitzi with respect—or maybe it was fear.

He wanted to form a relationship with Rowan, and she

thought—she knew—he cared only because his son had been killed. If he still had a living child born in wedlock, a son, she would be nothing, a mere extraneous piece of woman flesh he might treat indulgently as long as she did as she was told.

"I gave you life!" Torval clearly thought that should cinch the deal.

"And you tried to take it away."

"Now I'll do everything to save your life. Maintain it. You won't ever have to live in fear again." He placed his hand flat on his chest. "I swear."

"What are the conditions?"

BeBée flipped pages more quickly.

His hand dropped. "Conditions?"

"As long as I obey you, you'll maintain me. As long as I live where and how you demand, I won't have to live in fear?" Rowan's voice rose, and she enunciated every word. *"What, my dear sperm donor, are your conditions?"*

He clearly didn't know what issue to tackle first. "It would be better if you—"

"No! No, no, no, no!" She waved his words away. "For fourteen years I've lived as I wished. I got my education. I've moved across the country, met people, ate different cuisines. I don't need your trinkets. I've earned my living—" she held up her beringed fingers for his inspection "—and I've bought myself jewelry, but none more precious than the ring my mother gave me. I am Rowan Winterbourne, and I don't need your protection."

His gaze dwelled on her hands, and when he looked into her eyes, his tone was sure and firm. "Nevertheless, I pledge to preserve your life by any means so you never live in fear again."

She looked down at the rings that encrusted her fingers. "I'd like to believe that is true."

"I recognized your mother's ring."

So she had betrayed herself by wearing it. But she hadn't realized that her last small link to the past would betray her.

She knew what Lorenze Winterbourne would say about *that* excuse.

"Yvonne always wore it." Torval tried to take Rowan's hand to look at the ring. She refused, closed her fingers into a fist, and he behaved as if he didn't notice her small defiance. "She loved it, and she wouldn't let me replace it with something better."

"I'll bet you hated that."

He nodded grudgingly.

From her perch on the desk, BeBée jumped and squealed. "Daddy, who's that?" She held up the magazine and pointed at a publicity photo of a long-ago, dashingly handsome celebrity.

Torval barely glanced before returning his attention to Rowan. "I don't know. Some actor from the nineties. Listen, Rowan, I'm not the man I was twenty-eight years ago. I'm not the man I was fourteen years ago."

"You're worse."

"With you in my life, I can be better!"

"Get rid of Doug Moore."

Torval opened his mouth, but nothing came out. Rowan could see his thoughts. Give up his best torturer, the man who produced the desired results while Torval kept his hands clean?

Rowan laughed incredulously, bitterly.

Torval raised his open hand.

BeBée interceded again. "Oh, Daddy. You're kidding me." She leaned forward, both hands flat on the desk, and displayed an impressive amount of cleavage. "That's you, isn't it?"

Her voice gushed with such pleasure, Rowan stared at her in shock. What game was BeBée playing? Torval wasn't going to fall for that. But when she turned back to him, he pulled his hand back. He looked at his palm, then at Rowan. Then at BeBée with a half smile.

BeBée had had given him the excuse he needed to disengage. He asked, "Why would you think it was me?"

"Same hair, same chin, and oh, those big eyes! I knew you

were hiding a secret past, but I never thought this! You don't want anyone to know, do you? They'd think you were a pretty boy." So clever of BeBée to apply flattery and sex.

Torval glanced at Rowan.

Rowan, who watched him with unalloyed contempt.

"Daddy…" BeBée dragged out the word like one long sigh of seduction. "Come here and let me discover who you really are."

Torval walked toward her, a man more than willing to appear manipulated to get out of a fraught situation which had no possible resolution that could please and appease.

Still in that crooning voice, BeBée said, "You'd better tell Rowan if she can take that book, or she'll have to stay here and *talk* some more."

Torval waved his hand dismissively at her. "Go on. Take it. I don't care."

BeBée winked at her and slid her finger between her moist lips.

As Rowan escaped from the room, she heard BeBée's tissue-thin gown tear. "My God," Rowan whispered. In her next life, she swore she'd learn how to handle a man like that. In this life, if she talked in that girly tone or performed that finger-in-the-mouth maneuver, she was pretty sure she'd be ridiculous. To the bodyguard, she said, "I wouldn't let anyone else in that room for awhile."

Diego grunted his understanding and moved to stand, a muscular bulwark, in front of the door.

Clutching the book to her chest, Rowan walked toward suite 425 thought hard about how to keep possession of Frances Sattimore's guest book. For when Torval recovered from his sexual exhaustion, he'd remember what he'd given away, and want it back. She couldn't take a chance on losing possession now.

She swerved toward the service quarters, looking for Szababos, and found him supervising the clean-up of the night's reception. It would seem after the scene in the lobby, the guests had mostly vanished. Probably they feared the fallout. Possibly they had re-convened somewhere else to gossip and speculate. Rowan didn't really care. She needed to speak to Szababos alone.

At her summons, he hurried to her side. "Did you come back to see the doctor?"

"What?" She glanced at her bruised and swollen wrist. "Oh. No. I know it's going to hurt tomorrow, but tonight I have more to be concerned about. Is there a way to send an item from Raptor Island via the U.S. Postal Service?"

"We have daily air deliveries and mail of course goes out."

"I'd like to mail this." She showed him the satin-bound guest book. "Torval gave it to me. I don't want to give him a chance to change his mind."

"All outgoing mail is inspected for…"

She stared at Szababos. *"Really?"*

"But you're Mr. Torval's daughter." Szababos bowed briefly. "I know he would want you to be exempt."

She smiled bitterly. There was a benefit she'd never imagined. "Do you have an envelope I can use?"

Being Szababos and the epitome of efficiency, he produced a USPS envelope in the correct dimensions to fit the bubble-wrapped and taped book. She addressed it to her P.O. Box in Offbeat Bay and handed it over. "When will it go out?"

"I'll send it tonight."

"Thank you, Szababos." She put her hand on his arm. "It's important to me." Turning, she hurried toward the suite she shared with Joe, and met him rushing toward the door from the other direction. "I got it!" she called. "I found the guest book and it's in a safe place, waiting for my retrieval."

He didn't seem to care about that at all. Instead he asked, "Where have you been? You were spotted headed for the pool, then here, then I don't know, and—" Abruptly he stopped a foot away from her. "I swear I didn't know."

It took her a moment to realize what he didn't know. "That Torval is my father?"

"It never crossed my mind that such a thing was possible. It's too much of a coincidence."

"It's not a coincidence at all." She opened the door to their suite and led the way into the sitting room. "Torval's owned—"

He gestured her to silence and clicked on the microphone interrupter.

When he nodded to her, she started again. "Torval's owned this island for how many years? Twenty-eight? Thirty?"

"Something like that."

"When my father—Lorenze—was released from prison, my mother had finished high school and passed the tests to join the Coast Guard. Think! The Coast Guard. I don't think her actions were an accident, do you? Then Lorenze did the same thing. Finished high school, passed the tests, joined the Coast Guard."

Joe followed her logic. "They wanted to be a thorn in Gregory Torval's side."

"Yes, and more—they wanted to destroy his organization. They knew, better than anyone, what Torval was capable of. My mom said she knew stuff about my biological father that made him dangerous to us. It makes sense that she and Lorenze used their knowledge to undermine Torval."

"Ah." Joe nodded slowly. "That does make sense."

"No wonder Lorenze knew what would happen when he shot Torval's son. No wonder he moved so quickly to save us." She almost mentioned her sister's name, but caught herself at the last moment. Just in case Torval *was* listening. "Whether I'm Torval's biological daughter doesn't matter. He is nothing to me, except the enemy who murdered my mother, the heart of my family." She whispered, "Bring him down, Joe. Please bring him down."

"You trust me to do that for you?"

"I do." She took in a slow breath and let it out on one breathy word. *"Please."* She saw the slow shift in his eyes, from anxiety to passion, as her message made sense to him.

He clarified, "Please?"

"Yes. Please."

He moved toward her slowly, with that grace of movement that reminded her of their dance in her kitchen. He encircled her waist with his hands and dragged her close into his body. The scents of soap, sex and passion rose off him in waves, filling her with heady need.

"Say it again," he instructed her.

"Please."

"And?"

"I trust you."

He smiled in slow delight. "I hope you don't have anything planned for the rest of the night."

"Don't you have some devious undermining of Torval's authority you need to perform after dinner?"

"I suspect your absence, and mine, at one of his command performances should be sufficient undermining of Torval's authority. At least, let's hope so." He pulled her into his arms. "Since we'll be otherwise engaged."

32

ROWAN THOUGHT THEY'D just rip off their clothes and do it. Really, after Joe's impassioned speech about being in her all the time, that seemed logical. Didn't it?

But Joe, being Joe, had other ideas. Gently he took her left wrist, looked at the bruises there, kissed them and said, "What you need after such a fraught day is...forgetfulness."

"Forgetfulness?"

"Forgetfulness so total you don't remember where you are, who you are, the dangers that surround you, your past, your present, your future..."

"Joe, it's just sex." Right away she realized she'd blundered. "I mean, between us we had great sex, but—"

He put his lips on her forehead and kissed her as if she'd expressed the most foolish belief possible. "Trust me."

"I do." She did, but he promised a miracle he couldn't deliver. She was Rowan Winterbourne. In all the years since the events that ended with her father's death, she had never been able to forget that, and sometimes, it seemed that oblivion would have been easier.

He placed his hands on the bare skin of her shoulders, found the gathered blue violet silk sleeves that clung to her smooth skin, and slid them down her arms. "You have that little frown line between your brows. Don't worry. Let me handle the details."

The lined, smocked and fitted bodice caught on her breasts, then slithered to her waist leaving her bare to his gaze. "I've plotted every moment in my mind," he said. "And already you've surprised me." His fingertips grazed the curve of her breast. "I observed and supposed you were wearing a bra."

"My B cup doesn't require a lot of structure and I'm able to get away with built in support." How had she managed to wander down this conversational road? "You're very detail-oriented."

"Yes, but in this instance I managed not to plot this out on my spread sheet." He flashed her a grin. "This is my chance to find out if my imaginings work as I hope. You will tell me if I blunder?"

"Um, sure." She had second thoughts. "But not in so many words!"

He laughed. "My ego is not fragile, Rowan."

No doubt about that.

"You'll tell me what you like," he said persuasively.

"You'll be able to tell."

"I like words. I like to talk during sex."

"I remember." She did, and the recall of that one night made her blush like a girl. He had asked questions. "Do you like this?" "How about this?" "Which is better?" "How does this make you feel?" If she didn't answer, he would pause and wait. Like she could speak and orgasm and make sense all at the same time.

Now, he cupped her cheek, kissed her mouth for a long, long time. He had a way about him, so leisurely she wondered if he even knew how to hurry, yet so driven she knew he lusted to the point of madness. Kisses were more than a preliminary; they were a sex act in themselves. When he pulled back, he whispered, "Would you remove your gown for me?"

He knew how. Yes, he did.

But being Joe she knew he would request her consent in words and deeds; he wanted her all in at every stage of this love play. Putting her hands on her hips, she slid the the silk down. The elastic smocking clung, then eased down her long legs to fall at her feet. He followed it to the floor, knelt before her, smiled at her beige boy short panties. "Practical cotton is no disguise, Rowan," he said, and pressed his face to her belly and breathed deeply.

He behaved as if the scent of her body was an aphrodisiac, and she began to wonder if he could possibly fulfill his promise of forgetfulness.

The mere idea shot a bolt of panic through her. Being aware with all her senses had kept her alive for fourteen years, and to abandon that ingrained habit, even in Joe's arms—

"What's wrong?" He stood and observed her posture, her expression, then pushed a curl of hair off her forehead and gazed into her eyes. "Trust, blind trust, is so difficult for people like us. We need to hold on to control, don't we? To do otherwise is to risk more than life. It's risking our very selves."

She nodded. She should have been relieved that he understood so well. Instead, she felt exposed, her soul stripped more naked than her body. Yet...

Forgetfulness.

Trust.

That night, Rowan found both in Joe's arms.

And she gave both. They were gifts to be exchanged by two strangers who were, as Joe said, alike. They had met and merged in their minds and their bodies. Before, they'd had sex. Now... now they were lovers.

In the wee small hours of the morning, when they rested in each other's arms, comfortable, sated, exhausted, she didn't know what came over her. Maybe she felt the need to show her trust to Joe by confessing her most guarded secret. She blurted, "My father is dead. Lorenze Winterbourne…is dead."

With her head on his chest, she heard his startled intake of breath. His embrace strengthened, as if he understood he had to hold her together. "I'm honored by your confidence, and sorry to hear of his death. I thought so…but I hoped not. I wanted there to be a someone in this world who always did the strong, right thing. And you loved him, and the people you've trusted enough to love have occurred too seldom in your life."

"Mr. Bandara…and I had to find him an assassin." Her voice broke under the cane of recent grief.

"Ahhh." Now Joe understood about the assassin.

She gathered her composure and her words. "After Dad—Lorenze—came to Raptor Island and accomplished his goal to save my life…we had plans. When she was a teen, Kealoha had worked on a cruise ship. She had connections. We were going to hire on, get to Hawaii where her family lived. Kealoha and I would work. Dad could recover. Beach, sun, warm weather, and no fear that Gregory Torval could find us, get to us." Rowan had never shared this story with anyone. Why would she? Her mission in life was to make Gregory Torval afraid, to taunt him with the belief that her father lived, that he was the blessed crusader of Los Angeles, credited with all good deeds.

Joe rubbed a slow palm up and down her spine. "That was a good plan."

"I know. I wish…" The grief of this had never diminished. "Dad made it as far as San Diego. In the morning, we were supposed to board the ship. He died that night in a motel. Kealoha woke me, and we…" Rowan's voice wavered.

"What did you do?" His calm, concerned voice steadied her.

"The car was a—you know—Land Rover. Our family camped a lot. Dad drove it to work on the day he shot Torval's son, and we hung on to that vehicle all the way through hell and back. It was barely getting light when we 'helped' Dad out of the room and put him in the back seat. No one saw us, we thought, but the motel was such a dive I wonder now if other people had been 'helped' like that and no one paid attention. We headed east. Got him into Death Valley, went off-roading. I mean, as off-road as we could, really rugged stuff. We're lucky we didn't crack the oil pan. When we reached some rocks, no signs of people, we got him out. Stripped him so the predators wouldn't have problems with their…meal. Laid him out." Her heart hurt as she remembered the look of her father's naked, tortured, mutilated body. "We tried to say a few words, have a moment, but the car temp read 123 Fahrenheit. We gave up and left him."

"Did anybody find him? Law enforcement? Hikers?"

"When we stopped and looked back, the vultures were already circling."

"That's good."

"Yes. He was a very practical man, and he…he would have approved."

"I am sorry he's not alive. His story inspired me, and I love that, after all these years, he still gets credit for the hero stuff."

She smiled a faint smile. "I like it, too. I thought as the years passed, he'd be forgotten, but he's grown in stature. His name has become a synonym for courage against all odds. Not a bad legacy to have."

"His daughter is following in his footsteps. He would be proud of you, Rowan Winterbourne."

"Thank you. I hope I can live up to his example."

"Tomorrow we'll both remember how Lorenze Winterbourne taught us to be heroes."

"Without the dying part?"

"That's the plan."

DAY THREE

33

THE PARTY STARTED when circus music blared from Joe and Rowan's room speaker.

Rowan sat straight up in bed.

A high, scary laugh pierced the air, and a clown voice screeched, "The parade starts at ten! Be early for the best viewing! Be there or be square!"

Rowan looked over at Joe, naked, facedown and unmoving. She leaned over and spoke in his ear. "Is your pistol loaded?"

He didn't open his eyes. "Yes. Why?"

"Because I want to shoot that clown." She thought for a second. "No, first I want to shoot the speaker and then the clown."

"His funeral procession would be very short."

"What?" She was confused. "How so?"

"All his clown friends would come in one tiny car."

She pushed her pillow over his face.

Laughing, he shoved it aside, grabbed her and rolled her over.

He looked into her face and started to say something. And stopped. And said, "Today's the big day."

"Gosh, yes." She widened her eyes. "Can't wait."

"When we finish this event, you can leave."

"Not you?"

"Probably not. You've escaped the island before. You know the way."

"The way my father escaped…is blocked. But I do have a way."

"I thought you might." He nodded, satisfied and admiring. "You'll take the address book and get the reward. After that, you'll able to go where you want and do what you want."

She sat up on one elbow. "How much is this reward?"

"Not enough to make up for your having to leave the lighthouse."

Bitterness quirked her mouth. "No. I suppose not. That has been…the next best thing to a home I've had since I was fourteen."

"I am sorry for this result."

"But maybe…if our being here changes the current reality… if that reality makes it possible for me to go back…"

"Maybe."

He offered little hope, and Rowan deflated.

"Maybe someday, you'll understand why this was so important. But today, dress for action and—do you have another pair of running shoes? Besides the ones ruined by mud?"

"All my shoes are made for action. In case you haven't noticed, I'm too tall to wear heels, and in this madhouse, much too sensible."

"God, I love you." He pressed a kiss on her that felt like truth.

She didn't take the words at face value, but she kissed him back and smiled at him. "I trust you," she answered.

"That's even better." He pulled back reluctantly. "Performance time."

★ ★ ★

As instructed, Rowan wore sensible clothes: a sleeveless gray-blue jumpsuit with a smooth, flowing line that made her look six feet tall, white tennis shoes and a broad-brimmed white hat trimmed with a blue ribbon. Joe wore jeans that looked as if they'd been custom-fitted to him, a cream shirt with sleeves rolled up to his forearms, and hiking boots. From somewhere he'd procured a cowboy hat, and he appeared to be the epitome of casual...and powerful.

She wished she knew the trick to that.

They followed the crowd and arrived at the parade ground, a mile-long oval running track, and were met by two of Torval's beefier bouncers. "Mr. Torval invites you both to sit with him on the judging stand."

"Invites?" Rowan questioned them.

But Joe beamed. "What an honor!"

Which startled Rowan, because she'd thought that, whatever he had planned, he would need time away from Torval to put in the finishing touches. Either he had it planned down to the nth or—as they were escorted toward their destination, she looked around at the crowd that lined the sidelines—he had accomplices.

Huh. Who could they be? Why hadn't she thought of that before?

A commotion ahead centered her attention on the judging stand. Mitzi faced her husband, berating, gesturing, obviously furious. As usual, she wore black: a black suit with a fitted jacket and pencil skirt, stiletto heels, a pill-style hat with a widow's veil pulled low over her eyes, and—this marked an unusual departure for her—a bloodred silk button-up shirt.

When she finished speaking, Torval barked one word at her. "No!"

She turned and stormed down the steps and across the parade ground toward the house. When she saw Joe and Rowan, she changed course and steamed right at them.

Joe squeezed Rowan's fingers, then freed his hand, she supposed to allow him to draw his pistol. Clearly under directions to protect them, the bouncers moved closer.

Mitzi came to a halt in front of them.

BeBée was right. Mitzi's cheek was bruised and swollen where Rowan, and her rings, had blackened Mitzi's eye. Now, face-to-face with her, Rowan braced herself for another attack, possibly physical, likely verbal.

Mitzi ignored her and smiled at Joe, a cruel slash of lips and red, red lipstick. "You can't always be there. You can't protect her forever." With a nod to him, she walked on, strolling now, knowing she'd left fear behind.

Sadly for Mitzi, Rowan responded badly to threats. She followed Mitzi, put her hand on her shoulder and spun her around. "I don't need protection. I protect myself." She reached out to touch Mitzi's black eye.

Mitzi yanked herself away, a knee-jerk reaction that admitted more than she would have liked. Catching herself, she pulled back her veil to allow Rowan to clearly see the damage she'd done. It was an insult and a challenge. "You have to sleep sometime…and I have friends you can't imagine."

Rowan knew now why Mitzi had dressed as she had. Like a poisonous black widow spider with a red-splashed warning for the world to see.

Joe watched Mitzi until she was out of sight, then took Rowan's hand again. "Come on."

Why haven't I thought that Joe might have accomplices?

Oh. Right. She'd been distracted by having guns aimed at her, by the wrenching memory of Lorenze Winterbourne, by the threat presented by Doug Moore, and by the horror of discovering she was Torval's daughter.

Never mind. She gave herself a pass. She'd been too busy and distracted to think anything through.

The judging stand was decorated as if this parade was an all-

American Fourth of July parade with red, white and blue banners draped across the rails and U.S. flags waving on every corner. Some poor sucker, or probably several poor suckers, had transported Torval's leather-upholstered throne from the great hall, hoisted it up on the stand and centered it among the wooden benches. Mitzi's smaller throne had been transported, too. It, of course, stood empty except for BeBée, who leaned an elbow on the back of it and watched Torval as he genially strode forward to greet Joe and Rowan. Joe he shook hands with. Rowan he forcibly embraced. Before she could think of an appropriate response—maybe a *No!* like he'd shouted at Mitzi—he stepped away and said, "We missed you at last night's festivities."

Joe smiled. "We celebrated our own festivities. I'm sure you understand."

Torval's gaze slid to Rowan, then quickly away, and although he didn't speak aloud, Rowan read his thoughts. *That's my daughter, you bastard.*

Again Joe released Rowan's hand. Perhaps he read Torval's thoughts, too.

Yet with forced geniality, Torval gestured toward the seating. "I've got it all arranged. Rowan, you'll sit on my right hand with Joe beside you. BeBée, you'll take Mitzi's place."

"No, Daddy." BeBée stood firm and solemn. "I'm not sitting on the queen's throne. That privilege isn't worth my life."

"It's not a throne. It's a chair. Just a chair." Torval glowered at the chair as if it represented Mitzi herself. "She's not the queen!"

BeBée was unmoved by Torval's vehemence. "No, Daddy. You can't protect me from her."

Which sounded uncannily like Mitzi's threat on the parade ground.

Torval's face turned red. He seemed to swell with rage, and for a moment, Rowan expected him to pull a pistol and order BeBée to sit or die. Instead he shouted, "All right!" He turned to the bouncers. "Take Mitzi's chair away! Pull the benches closer!"

As the men moved to get the chair, one of them mumbled something about a hernia.

"What? What did he say?" Torval pointed a shaking finger.

The other bouncer answered. "He's new, and he said he was glad to do whatever you want, Boss. We're all glad for the jobs. You know that. Glad."

The mumbler nodded his head stiffly, as if he had just now realized he was expendable.

In the last five minutes, Torval had been crossed too many times. "That better be what he said. He better watch his mouth!"

The mumbler bowed and bowed again, jerky with fear. He picked up his end of the throne and, with his bouncer-handler, lugged the heavy chair off the stand and down the stairs.

Szababos arrived on the scene, casually dressed couples trailing after him. "Mr. Torval, are you ready for your guests?"

"Sure. Get 'em seated in their right places." Torval pointed to the bench on his left hand. "BeBée, you sit there."

"Okay, Daddy." BeBée seated herself so obediently she might never have defied him, and she patted his throne. "Come and sit with me. You know how shy I am without you."

Rowan rolled her eyes at Joe.

He grinned back at her.

They understood each other without words, and when they looked around, the other guests were watching them.

Gregory Torval was looking at them—and he was not pleased. He went to his throne and sat down. People scrambled to the seats to which Szababos directed them, and the parade began with a resounding crash of cymbals.

Somehow BeBée and Mitzi had assembled a non-high-school-affiliated marching band with a dancing drumline and widely, painfully smiling majorettes. The band pulled up in front of the stand and performed a special number that included a series of crotch-splitting cheerleader acrobatics and a rendition of "Happy Birthday, Mr. Torval."

They marched on around the arena, followed by classic 1950s and '60s convertibles loaded with people. The pretty girls wore crowns and sat up on the top of the back seats and waved and blew kisses. Men rode in the front seats and walked beside the cars. The convertibles were followed by a single tiny car with darkened windows. It stopped in front of the judging stand. Son of a gun, one of the miniature doors opened, an oversized red shoe appeared, followed by a long red-and-white-striped leg, followed by a sinewy body, followed by a painted face with oversized ears...and before it was over, a dozen clowns had exited the miniature car.

Rowan jabbed Joe with her elbow.

He grinned at her, all cocky like he'd been expecting it.

Torval forgot his displeasure and laughed and clapped.

BeBée slid off the bench, tiptoed behind him and crawled up behind Rowan. "The band and the clowns we hired. The people in the cars are Torval's people on the streets. I figured this was the best way to involve them in the celebration."

"Were they searched for weapons?" Joe asked out of the corner of his mouth.

"Before they got on the ferry and before they got off. It's amazing how much security managed to collect in the second search."

"Great." Joe watched two clowns who stopped to make a giant balloon animal, an elephant about half the size of a real elephant.

Torval was delighted.

They tied it to the railing, where it bobbed in the breeze, and then—a real circus elephant stomped into the arena carrying a trapeze in its trunk and acrobats on its back.

Everyone applauded wildly.

BeBée murmured, "We had to get an elephant out of retirement at a wildlife park. Apparently Peanut misses the applause and regularly performs for the tourists who visit the park."

Rowan laughed. "Of course he does." She watched as the

elephant strode to the center of the ring and helped the clowns set up the trapeze.

"Got to go back. It's time for the grand finale." BeBée scooted back to her seat.

The clowns did their magic tricks. The acrobats performed. With a great blast of trumpets, Peanut stood on his hind legs and waved his trunk.

The crowd gasped and cheered.

With another trumpet blast, a series of fireworks went off all around the jogging track.

Torval was ecstatic. "Did you enjoy it?" he asked Rowan. "Wasn't that fun?"

Did he think this was the equivalent of taking her to the circus as a child? Or imagine he had somehow overcome the murder of her mother? Rowan wanted to shout at him, and at the same time…she felt sorry for him. He had everything and nothing: all the money, all the power and no friends, no family, and a string of vultures waiting for him to fall so they could pick his bones. In some corner of his mind he knew it, and like a child, he thought if he bought her the right trinket, entertained her the right way, she'd be his daughter.

Never gonna happen.

But she looked past him to see BeBée staring at her with sad, pleading, puppy eyes and knew she was begging for Rowan to be kind. So for BeBée's sake, not for his, Rowan said, "Yes. Excellent entertainment. BeBée should be commended for arranging such a birthday celebration for you."

It wasn't a little girl's excitement, but it was enough for Torval. He grinned and stepped forward for another one of those forced embraces. She was ready this time and fended him off with an elbow jab to the chest. He took it, spun and hugged BeBée instead. "Did you hear that? You did a great job!"

"All for you, Daddy. All for you." BeBée smirked at Rowan over Torval's shoulder.

With a start, Rowan recognized an eerie similarity between BeBée's expression and Mitzi's. That made her wish she was home safe in her lighthouse…where she would never be really safe again.

34

FROM THE GROUNDS around the mansion, a cowboy dinner bell rang loud and long.

Torval stepped up to the mike and announced, "Lunch and liquor in the garden."

The folks around the arena cheered.

"Proceed in an orderly manner. Or else." Torval lifted one arm and pointed. "Follow the elephant!"

Peanut lifted the acrobats onto their perches on his back. Torval's street people piled into the convertibles, and when they were full, the remainder of them walked. Clowns made balloon animals and passed them out. The scene was silly and charming until Rowan remembered who and what these people were: killers, thieves, drug pushers and pimps. They, combined with the silly, friendly circus atmosphere, seemed off-kilter and sad, bizarre and pathetic, the innocence of childhood celebrated by the depraved and corrupt.

Torval turned to everyone on the stand. "As soon as the crowd clears, we'll head back into the throne room, where we'll enjoy a live band and dancing, then a sophisticated buffet, and I'll cut the massive cake I've been hearing about."

"Oh, Daddy." BeBée pouted. "I wanted the giant cake to be a surprise."

"I'll be surprised," he promised and winked.

Rowan overheard Savannah say to Wadell, "Torval looks a little tired."

"You'd be tired, too, if you'd been up all night banging BeBée," Wadell replied.

"I'm never tired." Savannah sounded snappish.

"What?" Wadell's voice held a lash.

"I…didn't mean anything by it." Savannah reached for him. "Forgive me, darling."

Wadell walked away and left her standing there.

She had fumbled her playing cards.

"The bus is almost here," BeBée announced.

Indeed it was, an open transport built to look like a red-and-gold circus carriage with three layers of elevated seats and a fringed tarp to protect the top passengers from the sun.

Rowan caught up with the disconsolate Savannah. "You can sit with us."

Savannah looked at Joe. "Is that okay?"

Rowan sighed in exasperation.

"Of course." Joe grinned at Rowan. From what he'd said about his mother, he understood the principles of living in the twenty-first century. Yay, him. Yet as he helped first Savannah, then Rowan up the stairs onto the bus, he murmured in Rowan's ear, "I'll get you and your friend to the next event. Don't worry your pretty little head."

She turned on the step above him, put her arms around his shoulders, and pressed her breasts into his face. "My pretty little head is thinking your snarky little mouth is going to be begging tonight."

For a mere moment, his eyes glazed. Then his formidable

brain snapped back into place. "I would walk across the world on my knees for you."

She ran her hands through his dark hair. "You are good."

"You know I am."

They smiled at each other. Broke apart. Climbed onto the bus. And found themselves the cynosure of all eyes.

Oh. The way for a female to be powerful in this crowd was to be on the arm of a powerful someone...who had a penis. *Great.* Rowan had it figured out now.

"Joe. Sit with Savannah," Rowan murmured.

He followed her thought without a hitch. "Shake things up a little?"

"Keep them off balance," she agreed, and sat in the seat right behind the driver. Give her enough time and she'd get the hang of this political gamesmanship crap. Heck, next she could run for US Congress.

They arrived at the mansion. The bus stopped at the grand entry. Wadell rushed to the front and helped Savannah off the bus. Mission accomplished; he had been knocked off-balance, his dominance challenged.

No one was paying attention to the birthday boy, Gregory Torval, and despite BeBée hanging on his arm and whispering in his ear, he was *not* happy.

Joe slid into the seat behind Rowan and toyed with the ends of her hair. "You are a genius. No one's watching anything except..."

"The balance of power shifting right before their eyes?"

"Right." When everyone had filed off and they were the only ones left on the bus, Joe stood and offered Rowan his hand. "Come on. Let's see what other distraction we can cause before we part."

She shouldn't have been surprised. "We're parting very soon?"

"Very soon."

"Then let's make these last few moments count."

35

WHEN THE BAND PLAYED, Joe and Rowan danced. When the buffet was served, they ate, and danced again. The circus theme continued inside with helium balloons, arcade games and cotton candy. Men tried to engage Joe in conversation, he brushed them off, preferring to spend his time with his arms around Rowan.

When the afternoon was waning, Joe looked at his watch and pulled her a little away from the crowd. Quietly he said, "In a few minutes, there'll be a commotion."

"All right."

"When I tell you, scream and run for the door."

"All right."

"Get off the island however you can."

"Not a problem."

He thoughtfully contemplated her. "It's the suitcase, isn't it? The yellow suitcase."

"That's right."

"What is it?"

"Hot-air balloon."

Joe threw back his head and laughed so long and loud everyone turned to look, and anyone suspicious who might have wondered about their low-voiced conversation was undoubtedly put at ease. Pulling her close, he kissed her hard. "How much I admire you!"

She grinned at him.

He sobered. "But you already had it made when I contacted you. What were you planning to do?"

"Come to the island. Wreak havoc. Get revenge."

The change from laughing Joe to sober Joe to horrified Joe was pronounced. "You would have died."

"Not if I did everything right."

"Woman. You terrify me."

"Don't get on my bad side."

"No. I promise I'll do my best to remain on your good side. For all the reasons." His warm voice and heated gaze made her eyelids flutter and her smile broaden. "Once you get to the mainland, take my car."

"I can't promise I'll land anywhere near your car."

"You can't steer a balloon?"

"Not a hot-air balloon. It drifts with the air currents. The prevailing wind is west to east, so I will make the coast." She shrugged. "I'm just not quite sure where."

He eyed her anxiously. "You'll make the coast?"

"Yes!" She was *almost* positive.

"Okay. If you can, get to my car and drive it. It's fast."

"Keys?"

"They're in the rear driver's side fender well in a magnetic key box."

"What?"

"Remember when I walked back to the car and—"

She did remember. "That was brilliantly played!"

"Thank you. Sometimes it's the easiest things that work." He smirked. "The box is locked with two fingerprints, yours and mine."

"Mine?" She was aghast. "How did you get mine?"

"The first night, I lifted it off your glass."

Him with her fingerprint, then Torval and Mitzi with her DNA. She hadn't even noticed. "You played me for such a sucker."

"Yes."

"I need to up my game." Or she would die.

He got very serious very quickly. "You need to stop playing."

She laughed sadly. "I wish that was possible."

"I'm working on it." He lifted her hand and kissed it, and looked into her eyes.

She looked into his.

And a muffled explosion rocked the floor.

36

AS IF BEWILDERED, Joe looked around. "What was that?" he asked loudly.

"It sounds like when I was in the war," Francisco suggested as loudly as Joe. "In Kuwait."

"You mean…a bomb?" Spencer's voice rose.

The words carried across the great hall on the force of fear. "A bomb?"

"What kind of bomb?"

"What do we do?"

Another explosion blasted, this one closer.

Torval stepped up to the microphone. In a forcefully calm tone he announced, "Folks, my security team is tracking down the source of this disturbance—"

Another explosion, farther away but still intense.

Voices rose on a tide of worry.

"Keep calm." Torval sounded like a man on the edge of fury. "We're going to figure out what—"

The boom this time was in the house and close enough to rattle the windows.

Joe gave Rowan a push toward the door and shouted, "Run, run! Get off the island!"

She filled her lungs, gave an ear-piercing scream, and ran.

That did it. Guests surged toward the exits.

From the podium, Torval shrieked, "Stop it! Stop now! I command you to stop!" He pulled a pistol and fired at the ceiling.

The stampede turned into a riot.

Rowan veered toward the balloon stand, dove toward the wall and the floor, gasped at the pain as she landed on her bruised wrist. She skidded into the clown trying to cram himself and his giant ears into the cubbyhole with the helium tanks. She stared at him, her nose to his red nose, and felt a desire to laugh hysterically.

"You're Rowan, right? Joe told me to keep a lookout for you." The clown's high-pitched voice had subsided into a smoker's husky tones. His breath smelled like a warped combination of cigarettes and cotton candy.

"Joe? You know Joe?"

"He's my boss." The clown grabbed a helium tank, a dark metal cylinder three feet tall, laid it on end, and picked up a giant iron wrench. "Watch this."

At the microphone, Torval bellowed orders no one could hear.

The clown lifted the wrench and struck the pop-off valve. Pressurized helium escaped in a roar that blasted the tank across the ballroom.

The screaming intensified.

Rowan viewed the clown in horror.

He explained, "Joe told me to add to the chaos if I could without hurting anyone. You have to admit, this is a great way to do it with the materials at hand!"

Rowan put her palm over her rapidly beating heart and nodded. She'd wondered if Joe had accomplices. Yeah, well, this guy wore a foolproof disguise.

"That one's a cool customer." The clown pointed.

Rowan looked around the stand.

BeBée stood listening to Szababos and a wildly gesturing server. She nodded and walked through the service door into the kitchen.

"She *is* a cool customer," Rowan said. "She'll take care of her staff."

"Somebody's got to." The clown lined up another tank.

"I'll leave you to your, um, chaos." She stayed low, peeked out from behind the stand, and saw Savannah and Li pushing at each other to get out the door first. From behind, Spencer grabbed them, shoved them behind him, and escaped.

Guests and staff ran, fell, were trampled, were dragged to safety. Explosions continued, some near, some far. Lights flickered, then went out, and only the sunlight that streamed through the tall windows and in the open doors lit the great room.

Joe was nowhere in sight.

A commotion, he called it. Right. This *was* a commotion.

She glanced at the stage. Szababos stood beside Torval, gesturing wildly.

Torval pointed his pistol at Szababos, who put up his hands and backed away.

She needed to get out now, while Torval was distracted. With a grunt, she lifted one of the smaller helium tanks in her arms and stood.

No good. Torval spotted her immediately. "You! Rowan Winterbourne! You're running? You're abandoning me? I'm your father!"

Moving toward the door, she shook her head and mouthed, *No. No, you're not.*

"Leave me when my back's to the wall. Damn you! I'll let Mitzi have you! She'll fillet you like a fish. She'll poison you, and you'll die writhing in agony." He aimed his pistol at her. "Or maybe I'll kill you myself. You have no respect for family!"

Even from here, she could see his brown eyes had turned that evil yellow of rage.

Would he shoot?

The clown set off another tank. The screaming around her grew in intensity.

No shots. Not yet.

She ducked into the crowd, using the helium tank as a battering ram to force her way through. She risked a glance back at the podium.

Torval stood and stared at the pistol in his hand as if he didn't know how it had appeared. Then he turned toward the wall and—vanished. Just disappeared without a trace.

She blinked. Where had he gone? How had he done that?

The force of movement pushed her into the corridor, and she had no more time to wonder. The hallway ran mad with shouting people going in different directions. An explosion rumbled overhead. Pieces of the ceiling fell.

Clutching her tank, she took a moment to look at the map posted in a frame on the wall, and as she traced her route, the classical marble statue behind her began to hum. She viewed it cautiously and backed away, and as she did, straight-line cracks began to show. It almost looked as if the statue had been assembled rather than carved... As the cracks widened, the hum became a sizzle, and she caught a glimpse of what looked like glowing circuitry. "Shit!" She stopped backing up, turned and raced down the corridor, the tank of helium heavy and slick in her arms. Behind her the statue exploded with a boom that rattled nearby windows.

Not all of Torval's art was real? Some or all of his art hid surveillance equipment, computers, explosives? She didn't know, but she was willing to bet Joe did. What she had to do now was find her way to their room and get out. *Get out!*

She avoided the elevators, climbed stairs, and ran down corridors empty of anyone except the occasional wide-eyed staff member or panicked guest fleeing the premises with their most precious belongings.

No one was going her way.

By the time Rowan turned into the empty corridor where suite 425 was located, she was running. She shifted the helium tank to one hand, pulled the card key out of her pocket, inserted it into the reader—and heard behind her the soft click of the door across the hall. She whirled to see Doug Moore…

Doug Moore, the torturer, as he tossed his wispy hair back from his face with his habitual irritating twitch. "Alone at last."

37

ROWAN FROZE, then slowly, carefully brought the helium tank to her chest and hugged it like a baby doll.

Moore wore that stupid suit with its stupid pin stripes and those subtly cruel drops of blood. His feet were bare. Always he imagined eccentricity set him apart and made him important. He wasn't important, merely a human monster among other monsters.

Noting her trembling fingers, he smiled in slow delight. With one step another, he paced toward her, a tiger on the hunt.

Her hands tightened on the tank.

"We're alone now, little girl," he crooned. "Your papa's not here to help you."

She didn't hesitate to make the claim that might save her. "My papa will kill you for hurting me."

"Torval? Do you mean Torval?" Doug Moore smiled in delight. "Who do you think sent me after you?"

That tender morsel of hope sank like stone in her belly.

"Gregory Torval's only use for you is as his obedient child, and you've proved to be a sad disappointment in all respects." His smile widened, and for the first time, she saw gaps at the back of his teeth where she had smashed his head with the steel bar. "If only you were a boy...but you're not. You're only a worthless girl-child. Do you believe that?"

"If Gregory Torval is that stupid, that's his loss."

"He's not only stupid, he makes enemies of his most valuable allies."

She pretended not to understand. "You mean Mitzi?"

Doug Moore's smooth, practiced smile crumpled into a snarl. "Me, you chip off the ol' block. Me. I'm going to kill Gregory Torval's only remaining offspring, and the woman who gave me this face. What do you have to say about that?"

She didn't waste any more breath. With a half twirl, she slammed the helium tank into Doug Moore's sternum. Something broke with an audible crack. A rib?

He screamed and stumbled backward.

The tank rebounded. She caught it, smacked the valve against the hardest surface she could see, the metal doorframe. As she leaped back, the helium exploded from the tank and propelled the tank into Doug Moore's legs. He fell. Blood spurted. His scream reached a new and higher pitch. He writhed—and he was still.

She stared at him, hardly believing the clown's trick had worked for her. She wanted to nudge Moore with her toe, make sure he was truly unconscious. But she knew better than to get close to those long arms.

In a shaking voice, she said, "You can hand it out, but you can't take it."

No reaction. No movement.

"Now you're nothing but a hideous, barefoot ex-torturer with a nervous tic."

Still nothing.

"It was me who smashed you in the side of the head. I've broken you twice. How does it feel to be such a loser?"

His chest moved a little, and beneath his closed lids, his eyes twitched. He was definitely alive, more was the shame, but fighting for breath or consciousness. She was weak, she guessed, but she didn't have it in her to kill a helpless man, and she didn't dare hang around. She had to go in the room and get her stuff. She groped for her key, saw it on the carpet beside the door, leaned over and winced.

What the—

On her right foot, she wore one red shoe. Lifting her pant leg, she saw a four-inch gash along her shin bone. Something— a shard of metal from the doorframe, a chunk of the valve—and blown back and sliced her, and she had been so wrapped up in fear and self-defense, she hadn't noticed. Now a slow, steady stream of blood trickled down her leg.

"Damn it, I don't have time for this!"

38

DOESN'T MATTER WHAT you have time for; you work with the time you've got. Lorenze Winterbourne's voice spoke in her head. Rowan hoped that hearing the voices of the dead didn't mean she had kicked the oxygen habit.

She used the magic card to open the door, limped into the room, locked and barred it behind her. She was pretty sure she'd disabled Doug Moore enough that, even if he recovered consciousness, he couldn't smash his way in. But pretty sure wasn't good enough, and she needed to tend to herself before she could escape this exploding house of horrors.

She dragged herself to the closet and found her backpack. Inside was the first aid kit. In the bathroom, she washed her hands, put her leg in the sink and ran water on the wound to flush it, and cried a little from the pain that was manifesting itself in increasing waves. She washed around the wound with soap and rinsed again, and probed with her fingers to see if there was any debris.

Nope. Whatever had done this had slammed in and out.

Gosh. What luck.

She used a quick clot agent. Then she spread a liquid bandage over the wound to seal it.

It leaked. She spread another coat, and another.

A deeper explosion rumbled through the mansion.

Smoke started seeping out of the ventilation shafts.

She had to make a decision between fixing her leg, or getting away before this place went up in fire and brimstone.

No choice. She fast-limped into the sitting room and extricated the propane canister and the fan from the closet and placed them beside the door to the corridor. Going back to the closet, she put her life vest around her neck and tied it around her waist. Taking the handle of her wheeled yellow suitcase, she dragged it after her.

With great stealth, she opened the outer door and checked Moore's prone body. He hadn't moved, but he still twitched, occasional violent trembles as if his nervous system sought to compensate for his helplessness. Blood soaked his pants and formed a pool under his thigh. Something white and sharp had poked through the material above his knee and…oh God. It was bone. If someone didn't find him, he was going to die. Which he deserved, and she was proud of her part, but…

She swore, went back into the room and to the house phone. She half hoped it wouldn't work, but it connected immediately to an unruffled voice. "This is housekeeping. How may I help you?"

"This is Rowan Winterbourne. Is BeBée around?" *Please, BeBée, be alive. Be safe.*

"Hold please." The operator connection broke. Elevator music played.

Rowan decided she'd give it exactly thirty seconds and—

"Rowan, are you okay?" BeBée sounded as calm as the operator.

"I'm fine." Rowan eyed her leg. "Fine-ish. Listen, Doug Moore is unconscious outside my door. I'm pretty sure he's got a compound fracture and maybe a few more broken bones."

"Did you do that, Rowan Winterbourne?" Rowan could hear the smile in BeBée's voice.

"He was going to kill me, so yes. But somebody needs to move him before this place burns down."

"Yes, we'd hate to have him suffer in the flames *before* he gets to hell," BeBée said ironically. "Don't worry, Rowan, I'll deal with Doug Moore."

"Thank you. Now I've got to go."

"You have a way out?"

"I do. How about you?"

"I figured out that way a long time ago. I was simply waiting for the right opportunity. Thanks to your Joe for that."

"Thank *you*, BeBée. Take care and let me know you got to safety. You know where I am, right?"

"Point Offbeat Lighthouse. But not for long. Maybe someplace new?"

"Probably."

"I'll find you. Wherever you go, I'll find you. I'll be in touch." BeBée hung up.

Rowan peeked out the door again. Doug Moore looked broken and as if he was still unconscious, not that she trusted him. She used the canister to prop the door open. Pulling her suitcase behind her, she hurried into the corridor and toward the bell tower.

A dozen steps and she stopped, returned, and picked up the propane canister in one arm. Across the hall, she heard a scratching. Doug Moore's fingernails were ripping at the carpet, and his eyes were half-opened and turned on her. But he didn't look really conscious, and with his leg like that, he wasn't going to chase her. Still she contemplated using the tank to give him one additional good slam across the skull.

But no. She wasn't getting close enough to his prone body

for that. She hooked the fan handle over her fingers, and more calmly moved toward the stairs that would take her to the roof.

Focus, Rowan! She had left two valuable pieces of equipment behind and had had to backtrack to recover them. She couldn't afford another mistake of that magnitude. She had to get off this island before the whole place blew apart, the Coast Guard landed—as she knew they would—and Torval sought hostages and placed blame.

It was three flights to the roof. Three flights that should be nothing, but she was losing blood, the propane tank weighed a good twenty-five pounds, and its weight had taken its toll. The fan bumped her thigh at every step, and when she got to the door labeled Roof, it was firmly closed—and locked.

But BeBée said she went to the top of the bell tower to view the world beyond the island, and that the roof door was kept locked and required a metal key. She said she could score one for Rowan, so…there had to be a way. Rowan searched with her fingers above the door, and there it was, the key with a thick paper tag on it and a childish scrawl that said, *For Rowan.*

She smiled at it. Bless BeBée!

She unlocked the door and stepped out onto the roof, and caught her breath. Here heating units, rainwater storage tanks and generators had been placed out of sight from the guests. With the wide views and brisk breeze, she was reminded of her lighthouse.

Not too much longer until she was home…and not much longer after that before she moved on.

With all she'd learned here and that had been learned about her, it was too dangerous to linger near Offbeat Bay. After so many years of roaming, of constant safety checks, she knew better than to be attached to a place.

Yet when she thought of leaving, she felt such a pang she put her hand on her chest over her heart.

She felt it leap in her chest when, at the far end of the roof, one of the generators exploded. She saw the flare, felt the flash of heat, heard the bell in the tower above her swing in the shock wave.

No time for sentimental pangs. No time to nurse the wrist Doug Moore had crushed or the leg that, despite her best efforts, still leaked blood. The generator was burning, and the roof was catching fire. Her advantage was that it had a long way to go before it reached her. Her disadvantage was— She felt a vibration in her feet, as if the whole mansion was a volcano trembling on the verge of an eruption.

From the ground she heard the gunning of motors as guests commandeered vehicles. Distant voices screamed in panic.

Kneeling beside the suitcase, she opened it wide. The balloon's envelope, of course, was just that—thin yellow silk she'd sewn herself, the smallest recommended to carry her weight and the weight of the propane tank. The plastic suitcase itself came apart to create the kit needed to launch the balloon, and she'd trained herself to assemble it in five minutes flat. She hoped she had those five minutes to do what she needed to do.

She finished in four minutes and twenty-two seconds.

The time required to ignite the burner and fill the envelope with hot air was her main worry. Fifteen to twenty minutes was the best she could hope for. She plugged in the fan, put it on High, and began the process of filling the balloon with air as she attached the propane tank to the tiny platform where she and it would stand. A hose ran from the tank to the burner, and by the time the balloon was sufficiently filled, she was ready. She held her breath as she clicked and clicked the lighter…and clicked and clicked…

She stopped. Took a breath. Told herself reasonably this was a new lighter she'd bought from the grocery store during the summer closeout barbecue sale, and all that was needed was for the butane to get to the spark and—

"Come on, you piece of shit!" She couldn't get to this point in this precisely planned balloon launch and be stopped by one little detail. She couldn't!

She shook the lighter hard and clicked and—the flame appeared in a whoosh. With a shaking hand, she lifted it to the opening of the balloon and lit the burner.

The air inside the envelope began to heat and expand the silk.

Additional plus: nothing except the burner caught fire.

She pushed the platform out to the roof's northeast side, where the wind blew briskly. She tethered it to the metal loop that had been used to lift the HVAC unit onto the roof. She stepped on the tiny, precarious plastic platform. She'd performed only a couple of balloon experiments—safety reasons—but she knew launching was really a three-man job, and launching the middle of what sounded like the revolution of a small country could not be a good idea, and—

Boom!

The HVAC unit blew.

When she opened her eyes, the tether had been severed, and she was floating four stories over the mansion's lawn in a hot-air balloon with...not-yet-hot-enough air to keep it aloft.

39

THE EXPLOSION PROVIDED enough lift for the balloon to clear the low wall around the roof and rise toward the sky. Everything was okay! Rowan had escaped Raptor Island!

Then—oh God—then the balloon started to descend. Slowly, majestically, it slid downward while floating west toward the line of tall cypress trees at the edge of the yard.

"No. No!" Rowan checked the burner; the explosion had blown out the flame.

The lighter. Where was the lighter?

She looked around the tiny yellow plastic platform. There were her feet and the propane tank. But! She was hanging on to the platform rail with one hand, and with the other, she still clutched the lighter. "You have to light!" She shook it once, hard, lifted it and clicked.

The lighter lit.

The burner lit.

The propane burned.

And she was still descending.

"No! Up. Up!" she coaxed and commanded as those trees loomed larger and taller. If she hung up in the tops of those trees, she'd be like a piñata waiting to be broken open, target practice for every person on Raptor Island with a gun. Judging from the sounds to the shots being fired in the distance, that was everybody.

She checked the propane valve. It was open all the way.

The balloon stalled, held by the doldrums in the space between the trees and the house, going neither up nor down, backward or forward.

She held her breath.

The balloon reversed course, ascending at an equally slow and majestic pace.

She stood on her tiptoes.

Which made no difference at all.

The ascent grew steeper. "Yes!"

The wind caught it. "No! Not yet!"

She was swept toward the treetops. She was going to hit. She was going to be caught—and the balloon made a sudden jump in elevation. Her plastic platform scraped the top branches—and kept climbing.

"Thank you, God." She put her hand on her face...and felt her eyebrows crumble against her palm. "Oh, no." She brushed at her face and hair. Her skin felt hot but not burned. But her brows and lashes and the ends of her hair were goners. Burned shreds rained down on her. She looked down at her scorched clothes, black, shredded, and faintly smoking, then farther down toward the ground.

Smoke spiraled up from the mansion's windows, and fire spread across the roof from multiple places. The road was crammed with vehicles that couldn't move and people on foot running toward the docks. The elephant and the circus people were moving across the track toward some unseen refuge.

Nowhere did she see a sign of Joe Grantham.

She concentrated on Torval's yacht, tied to its own dock, and

the single file of people boarding. They were all dressed alike…
They were Torval's staff. And the elegantly clad figure that waved
them aboard was BeBée!

How had BeBée done it? In the approximately forty-five minutes since Rowan had left her room, how had BeBée managed
to corral the people who worked for her, bypass the traffic jam
and get them down here?

For one thing, she hadn't done as she promised and rescued
Doug Moore. Or…wait. What was it BeBée had said? *I'll deal
with him.*

Oh. *Ohhh.*

Rowan could still hear gunfire, but she was high enough that
she could no longer hear the shouting.

Someone on the yacht pointed her out. BeBée glanced up and
waved energetically, then bounded up the gangplank and pulled
it in as Torval's top-tier guests, the ones who had ridden the
yacht to the island, arrived on the dock. Rowan could see them
jumping up and down and trying to command BeBée to bring
them on board. She could imagine the shouting and cursing.

Out to sea, Rowan spotted Coast Guard vessels approaching.
She leaned over to yell, "Better hurry, BeBée!" The tiny gon-
dola tipped with her. She rapidly righted herself. None of that.
For this trip, she had to remain upright.

The northeast wind picked up and carried her away. She left
Raptor Island behind and traveled across the sea. Sure, she was
up higher than most people wanted to ever be. Yes, she had no
control of her destination. But this experience was, in its way,
glorious. She rode on the wind, so she didn't feel a breeze. The
Pacific rocked beneath her, sending salt and scent and wildness
into the air like a blessing. Up here, she was safe…except for her
leg, which hurt and burned and slowly leaked blood. But that was
such a minor thing. For the first time in the last fourteen years,
she felt truly safe.

She thought, hoped, she might land on a beach within walking—or limping—distance of the lighthouse. But she'd used up her luck during the launch; about halfway between the island and the continent's edge, the wind changed to due north and carried her and the balloon parallel to shore while the propane tank drained to its last gasp.

The flame went out, and holding the lighter up didn't do the job of heating the air in the envelope and keeping the balloon aloft. She knew that because…she tried.

Slowly and irrevocably, the balloon drifted downward, and when the wind changed to westerly, she was five hundred feet off the California coast and miles north of her desired destination. Her leg had been cold and numb for several hours, and the sun was setting across the ocean. She wasn't going to make it to a beach before she hit the water, and she was pretty sure she wasn't going to survive much time in the Pacific Ocean… even in her life vest.

She looked into the setting sun and thought about her mother, Yvonne, and her father, Lorenze Winterbourne. Out loud, she wished her sister well and told Joe that she loved him and, yes, trusted him.

She hit the water.

40

ROWAN'S PLATFORM SKIPPED across the waves like a stone…
and sank. The slice on her leg burned in the salt water. The *frigid*
salt water. In sunny central California, although it should never
be, the Pacific Ocean was always glacial.

She fought herself free of the silk balloon material, felt the
ocean's current seize her and carry her onward. She prayed for
salvation and hoped for nothing.

To her astonishment, less than fifteen minutes later, when she
had been slapped by froth, submerged by waves, and yet was
still fighting to remain semiconscious, strong hands grabbed her
under the armpits and dragged her onto a beach.

She coughed and spit salt water, looked up at her savior, and
wondered if she was hallucinating when she heard, "I'm Madame
Rune, the psychic of Gothic. You've probably heard of me."

She shook her head. Madame Rune looked like a man in a
gypsy fortune teller costume and sounded like Julia Child. Why
would she have heard of him? Her? They?

Madame Rune sighed heavily. "A prophet in her own country is never respected. I predicted the arrival to this very beach of a person in need."

"Well, sure." Rowan coughed again, the salt and sand rough in her throat.

Madame Rune handed her a refillable bottle. "Sip on that. It's a hydrator mixed with water, and that'll help with everything."

Rowan sipped. Strawberry flavor wasn't her favorite, but the water cleared her throat, and the electrolytes almost immediately gave her a boost. "Thank you," she rasped.

"Can you hang on?" Madame Rune asked. "Your balloon is coming in on the waves."

Rowan nodded. "Please, bring it in."

While she rolled onto her elbows and watched, Madame Rune discarded her fringed shawl and her headscarf, removed her shoes and plunged into the water. When she was waist-deep, she grabbed something and began walking backward, and after a struggle against waves and currents, dragged the tattered, sopping remnants of Rowan's hot-air balloon out of the ocean, onto the sand and above the waterline.

The beautiful bright yellow silk looked stained and dingy. Half of the ropes had been severed by waves and rocks and who knew, maybe sharks? She was proud that the balloon had worked so well, and yet a vague sadness tugged at her to see it broken after its valiant efforts.

Madame Rune dragged the battered platform in last, got tangled in the plastic, fell over into the waves, lumbered to her feet, cursed like a sailor and still managed to tug everything far up on the beach.

Rowan sat up. "Is that all?"

Madame Rune stood wringing out her skirt. "Isn't that enough?"

"The propane tank is gone." Rowan rubbed her forehead. "Like we need more trash in the ocean. I really did intend to touch down on land."

"Maybe that's what you intended, but that's—" Madame Rune gestured "—a pretty flimsy excuse for a balloon."

Don't overexplain, Rowan. "Homemade." She sipped her water. Never mind the strawberry flavor; this was the *best* water she'd ever tasted. She drank again.

"You took to the air in a homemade hot-air balloon?" Madame Rune was clearly horrified.

"It was perfectly safe." If one blurred the definition of *perfectly* a bit.

Madame Rune was having none of that. "You landed in the *Pacific*. If all the ocean currents in the area didn't lead right to this beach, you'd still be out there somewhere!"

"I landed where the winds took me. The important thing is, the balloon went up and remained aloft for hours!" Rowan started to grin. She had done it. She had really done it! "Not bad, huh, madame?" She offered a fist bump.

"Call me Rune." She bumped. "The road's up there." She pointed toward the top of the cliffs that surrounded the pocket beach. "Do you think you can climb that far?"

Still carried on a tide of exaltation, Rowan laughed out loud. "It beats drowning."

"Yes." Rune surveyed her. "Once up in the village—possibly you've heard of Gothic?"

"That's the woo-woo place."

"Right. 'On stormy nights, Gothic is said to disappear, and on its return it brings lost souls back from the dead.'"

A little of Rowan's exhilaration faded. "That's creepy."

"Prophetic. Gothic did *not* disappear, but you're here, and you're looking a little worse for wear. Your clothes are singed, and you don't have any brows or lashes."

Blithely, Rowan said, "Had a smidge of trouble lighting the flame to heat the air."

"Right…" Rune knelt beside her. "That's not what happened with that leg, though, is it?"

Gingerly Rowan lifted her pant leg to view the damage more closely. The gash looked waterlogged, and although the blood flow had slowed, probably from the cold water, it hadn't stopped. The sandy beach and the steep climb to the road weren't going to help it, either.

Rune winced. "That looks bad. What'd you do?"

Rowan took a long swig of water. "You wouldn't believe it if I told you."

"You'd better think something up, because once we're up in Gothic, we'll transport you to the hospital in Salinas to have that stitched and get a shot of antibiotics, and whatever else the medical folks advise, and they're going to ask."

"Of course they are." Rowan had premade stories to fit a lot of scenarios, and she ran through them in her mind.

"Taking you to the hospital isn't woo-woo, simply practical, but does that sound all right to you?"

What an odd question! "Of course. That's the logical thing to do. Who wouldn't want that?"

"What's your name?"

Rowan stared at Rune for a long minute, grappling with an odd sense of disorientation.

"No, not again." Rune put her hand to her wet, tangled hair. "Please tell me you remember."

"Of course I remember. It's not amnesia." Three days with her own name and she was reluctant to claim her pseudonym? *Really, Rowan, get a grip.* "Helen Lamb. I'm Helen Lamb." She hoped she didn't sound defensive.

"I'm glad to meet you, Helen Lamb, glad you remember your name, and glad you're willing to go to the hospital for treatment. With that leg and the dunking you've had, if we didn't get you medical care, I suspect you'd soon receive front row tickets to a live Elvis concert." Rune stood and helped Rowan to her feet.

Even with Rune's help, Rowan had to stop to allow the pain

to wash over her. "Join the choir invisible," she whispered, took her first step, and stopped again.

Rune supported her as she took another step, and another. "Signed off online…permanently."

Rowan chuckled and began the slow process of muscling through the pain. "'Sleeping with the fishes' would be most appropriate."

"Right you are." Rune headed them toward the path. "Looking at the waves from Davy Jones's locker."

Rowan and Rune made it up the cliff by topping each other's bad jokes about death, laughing and ultimately crying, and when Rowan reached Rune's ATV, she got in the seat and fainted.

Being alive had cost her dearly.

It was a debt she was willing to pay.

NEVER GO HOME AGAIN

41

THE HOSPITAL STITCHED Rowan up and gave her a huge shot of antibiotics, and all the time the policeman yapped at her about how she got that cut and why her hair was burned and how she washed onto the beach…in a hot-air balloon…from…where?

She mostly answered with the truth. She told him her name was Helen Lamb and she lived in the lighthouse outside of Offbeat Bay and she'd been experimenting with a hot-air balloon and it carried her farther north than she expected and she'd run out of propane and gone into the drink and something in the ocean sliced her open…

The cop was able to verify her identity and her place of residence, and if the doctor who worked on her looked at her bruised wrist and shook his doubtful head, that was okay.

Madame Rune drove her back to Gothic and handed her over to Angelica Lindholm, the wealthy celebrity who lived in the huge Dracula's castle of a residence at the top of the hill above the village. Angelica got Rowan settled in a lovely guest room, assured her her assistant was dealing with the difficulties of getting Rowan a new driver's license, and left Rowan strict instructions to call for help if she needed it. Angelica's personal maid helped her shower and wash her hair and get into a nightgown and into bed.

Rowan woke in the middle of the night, realized her leg was swollen, red and puffy, and picked up the phone.

Angelica herself answered.

When Rowan stammered an apology, Angelica dismissed that with the comment that she was a light sleeper, and Rowan was on her way back to the hospital with Angelica's driver at the wheel and Angelica beside her in the back seat.

This time, the medical professionals checked her in and put her on intravenous liquids and antibiotics. She was there for three interminable days, watching local TV news, searching for information about the events on Raptor Island. An excited helicopter reporter showed footage of smoke and flames rising from Gregory Torval's mansion, of unmarked vessels fleeing the scene and later, Coast Guard vessels guarding the harbors. According to Coast Guard officials, drug and crime lord Gregory Torval's island fortress had been infiltrated by "persons unknown," and the Coast Guard and federal agents had taken control. The whereabouts of Gregory Torval was unknown.

Then the news switched to a story about the shortage of dishwasher soap in local stores. Rowan glared evilly at the screen, and slipped into one of her many unscheduled naps. The infection was playing havoc with her concentration.

When she was released, she returned to Angelica's house, where Angelica handed her a new iPhone. When Rowan said it was too expensive to accept, she discovered Angelica was a force of nature.

"Think nothing of it," Angelica said. "You lost yours in the ocean—"

Not true, but Rowan didn't correct her.

"—and you're in no shape to get yourself a new one. I keep my older models around in case of this kind of emergency."

Rowan looked at the iPhone, the current model, and wondered what Angelica's new phone could be. "Thank you so much. I'll make sure somehow you're paid."

"It's set up in my name and with my service. When you get on your feet—literally—" Angelica indicated Rowan's leg propped on pillows "—you can transfer it to your own service."

"I will," Rowan vowed.

Angelica stayed for a brief inquiry about Rowan's needs, then looked at her watch. "My film crew is here. I must run. Don't hesitate to call if you need anything."

"There is one thing. I had my mail held for me at the Offbeat Bay Post Office. If I can make arrangements to have it delivered here...?"

"Of course, you can do that online. My intern will get you the address." She turned to leave.

"I'll have to call and speak to them about including the contents of my P.O. Box." Now Rowan was thinking out loud, trying to figure out how to best insure she'd received Frances Sattimore's guest book and that it remained safe.

"Because your box key also went down with you. Is there something of importance you need?" Angelica asked. And then answered herself, "Of course, or you wouldn't be concerned. Make your call. Explain why you're delayed and that I'm sending someone down to collect your mail. Harper is available, so write a note, giving Harper Addison permission to pick up your mail. Sign it with your legal signature, and if you know anyone at the Post Office—"

"My mail carrier is Bill."

"Aptly named. If you could mention him, it might help relieve any lingering worry about one of my assistants doing your errands. Anything else?"

"No. Thank you for handling this so efficiently."

"That's what I do." And she was gone, a busy woman who went out of her way to care for those in need.

Rowan only wished Angelica's brisk manner didn't make her feel so acutely like a beggar at the feast.

Rowan's first search on her new phone was for the now old story of the fall of Gregory Torval's crime network. She turned up more videos of the mansion with smoke pouring from the windows, then of walls collapsing, but nothing about what had happened to Gregory Torval himself or those "persons un-known" who had infiltrated Torval's operation.

She googled Joe Grantham and got a big fat zippo, which didn't surprise her, but did leave her feeling frustrated and used, and disgusted with herself for her own reactions. What had she expected? That he'd be in the online phone book under the subject head of Mercenaries?

Actually, unless Torval and his cohorts knew exactly where to look and what alias to look under, Rowan Winterbourne herself had pretty much disappeared off the map. Taking a fortifying breath, she tapped into her cloud and her personal apps, specifi-cally the one that provided security for the lighthouse. Sensors and cameras had recorded mail delivery on the weekdays and Saturday, and yesterday, one unscheduled visitor: young Elijah from MVP's Grocery. He parked, walked hesitantly to the front door and ran the bell, and when he got no answer, he walked around the building and up the path to the Outlook Point. When he didn't find her, he scribbled a note and stuck it under the windshield wiper on her car, hopped in his car, and drove toward the lane that led to the highway. He stopped, backed up into the parking area, got out, removed the note...and left. Odd behavior, and she might have looked for dire motives if not for Joe's observation that Elijah had a crush on her.

She really hoped that was it. She didn't want to believe Elijah had been bribed or threatened or lured into criminal activities.

Other than that one visitor, to all appearances, the lighthouse was secure, undiscovered by Gregory Torval and his band of killers, drug sellers and torturers. She shouldn't have felt such a profound sense of relief, not if she really intended to leave for her own safety, but that night, for the first time since her escape from the island, she slept well.

In the morning, Angelica's intern appeared with the small stack of mail and one package, mailed from Raptor Island; the guest book had arrived unharmed. Rowan unwrapped it, and found she couldn't stop smiling. Using one of Angelica's computers, she searched for Frances Sattimore and found her in Grass Valley, California, a small town in the Sierra Nevada mountains. She emailed Frances, got a prompt and pleasant response back, and arranged to return the guest book as soon as possible.

Because she couldn't *not*, she peeked in at her sister's social media. Irena had posted a video of her first welding art lesson. She was supposed to make a bird on a perch. As she ruefully pointed out in the end, it looked more like a dinosaur crumpling a telephone pole.

Rowan smiled for the rest of the day.

After a week of recovery, she was transported back to the hospital and declared healthy enough to live on her own, and told for a complete recovery, she should arrange for physical therapy. When she returned to Angelica's mansion, Angelica was there to hand her her reissued California driver's license, a credit card and several hundred in cash. As before, Angelica waved away her objections.

"You can't go out into the world with nothing. You need cash and credit. As you can see, it's an Angelica Lindholm corporation credit card issued to Helen Lamb. I'll take care of the payments until you can get back to your home, get settled, get well. You own The Fixer, you have a reputation for hard work and honesty, and I have faith that you'll pay me back." Angelica smiled with real admiration. "I appreciate a woman who climbs the ladder by the sweat of her brow. I appreciate men who do that, too, but I must always factor in the knowledge the world is kinder to men."

Rowan thought of Raptor Island, and how that primitive social structure catered to the males. "It's true. Thank you."

"My assistant has picked out clothing and shoes from the Angelica Lindholm collection and packed them in this bag." Angelica indicated a backpack. "It's not much, just enough to replace your ruined garments and get you through the next few days. Madame Rune has asked to drive you wherever you wish to go." She smiled fondly. "I believe she foresees something remarkable in your future."

Rowan laughed out loud. "As long as she didn't foresee my move to Clay County."

"I'm not familiar with Clay County. Is that an unpleasant place to live?"

Rowan tried to figure out how to explain to this humorless woman that, to divert her from her pain, she and Rune had cracked jokes about death all the way up the path from the beach. Finally she settled on, "There's a lot of underground in Clay County. Thank you, Angelica, for everything." She offered her hand.

Angelica shook it. "Take care of yourself. I suspect you haven't told us your whole story and that it may include peril both past and future. Be safe, and call if I can help in any way."

Rune picked her up and drove her south to the beach where Joe had parked his car.

At the sight of the metal gate, Madame Rune braked. "That's disturbing."

It looked as if someone, in their rush to escape, had driven a truck through it. In fact, Rowan was fairly sure that was what had happened. "Let's see if the car is there and unharmed."

The silver Camry, crunched right front fender, sat in the same spot Joe had parked it, the paint and glass duller with the onshore salt and sand breeze.

"Is that yours?" Madame Rune asked.

"A friend's car. He's letting me use it."

Madame Rune drove in and parked next to the Camry. "I dragged you out of the ocean. I know you can't have a working key of any kind."

"My friend told me where he hid it." Rowan opened the door. "Hopefully it's still there." She walked around Joe's car to the driver's side rear wheel well, knelt, and cautiously groped around. She found the small magnetic box, pulled it free and pressed her index finger on the button.

It popped open. Joe wasn't kidding. He really had obtained her fingerprint and programmed it in.

Something she needed to file away under *spooky stuff to watch out for.*

She took out the key and started to hit the automatic door opener. Then Joe's conversation with Torval's guard Tyler buzzed through her mind. *The car is mine. I don't want it driven. I don't want it moved. I don't want it bugged or bombed...*

Rowan leaned into Madame Rune's open window. "You might want to go park over there." She pointed to the other side of the gate.

Madame Rune viewed her in horror. "What are you afraid of?" She held up both her hands. "No. Don't tell me! But now my psychic senses *assure* me you didn't launch your hot-air balloon as recreation. Hop in. You can try the door locks from there."

Rowan agreed, and hopped. When they were a relatively safe distance away, Rowan remotely unlocked the car—and they both flinched.

Nothing unexpected happened. The lights blinked. The car remained whole and unharmed.

Rowan got out again. "I think we're good."

"I'll follow you up the road," Madame Rune said. "To make sure."

"Thank you." Rowan got into the car. It started. The engine

purred as it had for Joe. She gave Madame Rune a thumbs-up, put it in gear and drove out the ruined gate and up the road to the highway. They both turned north, one after another, until they reached the turnoff for Gothic. With a mutual wave, Madame Rune turned east and Rowan drove north toward Carmel and Monterey and the highway through Sacramento and up to Grass Valley, where she would meet Frances Sattimore and return the address book.

Rowan didn't have to be psychic to know she would meet Madame Rune again.

42

ROWAN STARED AT the note in her hand, then at address on the townhouse. It was nice place, but "extremely wealthy" was not a term she would have used to describe this part of the subdivision. Upper middle class, maybe, but the yards needed work, and the townhomes needed paint. "Joe," she muttered, "you better not have lied about this, anyway." Not that he'd lied to her about anything that she knew of, but still...

She walked up to the door and rang the bell.

A woman's voice came through the intercom. "Come in, dear. I was expecting you. The door's open."

Rowan followed directions and found herself in the entry hall.

"I'm back here!" the voice called.

Rowan walked through the living room to the back of the house and out the open door onto the deck. The ground dropped off here, the deck was elevated, and the view looked over a bike path and into the forest.

"Isn't it beautiful?" the woman asked. "I love to sit out here on warm days and watch the hummingbirds come to the feeder and listen to the kids shout as they ride past."

Rowan turned to the lady. "Mrs. Sattimore?"

"Call me Frances. Joe has told me so much about you, I feel as if I already know you!"

Frances was much older than Rowan had expected, a tiny, stooped, skinny woman who wore a colorful caftan and smiled at Rowan with such delight that Rowan felt as if she'd been welcomed as a friend. "Joe talked to you about me?"

"Indeed he did. We had a Zoom." Frances dimpled. "He likes to check on me, bless him. I've known him since he was my nephew's best friend, and I've never before seen him smitten. You take good care of his heart. He's never given it to anyone!"

Good to know, but—"I'm not sure that I'm going to see him again."

"You don't like him?" Frances was clearly appalled.

"No, not that. I mean, after we retrieved your guest book—which I have here—" Rowan dug it out of her bag, removed it from the plastic and passed it into Frances's eager hands. "We separated, and I haven't seen or heard from him."

Frances lifted the book and pressed it to her forehead as if imprinting it into her brain. "You know what it's like with his job."

Rowan didn't have a clue.

"He told me he would be able to wind up his part of the operation and in a couple of weeks come by for a visit." Frances lowered the book and smoothed her crooked, withered fingers across the yellowed silk of the cover. "You'll hear from him then, I haven't a doubt. Would you join me for supper? I know we're going to get along!"

Rowan never stood a chance of maintaining her reserve. She shared two beers and the chicken enchilada casserole Frances's daughter had made for her and listened as Frances leafed through her guest book and reminisced about the family and friends who had visited. There were more than a few celebrities; with her welcoming personality, she'd made close friends of many of them, although she didn't hesitate to offer a critique of a few of the Evils and Egos, as she called them.

As Rowan cleaned up the kitchen, she asked, "How did Gregory Torval get your book? And why? What you've told me is interesting, but I don't understand how he laid hands on it. Did he break in and steal it?"

"No. Not that he isn't adept at breaking and entering, but he didn't have to. I know him. I opened the door for him. It's a long story." Frances sighed.

"I'm listening." Rowan was about to hear something of her biological father's real story, and that made her...queasy. As she loaded the dishwasher, she kept her face turned away, afraid Frances would read her expression.

"That boy," Frances said. "He was a bad seed. His mother, Edna, was my youngest sister's best friend in high school."

"Your youngest sister's best friend," Rowan repeated.

As if keeping up with her youngest sister's best friend was totally normal, Frances nodded. "Edna was a beautiful, warm, lovely human being who got pregnant by an absolute son of a bitch. I don't usually use that kind of language, but if you knew him..." She grimaced. "He was twenty-four. She was sixteen. He wasn't going to stick around, but her father had a shotgun and he wasn't afraid to use it. Poor Edna had to get married to a monster. Luckily, even before Gregory was born, her monster husband brought a knife to a gun fight and got whacked."

Rowan hid a smile as she filled the sink with soapy water to wash the delicate hand-washables. Frances had a way with words.

Frances continued, "But it was too late. The damage was done, and Edna produced her own monster. I employed her, watched Gregory grow up, and I knew... From the time he could toddle, he was greedy. He wanted what anyone else treasured. Edna grieved when he became the worst sort of criminal, and she grieved more when he married that woman. I figured he got what he deserved with *Mitzi*." Frances's tone dripped with contempt. "I never imagined Mitzi would allow her perfect, skinny body to become a vessel for a child, and when she did... That kid was doomed. So many bad genes. But Edna loved *him*, too."

Rowan found herself squirming. "I suppose. Yeah. It was her grandchild."

"Exactly. When Edna was in hospice, I kept her here, and the hospice people let me help care for her. Lovely people! I can't say enough good about them."

Rowan nodded. She knew. She had had to arrange hospice for one of her clients.

"I was only eighty-seven, and a lot more spry then. For goodness' sake, Edna was in *hospice*, and when Gregory didn't visit, I may have called and told him he was a lousy excuse for a human being."

"You may have?" Rowan washed, rinsed and stacked plates in the dish rack.

"All right. I did."

Rowan thought that figured.

"Edna loved her boy, and she didn't have long to live, and I wanted him to come and act like he cared. He came, he acted, and she died happy holding his hand, but when he left, my guest book went with him. That little shit didn't want it. He simply knew I loved it, and he loathed me. He knew I saw him for what he was."

"I heard from Torval's girlfriend that your ex-husband hired him to take the book."

Frances stared at Rowan, stricken. "Gregory got paid for being a thieving little shit? Talk about positive reinforcement for bad behavior!"

"Yes. And… Gregory Torval is my biological father." Rowan froze, her hands in a sink of soapy water.

Had she said that out loud?

43

THE SILENCE FROM the table was profound. Shocked, perhaps.

"My mother was his teenage mistress." Rowan explained because now that she'd made the dreaded confession, she had to say more. Explain more. "When she knew she was pregnant, she broke free and made a life for herself. Married the man I consider my father. His name was Lorenze Winterbourne."

Rowan heard the intake of breath; Frances recognized that name. "Your mother was Yvonne?"

"Yes. How did you know?"

"Come and sit down with me." Frances patted the table. Rowan dried her hands and sat, and Frances clasped her fingers. "No doubt you know Gregory uses women horribly."

Remembering Kealoha, Rowan nodded yes.

"In her way, Mitzi controls him, and although he's been a profligate, no woman had ever caught his attention, so Mitzi had never had reason to worry." Frances squeezed Rowan's fingers. "She worried about Yvonne. Yvonne captivated him, and when she left, he was livid. Gregory Torval walked away from women, women didn't walk away from him. As far as I knew, after a few howling tantrums, he settled back to normal. Did he know she was pregnant when she walked?"

"No. But I look like my mother, height and—" Rowan gestured at her figure "—yet I do resemble him a little. I can see it now that it's been called to my attention, but my mom never told me exactly who my biological father was, only that he was a...a bad man." She strained to analyze how Torval had figured out. "I think when he saw me, he may have had a stirring of suspicion. But Mitzi is the one who nailed it."

"That must have driven her toward the deep end of the poison pool."

"Heh." Rowan took a moment to appreciate the euphemism. "Yes. She went wild. After that, he recognized my mother's ring and made his own assumptions and investigations."

"Of course he did. He had no offspring now...except you."

In the presence of this woman's kindness, Rowan could express her confusion. "Why would he care so much for someone who has no impact on his life? DNA be damned! I'm nothing to him."

"He's a tyrant. A dictator. An emperor in his own mind. And in the definition of those very traditional male roles, we find a man who works for one goal: to give the world to his own offspring." As she spoke, Frances seemed to be dissecting the issue. "You're his hope for the future."

"Will he keep me from harm if that harm is his beloved Mitzi?"

"That woman. Yes. You're right. He's a man conflicted."

"Despite threats, Mitzi hasn't killed me yet, and if the world is just, she'll have the chance to enjoy a long cooldown in prison."

"Sometimes the world is just." Frances seemed to listen to an otherworldly source Rowan couldn't hear. "But being the world and not bound to anything but God and the universe, it takes its own sweet time."

"I suppose it does." Rowan realized the explosions and cleanup of Torval's house had been justice for Lorenze, and she'd been a part of it. The price she'd paid was dear, but worth every bit of pain and heartache.

"Could there be a doubt that Gregory lied? He's a notorious liar."

"He challenged me to a game of pool."

Frances tapped her hearing aids. "What? A game of...?"

"A game of pool."

"That's what I thought you said."

"My mother was a natural. A master."

"Oh, dear." Frances could see where this was going.

"I'm also quite good. While I was shooting—"

"Beating him?"

"Why, yes." They exchanged a smirk. Then Rowan's smile faded. "He sent my champagne glass away to be analyzed for DNA."

"What unbearably conniving people they are."

"Unscrupulous, deceitful, scheming." Rowan gritted her teeth when she remembered how she'd been manipulated. "It never occurred to me to worry about what traits I may have gained from my genetic father. Does vile corruption creep through my veins, waiting for the right trigger to erupt?"

"I know you're thinking about what I said about genetics, but because your mother left Gregory to raise you on her own, her bravery cancels all of Gregory's cowardice. When you add Lorenze Winterbourne into the equation, your stepfather's training and sacrifices, what could you be but an exemplary woman?"

"My parents led by example. Yet now I've discovered I carry the genes of the man who killed my mother, and I...don't know how to deal with that." Rowan realized how true this was, and how difficult. "I just...don't know."

Frances gave Rowan's hand a firm pat. "Your quandary is not whether these things happened. They did. They're a part of you. What you must decide now is how to process them in your mind and heart. You'll have to decide whether to let these issues drag you down or give you strength. In a few short hours, I feel I've come to see into your soul, and I'm sure you'll grow strong."

Rowan thought Frances was old enough to see into her soul if she wished.

Afterward, she sat with Frances in the beautifully decorated living room and watched an old, old episode of *The Tonight Show Starring Johnny Carson*. She helped Frances to the bathroom and then to bed. The evening felt oddly like visiting with Mr. Bandara, homey and warm, and made her parting from him a little less sad.

As she took her leave, Frances held her hand and smiled. "I have a lot of company, but I don't make many new friends anymore, so this has been the most delightful evening I've had in a long time. You will come back?"

"I'd love to."

"Dear girl, that's wonderful. Would you turn out the light on the way out? I'll lock the door from here with this clever app my daughter put on my phone." Frances started to lie back, then abruptly sat up. "I forgot! Why didn't you say something? Your check is in the envelope on the entry table."

"I forgot, too." Incredibly, that was true. "This wonderful visit drove it straight out of my mind. Thank you, Frances, sleep well." She used the light switch on her way out of the bedroom, collected the envelope, opened it and looked at the amount… and hurried back into the bedroom. She flipped the lights on.

Frances struggled up on her elbow. "I made it out to your business. Was that wrong?"

"No. The Fixer. That's it. But this is too much!" Rowan held the check at arm's length.

Frances's surprise appeared genuine. "It was the agreed-on amount."

"I didn't agree to this!"

"Joe said this was a dangerous mission, dangerous especially to you. And you were hurt, weren't you?"

"I...yes. How did you know?"

"You look a little drawn, like someone hearty who has been unexpectedly ill, and you list a little to one side."

The listing had to stop.

"I don't lightly ask people to risk their lives." Frances was quite firm. "In fact, if Joe had told me all the circumstances, I would have found another way to get my book back from that lousy little weasel, Gregory Torval." Then she looked stricken.

"Do you mean that lousy little weasel, Gregory Torval, my father?" Rowan asked lightly.

Frances sat up and fussed with her blankets. "Come and help me plump my pillows, dear."

Rowan did as she was told, and when the pillows were arranged, she helped Frances relax back on them.

"Sit down." Frances patted the mattress beside her, and when Rowan sat, Frances said, "I hate to admit it, but you need to know that Gregory had his shining moments. Edna finished life in a difficult and ugly way. There was a catheter, coughing and bringing up body fluids, inescapable pain and tears. Before it was over, that lovely woman was a living skeleton. She didn't want him to stay. Remember I said she died holding his hand? He insisted. Once he was here, he ignored frantic messages from his organization and nasty phone calls from his wife, and he was here, body and soul, for Edna."

"Well," Rowan said awkwardly. "That's good to know."

"I wish that had been my last memory of him, rather than him stealing my guest book. I don't like thinking ill of people. It takes too much energy, and while I'm being cranky, they're out drinking and dancing. In his case, fornicating."

Rowan winced, not because she didn't agree, but because hearing this ancient little woman talk about fornicating made her feel awkward.

But Frances charged on. "It's such an unfair exchange, don't you think?"

Rowan nodded.

"Also, my dear, the online news about Joe's operation and its success has been unclear. Raptor Island is ripped asunder. But is Gregory Torval still alive?"

"I don't know." Frances had unerringly hit on the one fear Rowan harbored in her heart.

"I don't either. It's not done until we know he's cashed his last paycheck." Frances heaved a mighty sigh. "Be careful, my young friend. Until you lift the eyelids on Gregory's body, and Mitzi's, and death stares back at you, you're not safe. You can't have inner turmoil about your birth and heritage until you have proof you have a future."

44

AS SOON AS Rowan got to Offbeat Bay, she went to the bank and deposited her check with her private banker. She tended to have a hefty bank balance—The Fixer was successful—but the amount of this check raised Lynette's eyebrows.

"I've been out of town on a job," Rowan said vaguely.

"I see that. A paper check for this amount...is going to take a little time to clear."

"It'll clear." Rowan never had a doubt.

"When it does, will you be coming in to invest it?"

"Yes. I hope you'll have some suggestions."

"I do my research. Would you like to make an appointment for Friday?"

They set up a time. Rowan left Lynette's office for the bank lobby and promptly ran into one of her Fixer clients.

"Helen, where have you been?" Alex Dixon asked. "I've been calling for two days!"

"I fell in the ocean."

He didn't blink. "Ohhh. Tough luck. Need a new phone?"

"Got one." She dug it out of her pocket and showed him. "New number. I'll send it out to all my clients."

"You can transfer it to your old number. You could have done that in the store. Still can. Go in and talk to them—"

"I'll send out the new number to my clients," she repeated. *And thank you for mansplaining cell phones to me, Alex Dixon.*

He made a face. "It'll be a pain to program in a new number."

Ah. She should have figured. Alex did not like to be inconvenienced. "I'll do that service for you for free."

He shrugged. "Whatever. I'm off on a business trip."

"When?"

"In an hour. Can you follow me home?"

"Sure." She had hoped to drive first to the grocery store and then to the lighthouse to make sure that, as her security app promised, it was still standing, but if Alex was leaving town, she was back on duty.

When she reached his house, he was waiting for her on the front walk. "New car!" he said. "Different, anyway. Where'd you get it? Private sale?"

"It's a friend's car. I'm borrowing it." *For who knows how long.*

"Glad you're just borrowing it. Kind of banged up. Engine purrs, though. I heard you left town with a friend. Where'd you go? Is this his?"

"Alex, you're nosy, and it's none of your business what I do, where I go or with whom." Those were the boundaries she always set, and he knew that very well.

"Okay then!" He stomped his way up the back stairs and into his kitchen, but he was too bursting with gossip to be irritated for long. "If you've been out of town, did you hear about old man Bandara? He was shot in his backyard!"

"I did hear, yes," she said steadily. "A couple of weeks ago. Did they ever find the shooter? Or a motive?"

"Nope. The town's finally calming down, but as it turns out, it was a blessing. He had cancer, did you know?"

"Yes, he…told me earlier that day."

"He was one of your clients?"

"He was. Nice man. I'm sorry to lose him." That ache of grief had been subdued by the weeks of shock, fear, pain, and action, but now, back in Offbeat Bay, the sorrow returned, and she worked to keep her feelings private. Boundaries, she reminded herself.

"If you need to fill the space," Alex said, "I've got a friend who's been chomping at the bit to hire someone like you. I could give her your number."

"How kind." *To think the only reason I'm sorry to lose Mr. Bandara is for the income he brought me.* "I have a list of clients waiting for a slot."

Alex took a breath to argue.

Hastily Rowan said, "But give me her number. I'll call and interview her."

"Right. I remember now. You do the interviewing. She's not going to like that."

Rowan looked at him.

"Or maybe she'll be impressed. Who knows with women? Look, I'm headed to Chile for two months." His backpack leaned against the wall, and his toolkit lay open on the table. He worked with a checklist, making sure each tool was secured in its proper place. "Do the usual."

She opened her app and ran down her own checklist. "Pick up your mail. If the job takes longer than you think, make sure there's enough money in your account for the bills. Monitor security. Deal with any issues that come up." She looked at him. "Not that they ever do. You're so OCD, you cover every base."

"Including having someone to handle an emergency." Something scratched at the door.

Rowan jumped at the sound and turned too quickly.

A dog. A dog stood on the back porch, looking soulfully through the screen.

Her reaction must have startled Alex, for he looked curiously at her, then moved to let the mangy beast in. "Do you want a dog? This showed up and it was starving, and as you can see, it's only got three legs."

She saw that now, although for this animal, it seemed like a small impediment.

Alex got a measuring cup, went into the pantry and came out with it full of dry food. "I tried to find the owner, but no luck. I figure someone dumped it. Anyway, I fed it, which I shouldn't have done, and now it's hanging around." He dumped the food into the bowl he had sitting beside the door.

She softened toward Alex, remembered why she'd taken him on despite his constant oblivious chatter.

He continued, "It's a nice dog, good manners, really smart. Not too big. Forty-five pounds? Poodle and husky, maybe? Doesn't shed much. Do you want it?"

She did. Of course she did. But if anything, this Raptor Island escapade with Joe had the potential to make her life even more precarious, and she didn't dare have excess baggage, especially not baggage she would come to adore in three minutes. "I would love a dog. I can't."

"Why not? You live in that lighthouse all by yourself. You could use some company, and I'm pretty sure this dog would protect you if anyone came around thinking to make trouble."

Smiling, she shook her head.

"You're pretty and you're single. Not trying to be an overly protective jackass, but when you travel as much as I do, you see things a woman like you can't even imagine."

"You'd be surprised."

The dog finished its breakfast and came over to introduce itself.

"Sit! Shake!" Alex said.

The dog *sat* and *shook*, looked at Helen with adoring brown eyes, and panted, displaying black spots on its tongue. She sat back and looked at its thick ruff. "Looks like some chow breed mixed in, too." She petted its head. "I live on the fourth floor. It can't climb down three flights of stairs every time it needs to piddle."

"It climbs the steps to the porch without a hitch."

"Anyway, I can't take it. I'm allergic." Nobody believed that, not even the dog.

"I tried," Alex said. "There's the last thing on your list. Take the dog to the shelter."

"Oh, no!" She sank her fingers into its fur. "It's got three legs. It'll never get adopted!"

"It's young and it's healthy. Maybe it will." He glanced out the window. "My ride is here."

She went from sad to fiery furious in point two seconds. "There's going to be an upcharge for this service!"

He took a breath to argue, then got a good look at her face. "I'm sure there will. Send the bill to my assistant. I'll see you in a couple of months." He leaned down and patted the dog. "Good luck, buddy. You deserve the best." The screen door slammed behind him.

Helen looked after him, then at the dog. "That flaming coward!"

The dog whimpered, hit the floor and put this head on its paws.

"I'm not mad at you," she reassured it, and leaned down to scratch its head. She sighed, went through the motions to close up the house, fed the dog again, let it out to do its business, and put it in her car. She stopped at Doggie Deli, got it a pupcake, and fed it to the dog one bite at a time. At the shelter, she handed the dog over, gave it a last scratch, shed a few tears, and walked away without a backward glance.

She hadn't even known she wanted a dog. Now she was crying about her loss and its fate.

It was the awful end of a thoroughly awful two weeks.

45

ROWAN WANTED TO go *home*.

She wanted to go *home* to her lighthouse. She could have; according to all reports, Torval's operation had been destroyed, and her app continued to assure her all was well. But if she was going to go home and stay, she needed food. In fact, she needed to eat *now*. She stopped at Offbeat Deli—people drove for miles for their sandwiches—waited in line, and got a club on rye to eat right away and a side of pasta primavera salad for later. Next she headed for MVP Grocery and pushed a cart up and down the aisles. She wanted to anticipate her every need over the next week so she could hunker down and be alone to recover from the emotions her recent ordeals had roiled up. To watch for trouble. To wonder if she was truly safe or if she was simply too weary and self-pitying to flee.

To prepare for her move to places unknown.

Yes, she knew she had to go. But one more night wouldn't hurt, especially when— She turned wrong and winced. Oh, yes. She needed a moment and a safe place to recover from her injuries.

She reached the cheese case and commenced her inner debate on whether to buy a round of goat brie or a lovely, melty fontina when her phone gave a *you've got a visitor* chirp. She pulled it out and keyed into the outside lighthouse camera. A black SUV pulled up to park beside her garage, and a woman stepped out.

A tall woman. A thin woman. Savannah.

"Shit," Rowan said quietly.

"What's wrong?" Elijah had been trailing her, holding a bottle of ketchup.

"Not sure yet." She shrugged at the boy clerk and tried to smile.

"Is there anything I can help with?" Joe had said Elijah had a crush on her. It looked as if he might be right.

"'Fraid not." *Because if I sent you to check things out and Savannah hurt you, I'd never forgive herself.*

Not that she thought Savannah was dangerous; Savannah wasn't overly athletic, and her handling of Wadell had been none too bright. Yet after the events on Raptor Island, Rowan was suspicious of anyone who showed up at her door. Because… how had Savannah found her?

On camera, Savannah walked toward the lighthouse door and rang the bell. Rowan zoomed in on her face. Savannah's mascara was smudged. She was biting her lip. She'd been crying.

Rowan caught herself before she said *shit* again.

Really—how had Savannah found her? She wasn't the harbinger of doom, Rowan was sure of that. Savannah couldn't punch her way out of a paper bag, and that was only the start of her self-defense deficiencies.

But did Savannah's appearance mean everyone who had been on Raptor Island during the last weeks had discovered her location? And how convenient that Savannah's arrival had occurred on the same day Rowan rolled into town.

Rowan tossed the goat brie and the fontina into her cart, and moved to the deli and ordered a quarter pound of thin-cut prosciutto.

Almost worse was the question of—*why had Savannah been crying?*

Oh God. She hadn't come to Rowan for help with man problems, had she?

No. Not even Savannah was that dumb.

Maybe she'd come to see if she could cull Joe from Rowan. Or maybe—Rowan straightened in horror—maybe she'd come to tell Rowan Joe had been killed.

Her mother's voice echoed in her head. *The Coast Guard taught me a lot about being aware, thinking ahead, not imagining what might be but seeing what is.*

Rowan would not imagine what might be. She would see what was.

She received her package of prosciutto and turned around to find Elijah lingering nearby, clutching the bottle of ketchup like an unassailable excuse. As soon as she met his eyes, he said, "I could go home with you. To make sure everything is okay. Not because, um…" He blushed bright red.

"It's nothing. Really." She settled on a version of the truth. "I have a visitor I'm not looking forward to seeing. But you know how it is—you can pick your nose, but sometimes you don't pick the right friends."

Elijah snorted, then covered his mouth. "My mom used to say something like that before she…left."

So maybe not a crush. Maybe a mother substitute. How deflating.

"I'll tell you what," she said. "I've been out of town—"

"I thought so! Is that how you got hurt?"

"Am I limping?" Because she needed to stop that tell right now.

"A little. I was watching really close."

Okay, back to the crush. "I didn't bring my reusable grocery bags. I'll have to buy them, right?"

"Right. Ten cents a bag."

"Do you have grocery bags with handles?"

"We have compostable plastic bags with handles."

"That's *perfect.* I'll finish shopping and you can check me out, and we'll put all my stuff in a compostable bag."

"Okay." He seemed uncertain what she was talking about.

"Um." She frowned as she thought about how to survive the next few hours if what she suspected was true. "Is there a hardware section to the store?"

"Sure. The end of aisle nineteen against the wall."

The overhead blared, "Elijah, to the front. Elijah, to the front," and he tossed the bottle of ketchup into the cheese cooler and ran toward the check stands.

Moving quickly, Rowan retraced her steps through the store, gathering twenty-eight-ounce cans of diced tomatoes, small cans of sliced black olives, glass jars of pickles and a half gallon of milk in a plastic jug. At the end of aisle nineteen, she looked at the plastic buckets, pipe wrenches, paint brushes—and *look!* A clip-on-your-belt lock-back utility knife equipped with a slide-out razor blade for cutting things like tape and cardboard and…stuff. The owner of The Fixer should carry such a useful gadget. In fact, she had one at the lighthouse in her toolbox, but hey. A girl could never have too many utility knives. She plucked it off the hanger and tossed it in her basket. As long as she was restocking, she grabbed a screwdriver too.

Later she'd have to return to do the real bulk of her shopping. If she lived through the next few hours, she would.

She hustled up to the front, got in Elijah's line, and unloaded her groceries onto the belt. Elijah alternated between staring at her face and checking while she bagged.

Damn Joe. Elijah had always been like this. She simply hadn't noticed, and she had liked it that way.

When Elijah got done with the checking, he said, "Rowan, um, let me help you. You're putting all that heavy stuff in one bag, and it's going to break."

"It's okay," she assured him. *It's perfect.* "I'll put my arm underneath it."

"You can bring the bags back, and we'll refund your ten cents."

She grinned at him. "I'm not worried about the dime."

"I'll double-bag it." He would not be dissuaded.

She let him do that and coughed up the extra bag charge. "Thanks, Elijah. You've been a huge help." She lugged the bag out to the car and put it in the passenger seat, removed the second plastic bag that Elijah had so thoughtfully provided, and used the utility knife to slice a couple of holes in the bottom of the loaded bag. She clipped the knife to her belt loop, added the screwdriver on the other side, then drove straight home…

No, not home. She couldn't think of it as home. That way lay heartbreak. Before she turned onto the lane that led to the lighthouse, she pulled over onto the shoulder of the highway and checked the camera feed again.

Savannah was still there, leaning on the side of the vehicle and looking miserable. Rowan didn't see anybody else in the vicinity or in the car.

Rowan drove the rest of the way down the narrow unpaved road and parked in front of the door. She gathered her grocery bag, got out and walked toward Savannah, making sure that she did not limp. "What a pleasant surprise! What are you doing here?"

"I didn't know who else to come to."

Time for the important question. "How did you find me?"

"I asked Joe."

"Joe's okay?" That was a little more swift and anxious than Rowan would have liked.

"Sure! Didn't you know? He always lands on his feet."

The way Savannah said it, as if she knew him well, gave Rowan a queasy feeling, and made her examine Savannah a little more closely. According to her body language, she was lying. Assuming if that was the case, why? What was she hiding? What did she intend? "I'd as soon he wasn't handing out my address to everyone."

"I'm not everyone."

No, you're not. You're someone who might possibly be smart enough to be able to track me because of my recent hospitalization and getting a new driver's license and…and.

Savannah said, "I thought you and me were friends!"

"You did?"

Tears welled in Savannah's eyes. "Yes. I thought…"

"Sure. We're friends!" *Go away, I'm desperate to be alone.* "What's wrong?"

"Wadell dumped me. I didn't know where to go. Joe said to see if you could help me find a place. He said you were really capable."

What a compliment…and that didn't sound like silver-tongued Joe at all..

"He felt sorry for me. Rowan, what am I going to do? No one wants an overweight, aging consort!"

For the love of God. "You're not overweight and aging!"

"I've already aged out of one profession. When I turned twelve! No one wants a former child actress who's going through puberty!" Savannah was snarling. "Do you think I don't know what aging out looks like?"

"You undervalue yourself. You're a beautiful woman who has lots of opportunities ahead of her."

"Wadell realized that I gained three pounds."

Rowan savagely hated Wadell for putting her into this situation. "Wadell has a lot to answer for."

"I'm twenty-eight years old. Past my prime!" Savannah burst into loud sobbing and collapsed against the car door.

When Rowan saw Joe, if she ever did, she was going to bust

his nose. Gingerly she moved close enough to pat Savannah on the shoulder.

Savannah threw her arms around Rowan, clutched her, and wept.

Rowan sighed and tried to disengage—and saw a movement in the reflection of the window: behind her, a woman's figure dressed in black and red.

Gripping Savannah in one arm, Rowan swung her around as a shield.

Savannah screamed and convulsed.

Rowan shoved her all the way onto the point of Mitzi's knife.

46

SAVANNAH SCREAMED AGAIN.

Mitzi screamed louder, a cry of maddened fury and frustration, and with a yank, she pulled the knife from Savannah's back.

Savannah collapsed, shrieking, "It's poisoned. It's poisoned. I'm dying!"

Rowan leaped over her convulsing body, stopped in the middle of the open space in front of the lighthouse, and faced Mitzi... close enough, but not too close.

Like some James Bond supervillain, Mitzi wore an all-black spandex cat suit and black boots with silver buckles. As always, her red nails had been sharpened to points. Smiling faintly, she kicked Savannah hard enough to make her moan and roll aside, and turned to face Rowan, blade pointed at her belly. "Sorry I missed the first time—child killer!"

So Joe hadn't given anyone her address. Mitzi had found her. Still clutching her groceries, Rowan waited...

Lorenze Winterbourne's voice spoke in her head. *Waiting is always the hard part.*

Mitzi gathered herself to spring.

Rowan swung the weighted bag at arm's length in a wide sweep. The combination of cans, bottles and milk hit Mitzi's midsection. Her breath oofed out of her. She bent double.

Gaining momentum, Rowan completed the circle's rotation. The power of the blow smashed into Mitzi's shoulder.

Mitzi staggered sideways and lost her grip on the knife.

The bag split open. Cans rolled everywhere, glass pickle bottles shattered, and the smell of vinegar, dill and mustard seed filled the air. The plastic milk jug flew like a missile and hit the SUV. The impact knocked the top off, and milk spewed like a geyser, wetting them both and dampening Savannah's cries.

Mitzi managed to keep her feet. Tripped on a rolling can. Fell to her hands and knees and screamed again. This time, as glass pierced her palm, it was a scream of agony.

Amid the cries of pain and panic, fury and furor, and an odd, loud, deep rumbling, Rowan ran toward the lighthouse and hit the hidden emergency button in the wall. The door sprang open.

Mitzi shouted, "I'll shoot you where you stand."

Without any thought except coming through this alive, Rowan dove low and hard for the dim, gaping entrance.

A bullet buried itself in the wall beside her.

That sucks! She'd hoped the gun was an empty threat. She jumped to her feet to get inside.

Her leg collapsed.

Pain made her grunt. Pain made her head spin.

Son of a bitch. She touched her calf, lifted her palm before her eyes. Blood. Dark red blood. Somewhere in the excitement, the struggle, and probably that last wild leap, she'd ripped her stitches.

She crawled.

Her world was rattling with noise: Savannah's screaming began to fade, but the thumping grew louder.

Another gunshot. Rowan covered her head with her arms.

Mitzi bellowed, "I'll kill you!"

I believe you.

"I'll kill you if you try to stop me now!" Mitzi's pitch shrilled so high, dogs must have been howling for miles around.

Really, I believe you. Rowan inched forward into the foyer, afraid, furious, and disbelieving that she had come so far and withstood so much…only to die at Mitzi's hand. Yet she couldn't give up, couldn't stop inching forward, dragging herself on her elbows. She heard a thumping in her head, thought it must be the pain, maybe onset of death, when a violent wind buffeted her and—

A helicopter. That noise wasn't in her head. It was a private helicopter, and from the sounds and the buffeting of air, it sounded as if it was landing on top of her.

She felt a stirring of hope, but she didn't stop crawling. She didn't dare a glance behind. She had to get inside. She had to survive. For a few more minutes. Survive… "Please be Joe," she whispered. "Please be Joe." Her body shook. Her vision grew dark with swirling specks. She had to halt, to breathe, to put oxygen into her brain and heart. She stopped crawling and risked a glance at the parking area.

The helicopter landed between her and Mitzi and Savannah, landed so hard it bounced.

Surely it was Joe. Or someone come to save her. Who else could it be?

Yet when the door slid open… Gregory Torval jumped out.

Cornered. Rowan was cornered. There was no Lorenze Winterbourne or Joe Grantham to help.

She had to save herself.

Again.

47

ACROSS THE DISTANCE, Rowan and Torval stared at each other. His face was angry, haggard, and even from here, she could see that his brown eyes had that deadly yellow tinge. "You!" He pointed a shaking finger at her. "You betrayed me!"

Mitzi had arrived to remove the person Lorenze Winterbourne had fought so hard to save.

Torval had come to remove the daughter he blamed for his downfall.

Rowan was *fucked*.

Mitzi yelled at Torval. "You worthless bastard, I told you *no*!"

"I told *you* to stay put, and you're my wife. You do as you're told!" Torval yelled back.

Mitzi's screech startled the birds from the trees, and honestly, Rowan didn't blame her. *You're my wife. You do as you're told?* Could you be more primitive, more conceited, more of a bullshit full-of-himself male prick?

Torval started purposefully toward Rowan.

She used the doorframe as a support, and lifted herself to her feet.

Her leg collapsed again.

No. She couldn't allow this weakness. Lorenze Winterbourne had dealt with much worse and managed to impress people with his strength. She could save herself. She would. She had no choice.

Another gunshot.

Rowan ducked and crawled toward the door that led to the spiral stairway.

A gunshot from Mitzi?

Yes, from Mitzi, but at who?

A scream rose above all the other sounds. A man's scream.

Rowan looked back.

Torval stood erect, straight, staring at his hip, bleeding and blasted from Mitzi's gunshot. He reached his hand toward Mitzi. His fingers touched her cheek. "My darling. My dearest. Why would you do this to me?" It was a lover's cry of anguish.

"You're my eternal mate." Mitzi caressed his cheek in return. "But you betrayed me and our son. You will die in agony." She dispensed her sentence like a venomous snake.

Dear God. Yes. A South American soap opera. Rowan had to get herself out of here before she became a dead prop in the play.

Again she pulled herself to her feet. Again she collapsed.

Unexpectedly, a strong arm slid under her arm and helped her up.

She looked around, not sure if she should strike or thank.

Elijah stood there, his brown eyes wide, sweat dripping off his forehead in an unsteady stream of terror. "Where do you want to go?"

She indicated the door that led to the spiral staircase, and when he had helped her there, she said, "Kid. Get out!"

He nodded, turned toward the outer door, and turned back to her, his complexion green with fear. "She's here!"

Mitzi had arrived.

So Torval was dead.

"That way!" Rowan pointed up the wide main stairs, the obvious stairs that led to the different floors and ultimately to the trapdoor into her apartment. "Third floor. Hunker down! Anywhere!"

If he followed her directions, he'd be okay among the shabby furniture she'd imported to fool any searchers into thinking that floor was her home. Each twist and turn was all a maze, a rabbit warren, with hiding places galore and, if Elijah was attentive, a few traps he could activate.

Poor boy. He probably would be too panicked to note the ways to activate those traps, but he did know how to hunker down…she hoped.

She hit the concealed button on the spiral stairs and pressed her ring finger print to the reader. The mechanism worked: the door swung open. Gripping the metal railing, using it for support, she ran up the first flight of stairs. Stumbled. Went down. As her knee hit the step, the metal clanged. The denim split on the rough tread.

Great. Now she was bleeding from her knee, too. Minor, but her foot had again grown cold. She was clumsy, in pain. Maybe she should have shut that door, but she told herself that would be nothing more than a temporary reprieve. She wasn't going to get better, and she needed to end this *now*.

She heard the thumps as someone flung back the outer door. Was it Mitzi? Was it Torval?

"I'm in here," she shouted. She didn't want any of these crazy, cruel, immoral people to accidentally head up the wrong stairs and stumble on Elijah. He would never survive that encounter, and she could never live with the guilt.

The door to the spiral stairs slammed against the wall, and Mitzi stepped inside. She looked up, pistol in hand.

Rowan leaned over the rail, stared into her eyes, and smiled. "Come and get me…if you can."

She had hoped to madden Mitzi.

Safe to say it worked.

Mitzi screamed in rage. Hand shaking, she fired wildly.

Rowan ducked.

The roar of the shot echoed up and down the metal tube. The bullet pinged as it ricocheted who knew where.

Rowan crawled up the next few steps, preserving her strength. With exaggerated patience, she called, "Mitzi, do you have to shriek *all* the time? You're my evil stepmother, and being shrill is *so* Disney."

Another scream, and she heard the thump of Mitzi's running feet on the steps.

The confrontation she hoped for, planned for, was almost here. With a last burst of strength, Rowan ran the rest of the way up the second flight of stairs.

More bleeding. Pain. Enough dizziness to cause vertigo. For one moment, she considered vomiting on Mitzi. The idea gave her enough of an amused boost to reach the next landing.

Mitzi gained on her every step of the way. "You're bleeding, bitch." There was pleasure in her tone, a purring satisfaction. "It's all over the stairs. Great blobs of sticky red blood that mean you won't even be able to give me a proper fight." Her feet thumped on the stairs. "How sad."

Rowan wanted to say something taunting, something witty, but Mitzi was right. Her own racing heart pumped out the warm blood in streams. She would save her breath for this, the final resolution.

Then, two stories below, the door slammed against the wall again. "Mitzi!" Torval bellowed. "I won't let you kill my daughter!"

The moment of silence that followed was profound.

Rowan didn't move.

Mitzi didn't make a sound.

Then all hell broke loose.

48

MITZI'S HIGH SCREECH erupted in an operatic blast of prima donna.

Rowan covered her ears. *My God, does the woman ever shut up?*

Torval roared back, a primal, deep-throated Titan challenge.

From the sound of it, Mitzi leaped over the spiral staircase railing and directly onto Torval. The smack sounded as if they had collided like two sumo wrestlers.

Rowan craned her neck, trying to see what was happening, but they fought directly below her. She heard a punch of fist to flesh. A scream and a grunt of pain. A shove. A crash. Something tore, flesh or cloth or vital organs; Torval roared again, but weaker this time.

Rowan dragged herself up the stairs, trying to distance herself from the horrors below. Nothing good could come of this. Even if Gregory Torval truly wanted to stop Mitzi, he loved and revered his wife. He wouldn't hurt her, not for any reason, certainly not for his newfound daughter.

Mitzi was *not* conflicted. She had lost her son. Torval failed to avenge him as she demanded. Rowan had sprung up, the daughter of Lorenze Winterbourne, and even worse, flesh of Torval's flesh. Mitzi would gladly kill them both. She bore a madness and a cruelty that went right to the bone, and when Rowan remembered the throne room, the explosions, the guests' riot and Gregory Torval's maddened shouting... He had cursed Rowan for fleeing. He had wanted loyalty based on nothing more than a genetic relationship. He had no one else; that was no reason for Rowan to support him. He'd spent half her life trying to kill her. He'd sent Doug Moore to kill her.

She had no chance but to hurry, to get into place and spring her trap.

The sounds below intensified. The meaty sound of boot meeting flesh. A crack. A shove. Someone tumbled down the metal steps, followed by man's weakened growl that faded to nothingness, and a she-cat's triumphant scream.

Mitzi had won.

Rowan hadn't even realized she held hope for Torval's success. But now...she was devastated.

Thump. Thump.

Mitzi was stomping up the stairs, sure she had Rowan hunted into the ground, too weak to flee, and she would die in fear and trembling.

Thump. Thump.

Mitzi reached the landing and laid eyes on Rowan one flight of stairs above. Her all-black cat suit had been dirtied by her fall onto the asphalt and rumpled by her efforts. She had blood smeared on her mouth and blood on her fingers from the knife work, or she'd used those claws on someone. On Torval.

But she smiled. Oh, how she smiled. "Look at you, cowering, hurt and exhausted. This is going to be almost too easy." She stalked up the steps, all preening she-tiger confidence.

When she was firmly caught in the trap, Rowan smiled back at her.

Mitzi paused in surprise and consternation.
Rowan pressed the release mechanism.
Triumph!
Except…nothing happened.

49

ROWAN GROPED, made sure she was in the right spot, and tried again.

Nothing.

The mechanism was stuck. Stuck! Why? She kept it lubricated. She tested it regularly. It worked like a dream. How could it be stuck *now*?

She groped the railing up and down.

Because damn it, the metal was dented. How the hell... Her mind replayed that moment when Mitzi stepped through into the stairway and fired. That bullet had ricocheted off somewhere in the upper depths.

Now Rowan knew where it had hit—it had bounced off the railing.

"Is something wrong, my dear?" Like a black widow spider on her web, Mitzi swayed from side to side as if testing the stairs. "Could it be your little plan, whatever it was, has failed you?"

No time to curse this setback; keeping an eye on Mitzi's advance, Rowan frantically jiggled the switch with one hand. With the other hand, she pulled the utility knife from her belt and, keeping it close to her side, slid the razor blade out of its sheath. "Come on, come on, come on, come on," she whispered encouragement to the mechanism.

No luck. It scraped as it moved…a little.

Mitzi kept coming, one slow step at a time. At last, grinning, she stood over Rowan. Red, pointed nails outstretched, she reached for her.

Rowan slashed with the knife.

The razor sliced Mitzi's lily-white skin. Crimson blood bloomed in a long line. Mitzi yanked her hand back, looked at it in astonishment, cradled it like a baby. "You dare." One black boot flashed out. She kicked the knife out of Rowan's hand.

Fingers smashed. Rowan groaned and gave the trap one more good jerk.

The stairway broke away beneath Mitzi, plunging her three stories down to—

Mitzi grabbed Rowan's dangling leg.

The sudden weight, the jerk, almost pulled Rowan off the landing. She grabbed an upright on the railing, hooked her elbows around it, braced her free foot on the landing and hung on for dear life.

All the while, Mitzi screamed curses and dug those claws into Rowan's leg. Rowan's already bleeding leg. The agony of the reopened wound, the damage Mitzi was doing, the weight and Rowan's weakness made her foot slip, once, twice.

Mitzi screamed, "I'm not going alone, daughter of Lorenze Winterbourne. I'm taking you to hell with me!" She let go with one hand and used it to swing for the landing.

The change in weight threw Rowan sideways. The weight on her elbows was agony. She was going to go down…with Mitzi. She tasted bitterness and triumph. Mitzi would be dead, one evil would be vanquished from the world, but what a hollow victory to die now!

She closed her eyes tightly, concentrating hard on keeping her hold on that landing...when from nowhere she heard her father's calm, deep voice.

"Rowan. Rowan, listen to me. You know what to do."

Rowan did know what to do. But— "I can't." Her joints were stretched to breaking. Her muscles screamed as they carried a load too big and heavy. Colored lights exploded behind her eyes, and she was faint with blood loss and pain. She couldn't perform another impossible task, run another mile, learn another skill. It was time to be at rest in the home she'd sought for so many years. "I can't."

"I'll help you."

The warm, bracing voice bolstered her courage. One more effort. What would that cost her? She opened her eyes and looked around, expecting to see Lorenze Winterbourne standing at her shoulder.

Instead, Gregory Torval stood on the landing below.

50

TORVAL HAD A crimson stain on his hip. His nose was broken, and bruises covered him, clearly from the fall down the stairs. Blood covered his face, his neck, clotted in his hair. Rowan thought, she wasn't sure, that one ear had been ripped away.

Mitzi and her claws. She'd tried to blind him, rip him to shreds, and she must have in part succeeded, for even now he pressed his index finger to his forehead as if pushing his skull back into place.

"Look. You're my daughter. You've survived because you've got my DNA, and Lorenze Winterbourne taught you the skills. You will continue to survive because I'm going to help you."

Transfixed, she stared into his eyes.

He was calm, as if the spirit of Lorenze Winterbourne had possessed him, as if his own life meant nothing and his daughter's meant all the world to him.

Mitzi clawed at Rowan's leg and shouted at him, "Shut up, you prick. You can't help her. You help *me*, you treacherous piece of—"

He nodded at Rowan.

She nodded back. If she was wrong, if she trusted him and he betrayed her, she was dead. But she had to believe, so she lifted her foot, the one braced against the landing, and kicked at Mitzi's face.

As Mitzi's head snapped back on her neck, Torval leaped and caught her dangling legs. The weight, the surprise made her release Rowan.

The scream, the terrible thud, the silence that went on and on and spoke of heaven and hell, that final moment of life and an eternity of nothingness...

Rowan shuddered. Her breathing grew labored, and her eyes grew dim. The efforts she had made, the blood she'd lost weakened her. Her crooked arms loosened on the railing. She caught herself in time...barely. Her body skidded off the step. She dangled over the dark chasm. Three stories to the ground, she knew. No one—not Gregory Torval, not Mitzi—had survived that fall. She had to pull herself up. But she could hear the thick, slow splash of blood dripping onto the concrete floor far below. *Her blood.* In her mind, the sound amplified like the approaching and ominous footsteps of death.

She swung her legs toward the railing. Missed. Tried again.

She didn't want to join Torval and Mitzi, to form that unholy trilogy...but she was tired. So tired. Her shoulders bunched with strain. Her arms were numb from her elbows to her hands.

Was she really going to die now? Now, when her death would be a betrayal to her mother and both her fathers?

"I've got you." A man's voice spoke from inside her apartment. He grasped her by the shoulders and dragged her, almost unconscious, up the stairs and inside, and placed her on the floor. For the briefest moment, she opened her eyes and saw the silhouette of the man with...she thought...an intense gaze and a sexy smile.

"Joe," she breathed, and slipped easily into unconsciousness.

When next she woke, EMTs surrounded her, police officers moved around the perimeter, and she wanted to tell them all to get out of her space and leave her alone with Joe. Yet she had IV tubes feeding into her arms. Strange faces were shining lights into her eyes, attaching patches to her chest, taking her blood pressure and speaking in serious tones. She could tell by the pain in her body she was badly injured, and she could tell by her otherworldly feeling she had been given drugs to...sedate her. Ease her agony.

She caught sight of a familiar face.

Among the EMTs and law enforcement, Elijah hovered in the background, looking young and scared and happy and brave.

Elijah. Sure. It was Elijah's hands on my shoulders that dragged me to safety. Elijah performed the final rescue.

Joe was nowhere in sight.

She closed her eyes and slipped away.

THE FIRST DAY OF THE REST
OF HER LIFE

51

ROWAN STOOD AT the stove, browning cut pieces of a whole chicken: the backs, the wing tips, the ribs. It was her first attempt to make her own broth, and if the worshipful way the dogs stared at her was any indication, it was going to be wildly successful.

When, after her rescue at the lighthouse, she was taken to the hospital, treated and kept, and finally released, her first stop had been at the Humane Society to pick up her dog. Little Miss Three-Legs with the Huge Wagging Tail was still there; Rowan had decided because of her intelligence and loyalty, she deserved to be called Lassie.

Lassie had collected an assistance dog to help her get around. That meant Rowan had also adopted Swag, a skinny, black-and-white street boy-dog whose first job was to make sure Lassie got up and down the stairs with no falls and whose second job was to step out onto the deck and bark at incoming traffic by sea or land.

Rowan didn't know why she'd ever bothered with a security app. Swag was so much easier.

As she added savory vegetables—celery, onion and parsley—
to her pot, something out at sea attracted Swag's attention, and
he darted up the stairs to the top floor, which housed the lighthouse light. The day was bright and warm, and while Swag
barked, Rowan added eight cups of water to her impending
broth, turned it to the lowest simmer, and said to Lassie, "I'm
not giving you the broth, so you might as well come up and see
what's he's carrying on about."

Lassie indicated her lack of enthusiasm by sighing and hop-
ping over to the stairs.

Rowan picked her up—forty-five pounds should be no big
deal, but Rowan's ordeal two months ago had left her dealing
with injuries that had incapacitated her and required twice-
weekly physical therapy to get her on her feet. The trek up the
stairs left her breathless.

Lassie licked her chin and wiggled out of her arms, and went
to stand next to Swag to stare out to sea.

Rowan went to the rail and looked out to sea, too. What she
saw made her do a double take. She grabbed her binoculars and
zeroed in on the white yacht bobbing in the swells.

Torval's yacht. In the wheelhouse—BeBée, binoculars pressed
to her face, waving enthusiastically.

Rowan's phone buzzed with a text message. Rowan dug it
out of her pocket and read:

Want to go for a ride?

She texted back:

Sure!

BeBée replied:

Meet me at the Offbeat Bay marina.

Rowan told the sad-eyed dogs they couldn't go, tied on her sneakers, got in the not-hers Camry, and drove south to the docks.

The yacht rode the waves BeBée leaned over the rail and argued with the officious manager, Mr. Inkpad, who ogled at her admirable cleavage and tried to articulate why she couldn't dock here and that he needed to view her papers.

Glancing up, she saw Rowan and said to him, "My friend is here. I told you she'd be quick. I'll take her on a quick run and drop her off later!"

As Rowan walked up the gangplank, Inkpad got his words back. "Helen, do you know this woman?"

Half the town hadn't yet gotten the word that Helen Lamb was now Rowan Winterbourne.

"I do know her."

"Is she always like this? No respect for authority?"

"Yes," Rowan said with fake sympathy. "Yes, I'm afraid she is."

"I need proof of ownership for this yacht and to see her license to drive this thing!"

"I'll tell her."

He must have sensed her insincerity. "You can't dock here!" he shouted at BeBée.

"I know. We're leaving. See you later!" BeBée winked at Rowan and dashed up to the wheelhouse, leaving Rowan to bring the gangplank in.

She did so with complete efficiency and an amused awareness that out here on the water with the prospect of a short cruise and a long talk, her low-level depression had lifted, and she felt better than she had in two months.

BeBée backed out, turned the yacht and headed out to sea. When the shore was a smudge on the horizon, she turned south and put it on autopilot.

Rowan joined her in the wheelhouse, and the two women hugged and laughed and hugged again.

BeBée put her hands on Rowan's shoulders and shook her. "I saw you get away from Raptor Island in that balloon!"

Rowan shook her back. "I saw you get away, too! With this, which is far more impressive than a balloon."

"Hell, yeah! Years ago, I had Torval put this in my name to save on his taxes. Because I didn't have an income. Heh."

"Aren't you clever? Do you have a license to operate it, too?"

"Of course, and the yacht has all the bells and whistles for me to operate it alone. I sent Inkpen a scan, but he was being such an ass that I didn't feel like showing him the original. Call me a rebel."

"You're a rebel!"

BeBée threw her arms into the air. "I know! I'm *free!*" She smiled invitingly at Rowan. "Want to be a rebel with me?"

Hmm. "I don't know. What does being a rebel entail?"

"I'm headed to South America. I've got a passport and a visa."

"Real, legal papers?"

"Close enough to pass for real!"

Rowan laughed. "BeBée, you're an amazing woman."

"I speak Spanish. I told you I had investments. I'm going to travel. I'm going to hike. I'm going to meet new people and do things I've never done before. Zipline! Skydive! Rappel! I'm going to visit all the cities and the monuments and eat all the food. I'm done with counting calories. I'm done with monotony. I'm going to live like a queen!" BeBée was gulping fresh air as if she'd never breathed before. "Want to come and live with me?"

Rowan understood what BeBée was asking. "I'd love to come and live with you."

BeBée's smile dimmed. "But?"

Rowan struggled to gently explain.

BeBée made the wise guess. "But you like driving a stick."

It took Rowan a moment to understand the euphemism for

preferring a male sexual partner. "Ah. Yes. Not that I expect much more in the way of men in my life. But BeBée, it's not merely that. Not really. I've had enough adventure for twenty lifetimes. I want to stay in my home with my dogs and live a boring life forever until when I die, my obituary calls me 'That crazy old lady who lives alone in the lighthouse.'"

"I don't quite see you condemned to a solitary life." BeBée smiled as if she knew something Rowan did not.

Rowan eyed her curiously. "I thought you were partial to driving a stick yourself."

"Male or female." BeBée performed her patented voluptuous roll from the shoulders to the hips. "I don't care one way or another. What I want for the rest of my life is to live with someone I love and respect. I do love and respect you."

Without reservation, Rowan hugged her. "I know. I love and respect you *more*."

BeBée pushed her. "Shut up, you."

"You need to be free, at least for awhile, to do your hiking and traveling and learning and skydiving and eating."

"You're right. I shall enjoy myself." BeBée sighed. "I'd enjoy my life with you, too. Maybe someday I'll want to settle down."

"Maybe someday I'll want to adventure again."

"Maybe."

They sighed in unison.

"You heard what happened to Torval and Mitzi?" Rowan asked.

"Of course. Big news for a couple of news cycles while people tried to figure out how those two escaped Raptor Island and what they were doing in a lighthouse smashed into tiny Gregory and Mitzi pieces on a concrete floor." BeBée didn't tear up, but she was somber and perhaps a little surprised at herself. "I don't miss them, and I like this life…but I lived on that damned island for over ten years, and surviving and helping others survive were my job."

"It's a good gap to have to fill."

"Exactly. I always knew when I went to the island with that shipment of girls and you vanished, then Doug Moore got slammed and Lorenze Winterbourne broke out... I always knew I'd see you again. I knew you'd do good by me."

Rowan embraced her, and they rocked together, and Rowan thought, *That answers that question. BeBée recognized me from the start.*

They broke apart, and BeBée asked, "Shall we turn around now?"

"Yes, let's. Promise you'll come back whenever you need a break from your adventures."

"I will." BeBée took the wheel and turned the yacht toward Offbeat Bay. She looked sideways at Rowan. "By the way, good job finishing off Doug Moore."

"I didn't! I told you to come and—"

"I was busy organizing the exodus, and sent one of my people. I got a photo texted to me. Moore had plastic smashed onto his face and a knife in his chest. I couldn't tell if he died of asphyxiation or he bled out."

Rowan contemplated that information. "You and me—we weren't the only ones who hated him."

"Amen, sister."

As they pulled into the harbor, Rowan asked, "How did you get my phone number?"

"Joe gave it to me."

"Seriously?" Rowan remembered Savannah saying Joe had told her where to find the lighthouse. Had he? She didn't know, but it seemed unlikely. "How did he get it?"

BeBée shrugged in exaggerated lack of knowledge and turned toward the open berth.

Inkpad ran out and stood there, shouting and waving his arms.

Rowan turned to BeBée. "Looks like I have no choice."

BeBée handed her a life vest and a hug. "You have a good life, Rowan Winterbourne."

"You, too, BeBée... Say, what is your last name?"

"Smith. It's BeBée Smith."

"That's perfect. Fancy and plain." Rowan climbed up on the railing.

Inkpad yelled louder, forbidding her to jump.

"And average!" BeBée yelled to Roman.

"You will never be average, BeBée!" Rowan put her hands over her head and dove into the bay. By the time she had swum to shore, Inkpad was apoplectic with rage and the yacht had cleared the harbor.

Rowan bought a towel at the marina shop and dried off, smugly aware that neither she or BeBée would ever be average.

The next day, Rowan came back from hiking the cliffs to find Bill, her mail carrier, sitting in front of her house, eating his lunch.

She shushed Swag's barking. "Bill, what's up?"

"I've got a registered letter for you to sign for. Since your car's here—" he indicated Joe's car "—I figured you couldn't have gone too far and thought I'd save you a trip to town."

Also, Bill had a well-deserved reputation as a snoop.

"Thanks." She accepted the clipboard, signed the back of the envelope and handed it to Bill.

He tore off the return label and returned the envelope, then waited while she examined the return address.

No wonder he was sticking around. It was from the IRS.

"Thank you, Bill." She turned the dogs toward the lighthouse.

"I hope everything's okay!" he called.

She hoped so, too. "Thanks for your concern." She shut the door behind her, got all the way up the stairs—she used the main stairs now—and into her rooms, gave the dogs their water, and watched them flop down, tongues hanging out, before she tore open the envelope.

"Well, hell," she said. So much for a peaceful life.

She held a letter assuring her that she was in no trouble, but she had been summoned to the Taxpayer Assistance Center in Santa Maria for a preliminary audit.

52

"I HAVE AN appointment with—" Rowan consulted her paper-work "—IRS agent J.G. Hamilton?"

The federal guard tapped on her computer, then nodded. "You're in Conference Room C."

"A conference room? How many people am I meeting with?"

The guard was smiling, but she shrugged. "They don't tell us details. Hardy will escort you."

A young man appeared at Rowan's elbow. "This way."

He led her toward the conference room, and he kept glanc-ing at her and smiling,, which was sort of mean considering she was coming in for a preliminary audit.

Rowan approached cautiously. The dogs were in the kennel, enjoying a woods walk every day and all the belly rubs the vet-erinarian-in-training kids could give them, so even if she was arrested, which she wouldn't be because she had done noth-ing wrong, they'd be fine. She had all her paperwork. She was lawfully allowed to earn a large lump payment for her work... assuming that the check from Frances Sattimore was what this investigation was about. Surely every single person called by the IRS felt uneasy and guilty even when they weren't.

Surely.

She took a breath, put her hand on the knob of the closed door, looked back at Hardy.

He smiled widely and made a shooing motion.

She turned the knob and walked in.

The large conference room had narrow windows, a long table, lots of chairs, and at the far side of the room on the opposite wall hung a huge dry board with markers in the tray.

Joe Grantham stood there, dressed in a business suit, looking every inch of an IRS agent.

Rowan stared at him, trying to decide if she was surprised or not.

Possibly not.

Probably not.

He gazed at her; his face warmed as if the sight of her gave him pleasure. Then he tilted his head to the side, toward the small group of people halfway down the table.

She didn't want to look away from him. But she did.

Three people stood there. A dad, a mom, and... Rowan's sister. Her sister.

Her sister.

Rowan's mind was stammering. She suffered from shock, memories, the fear of rejection... So many thoughts and emotions battered her she didn't know how she could... Her voice was not even a whisper. "Linden?" Wait, that name was wrong. "Irena?"

"Rowie?" The girl paced toward her, her whole body posed to embrace, to welcome. "Rowie, do you remember me?"

Rowie. Oh, God. *Rowie.* Somehow, this girl, this young woman who hadn't seen Rowan for fourteen years, remembered her nickname for Rowan, for her big sister.

All the years of careful restraint, of loneliness, of setting herself apart…all the years of tragedy were pushed aside by a surge of joy and connection, and Rowan flung herself into Irena's waiting arms.

The sisters hugged. They laughed. They exchanged incoherent words. Somehow…somehow, Irena remembered Rowan. Only fragments, bits of memory, of family and love and real life tidbits. She didn't recall anything of the massacre at her school, or of Lorenze and Rowan taking her to an orphanage and abandoning her there. But she talked about being rocked in the blue rocker and Daddy and Mommy singing "Rowie Rowie Rowie your boat" while Rowie pulled Linden's blankie with the purple bear over her head.

Irena's parents moved closer, and soon Shane and Dana Tremblay took part in the embrace while Rowan tried to thank them for their care of her sister and Irena tried to introduce them and explain who they were and what they were like, and Rowan finally had to admit she'd been spying on them.

That caused a moment of consternation. Then all agreed that was good and natural and showed her concern for her baby sister. There was so much warm family stuff, Rowan felt as if she'd been wrapped in a fuzzy blanket and fed stew and chocolate chip cookies and baked mac and cheese and garden-fresh tomatoes and placed before the fire of love to warm herself.

Probably an hour later, or maybe it was a lifetime, the Tremblays announced they were going out to lunch to plan a family reunion that would introduce Rowan to the rest of the Tremblays, as well as the maternal Roderiguez members and all the various widely spread cousins and aunts and uncles and offspring.

About that time, Rowan remembered Joe…but he had vanished. That made her feel disoriented and disconcerted, as if he'd been appearing and disappearing out of her life like a Robin Williams genie who averted disasters she hadn't dared imagine and granted wishes she hadn't yet formulated.

Had she imagined him?

No, she hadn't. Not this time. Shane and Dana assured her when that IRS agent J.G. Hamilton had contacted them, they'd been freaked out about some tax misunderstanding, but he'd assured them he was on unofficial business and explained that he was acquainted with Irena's sister and would like to engineer a reunion in a neutral location.

Rowan gestured at the conference room. "In an IRS building?"

Dana laughed. "I know, right?"

But Shane said, "I believe Joe thought it would be best to undeniably establish his identity in Rowan's mind."

"Shane's always right," Dana said to Rowan. "Remember that when you get married and it'll save you so much argument."

Irena mouthed to Rowan, "No, he's not."

"I saw that, young woman!" Shane hugged Irena and Rowan, and smiled at his wife. "Come on, I'll buy you ladies lunch and we'll plan a family reunion."

As they walked out of the Taxpayer Assistance Center, Hardy, the guard, and apparently quite a few other people who had known what was happening gave them a round of applause.

After the planning lunch and upon the Tremblays' urging, Rowan called the kennel and asked them to keep the dogs for the night, and she stayed at their house in Paso Robles. The number of friends and relatives who dropped by casually bearing casseroles and staying for dinner was *not* the official family reunion.

Irena begged Rowan to sleep in the second twin bed in her bedroom. "It'll be like old times," she said, and reminisced about climbing out of her crib on weekend mornings and coming to snuggle with Rowan.

Tears sprang to Rowan's eyes again, and she discovered the Tremblays and everyone related to them were enthusiastic criers, for everyone burst into tears along with her.

The emotional day needed only one thing to make it complete.

Dana asked if she could come in and tuck them in.

"Oh, Mom!" Irena was teenagerly embarrassed. Catching sight of Rowan's expression, she changed her mind. "Sure, Mom!"

Dana tucked Irena in, then came over and tucked Rowan in and sat on the bed. "When Irena came to us, she was obviously traumatized. She cried when we popped corn or if someone shouted on the television. She had night terrors about 'the men.' We thought maybe that she'd been abused, but no. Obviously, too, she'd lost a family she loved very much. She cried for her mommy and daddy, and she cried for Rowie. We thought maybe Rowie was her teddy bear or her blankie."

Rowan chuckled sadly. "No. No, when she was tiny, she couldn't say Rowan. First she called me 'Owie,' which made Rowie sound pretty good."

Dana took her hand and squeezed it. "Her whole childhood, she would sing, 'Rowie, Rowie, Rowie your boat,' and finally, when she was older, we asked her what that meant."

"What did she say?"

"She was startled, as if she'd never thought of it. She said, 'I don't know what I means, but it makes me happy.'"

Rowan's eyes and heart overflowed. "Thank you for giving my sister such a happy, secure upbringing. Watching from afar has given me so much comfort, knowing she had you."

Irena jumped out of bed and ran over to throw her arms around Rowan, and the three women cried until Shane showed up, took Dana away, and told them to go to sleep.

The next morning, Rowan insisted she had to go home. She used the recently adopted dogs as an excuse, promised to come back, and for a short respite escaped the emotional turmoil.

But she had one more thing to do before she returned to her pets and her lighthouse. She went to the IRS building to see Joe. She was told by the guard, who remembered her from yesterday, that after his recent triumph over organized crime, J.G. Hamilton had resigned from the IRS and was now working for the MFAA, unofficially known as the Monuments Men, an agency headquartered in Washington DC.

She thanked the guard and drove home in Joe's car, cursing his name, or rather, all of the names she knew of, all the way.

53

AMID MUCH REJOICING, the first autumn storm rolled off the Pacific with winds and a deluge that California always needed and craved. Rowan stood out on the deck. She faced into the teeth of the storm and remembered that day not so long ago when she arranged Mr. Bandara's death and wondered if that blistering storm had been the universe's vengeance on her.

Yet the night had brought her Joe, and somehow she wasn't surprised when her app went off and Swag barked—she wasn't nearly as aware of security as when Gregory Torval had been alive, but she was still a woman living alone—and she checked her camera to see a silver car turn into her driveway.

Coming in, she stripped off her rain gear and hung it on the hooks. She blotted her face and toed off her rain boots. She dried the dogs with the old towels she kept for that purpose. Opening the door to her apartment, she followed the dogs down the stairs. She went to the bathroom, used the toilet and ran a comb through her damp hair.

She watched as the car parked in front of the door and a man in a dark raincoat got out, came up onto the porch and rang the doorbell. This time, his fingerprint registered in her database.

J.G. Hamilton in the flesh.

Since her return from the second hospital visit, she'd taken to wearing T-shirt dresses, mostly maxi-length, for comfort and to cover the bruising and scars. Today she wore a long cotton ombré in off-white and autumn orange. The colors made her cheerful, and she knew the loose fit would be a disadvantage in case of fight or flight; wearing it reminded her that she was no longer being hunted.

She opened the newly designed and professionally installed third-floor entrance to her home—no more jumping from the top step—which included a locking door, stairs going down to the now primary wide stairway, and a landing.

Swag took the lead, dashing down and barking all the way. Rowan and Lassie followed, taking their time. J.G. Hamilton could damned well wait until they got around to letting him in.

By the time she opened the door, Joe was getting back into his car.

Swag ran out, barking furiously

"Sit!" Joe said.

Swag responded to the voice of a master. He sat.

"What's the fuss about?" Joe leaned down and scratched his head. "I know you're a brave dog, but also you know this woman can protect herself. And you."

"Swag is my warning alarm. My protector is Lassie." Rowan indicated Lassie, who sat at her side and watched Joe in a forbidding silence.

"Will she let me in?" Joe asked.

"If I tell her to."

"Will you let me in?"

"Of course. Because no harm ever came of inviting you in." Rowan ladled the sarcasm into her tone.

He reached into his car and brought forth bags marked with

the logo of the best Chinese restaurant in San Francisco. "I brought dinner this time."

Smart guy. "Then you can come in, Joe." She put her hand on Lassie's flank to let her know she could relax her guard. "It is Joe, isn't it?"

"Yes." Joe got another bag, a plain brown bag, out of the car, and a computer case, which he swung over his shoulder. He called Swag to heel—who knew the dog knew how to heel?—and when they were inside, he shut the door with a bump of the hip. He wore jeans that fit him like a glove and a starched button-up shirt, sleeves rolled up to the elbows, in a blue that made his eyes pop. His dark hair was shorter and spiky. His running shoes looked new. Compared with his first visit, he was slightly more formal, as if he were paying a call where he wasn't sure of his welcome.

That suited Rowan's mood.

As before, he gestured her ahead, and as before, she returned the gesture.

He nodded his understanding. "You don't trust me anymore."

"No." She felt the urge to explain why: he'd been gone too long without a word, he'd been nowhere in sight when the lighthouse had been attacked, he'd used an alias, he'd changed jobs as soon as he'd contacted her... The list went on and on. But he was an intelligent man. He at least had his suspicions.

He didn't budge. "Can I earn back your trust?"

"I don't know." She lifted her hem and showed him the ugly scar left by the exploding helium tank and Mitzi's pointed nails.

"That's so much worse than I—" He started toward her.

She held up her hand.

He halted.

She waved him up the stairs.

He climbed them, Swag bounding happily after him.

Maybe that was why Swag obeyed him. They both understood hand commands well.

With Lassie sticking close to her side, Rowan climbed after them.

"You don't use the spiral staircase anymore?" Joe indicated the metal tube that contained it.

"No. I wasn't here when they brought the bodies out. Torval and Mitzi, I mean." Rowan had been on the surgical table while a specialist reattached muscles and tendons and bones in her leg. "But law enforcement informed me the parts were so mashed together and entwined they couldn't easily distinguish one from the other. Which is right for them, but I don't wish to remember those events, so I keep that way closed. When it's time, I'll have it torn out." They reached the top of the stairs. She used the keypad to unlock the door. She held it open for him and his bags… and the dogs, who bounded in and headed for their food bowls.

"Nice remodel on the entry." Joe walked inside. "What if someone breaks in and threatens you again? Will you use the spiral staircase?"

"Of course, if the trap hasn't been dismantled, I wouldn't allow superstition to keep me away from the place that'll save me." Although she was considerably more superstitious than she'd been before she'd first met Joe. The moment Gregory Torval spoke with her stepfather's comforting voice was the moment she'd learned to believe in ghosts.

Joe went to the round quartz stone kitchen table and unloaded a variety of white paper boxes and containers from his bags.

Rowan inhaled. Her irritation with J.G. Hamilton faded under the influencing scents of toasted sesame oil, five spice powder, mint, basil, Sichuan peppercorns and barbecue pork. For the first time in a long time, her stomach growled.

Points to Joe.

Swag hurried to Joe's feet, sat and looked up at him worshipfully.

Rowan assured Lassie, "It's okay, girl," and the dog joined her assistant dog in staring at Joe as if he was the God of Chinese Food Delivery.

"I'd better feed these guys," she said to the room.

As she did, she was aware how very comfortable this was: out-side the storm lashing the windows, inside the dogs, the food, the conversation. Beneath the motions, the sounds and the scents hummed her low-level awareness of Joe and his probable reasons for coming here (sex) and his possible reasons (love, according to Frances Sattimore).

But he had been absent for all her ordeals, so—how did she feel about Joe?

54

JOE APPEARED BLISSFULLY unaware of Rowan's quandary. He got out the plates and silverware and set the table. He placed the spring rolls on a plate and opened the small accompanying container of sauce. "Sit. Talk to me while I heat the rest of this up."

She sank down in a kitchen chair, helped herself to a roll, savored the shrimp and herbs in a rice wrapper and dipped in peanut sauce. "What do you want to talk about?"

"How do you feel about Gregory Torval now?"

Way to jump right back into the big issues. No subtlety points to you, Joe. "That's difficult to quantify."

"I can see it would be."

Choosing her words carefully, she said, "When Torval landed in his helicopter, his eyes were burning yellow."

"Cat-piss yellow." Joe used BeBée's phrase.

"Yes." Even now, her fingers trembled; peanut sauce dripped onto the table.

Joe handed her a paper towel.

As she wiped the spot, she didn't look at him. "He was furious at me for collaborating with you to bring him down."

"If I had him here now, I'd assure him you weren't a collaborator. You were the distraction." Joe rattled around in her cabinets, collecting pots and pans and microwave containers. "What we planned was total elimination of his operation. We lost Torval early. One moment he was shouting in the ballroom. The next he vanished."

"We all had our escape plan, didn't we?" she asked in bitter irony.

"Since Mitzi escaped, too, and we don't know how, I'm forced to agree." He began to heat up food on the stove, in the microwave. "Torval's helicopter landed *here*. Delivered him *here*. What kept him from going mad and killing you?"

"Maybe if Mitzi hadn't attacked him, he would have."

"Could have, would have." Joe mocked her gently.

"I know. So many could-haves and would-haves and if-onlys..." Rowan's mouth dried with remembered fear and angst.

Joe put a glass of ice water and a bowl of salted edamame in front of her.

She sipped, cracked open the pods, ate, and pushed back the memories until she could speak again. "When I was dangling four stories above the floor, with Mitzi attached to my leg and screaming she was going to take me to hell with her—"

Joe blanched. "Dear God."

"—in the midst of that terror, pain and sweat, I heard my father's voice. Lorenze Winterbourne. My heart father. My life father. But there was only Gregory Torval, there on the stairs below, covered with blood. He jumped, grabbed her, and they went down together."

"He died for you."

"Yes. He could have gone away and left Mitzi and me to perish. Before...on the island... BeBée said he understood what was owed to family. I didn't believe her. I didn't believe he had a single decent impulse, but he had…one."

"At least one. Thank God for that. Thank God." Joe took her hand, bent over it and put it to his lips. And stayed there for a long, long moment, until the microwave dinged. He headed for it. The pan on the stove overflowed. He jumped for that.

Rowan probably ought to help him, but…nah. Watching was too entertaining. Perhaps she *did* cherish a bit of a grudge for all he'd put her through.

When he got his food-heating-up back under control, he said, "After the screaming and dangling and bleeding, you crawled up into your apartment."

"Not exactly. I was so depleted. I had no more reserves left. I realized I'd have to die after all, fall on top of Torval and Mitzi like some sacrifice to evil. Then someone, a man, grabbed my shoulders and pulled me to safety." She stared at him.

He stared at her.

She came to her feet with a shout. "It *was* you! I thought I'd hallucinated it. You were there. You did it!" She hurried toward him, hugged him.

He hugged her back. "I did it." He sounded as if even the memory left him breathless.

"How did you get here at that moment?" She pulled away.

His arms tightened.

"You'd better get that pan off before rice burns," she advised.

He released her reluctantly, pulled the skillet off and onto a hot pad on the counter, then prepped another pan for string beans with garlic. "We were sure Torval and Mitzi were somewhere on the island. A bunker, a cave… We got cocky. How could they get off without us knowing? The next thing I hear is our guard on Torval's helicopter is unconscious and Torval's at the controls headed for Offbeat Bay. I knew… I mean, I didn't know. But I suspected so strongly that I dropped everything and came here as quickly as I could."

"You knew where I was?"

He handed her a crispy imperial roll on a napkin. "Once you surfaced in the hospital as Helen Lamb, we kept you in our sights."

"Humph." She bit into the roll; it was so good she closed her eyes to better savor it.

"For your own safety." From the plain bag, he removed a bottle of Pommery's Springtime Champagne Brut Rosé and two elegant cut-glass champagne flutes.

"Humph."

"I didn't get here in time to do anything but drag you to safety." He pulled the cork. It popped. "Thank God for that, but I would have helped you earlier."

"Would have, could have," she gibed at him. "Afterward, why didn't you stick around?"

"The cleanup on Raptor Island was ongoing. I was needed. And the Torvals' escape all too clearly illustrated we hadn't won a complete triumph yet. Forces we didn't understand were still at work."

"Okay." She already knew Joe was driven by duty. He wouldn't be Joe if he wasn't.

"That kid, Elijah, he'd already called law enforcement and an ambulance. He's got a cool head, and he's brave under fire." Joe filled the flutes with sparkling pink and handed one to her. "Doug Moore is dead."

"So I heard." She sipped.

"Rumor is you did it."

"I hurt him enough for someone else to finish the job."

Joe smiled proudly. "That was only thing that kept me sane when your balloon disappeared off the coast. You're so good at handling all the challenges, triumphing over every circumstance. You don't need me." He toasted her. "Damn it. So before I came, I talked to my father."

She blinked. That seemed apropos of nothing. "About?"

"About how to woo you."

"Woo me." She grinned at that quaint phrase, and sipped again. "Not that I know much about champagne, but I like this. What did your father say?"

"He said—" Joe put his glass down on the counter and walked toward her "—grovel." He took her glass, put it on the counter, knelt at her feet, wrapped his arms around her waist, and pressed his forehead to her belly. "I'm sorry I involved you in the operation. I'm an analyst, into math and patterns, and all the patterns projected no more than fifty-fifty success in the operation to bring Torval down. We needed a wild card."

"So far, I'm not impressed with your groveling."

"I decided we had to use you."

"And use me you did." She wished she had her champagne back. A little alcohol would take the edge off a conversation that had more than a fifty-fifty chance to bite deep into her fears and conflicted feelings.

"Not...like that! You do know I didn't sleep with you because you were convenient?"

"The first time?"

"Never."

She remembered his tantrum in Torval's corridor, the words he used to express lust, desire, sex, eternity. "Yes. I do." She taunted him, "We're going to be a hundred years old and still going at it like rabbits... You romantic devil."

"I did apologize."

"You meant what you said, but you apologized for saying it."

He looked up. "I'm glad you understand." He looked back down again, probably so she couldn't read his expression, which was not at all grovely. "After you were out of the hospital, you got the dogs, and I thought—she knows she's safe now."

"Yes. I never would put an animal's life at risk if I thought they would die for me."

"And I wanted to give you a gift."

"I got the money from Frances."

"Not a reward. You earned that. A gift. So I contacted the Tremblays, and you know what happened."

"Right. That. Irena. Meeting her. No. I…no, I hadn't made a move in that direction." She stumbled across her words, trying to explain how she had felt. "I haven't had good luck with family, and I was…"

"Afraid."

She shoved at his shoulders.

He wouldn't let go.

She sighed and let him keep clutching. "Yes, I was afraid. Of being rejected or ignored or not being… I don't have any experience being a sister!" She smiled a crooked smile. "But it didn't matter. Irena didn't either, and we're figuring it out."

"I'm an interfering asshole, aren't I?"

"Yes." But she smoothed his hair.

He stood, opened the plain brown bag, pulled out a box and put it in her hands. "Replacements for the running shoes you ruined on Raptor Island."

She opened the box and looked. These shoes were the newest model, approximately the same color, and of course the right size. "Thank you. I appreciate your thoughtfulness." She honestly did; she hadn't given the shoes another thought, and he'd made sure he memorized her shoe size.

"Thank *you*. We couldn't have done it without you. My new boss at MFAA wants to hire you. I said no."

She felt the prickles of resentment start. "Why did you tell him that, Joseph Grantham Hamilton?"

"Her. I told her because I can't stand to know you're in danger."

She put the shoes to the side. "*You* can't stand?"

He hit the floor on his knees *again*, pressed his forehead to her belly *again*. "Will you forgive me?"

"Yes. Stop breathing on my pubes. Whatever you're trying to do, it's not going to work."

He didn't look up, but she could feel him smile. "I'm trying to soften you up so I can ask you a question."

"I'm soft."

"Ummm." He kissed her belly.

Don't even try to tell me that's not foreplay. Whatever would he do next?

Not what she expected. He started shifting from knee to knee, as if he was kneeling on a bed of nails. "I, um, want to ask you if you, um, would like to… You did really mean you've forgiven me? Yes. I mean, you say what you mean. Okay. Okay. I can do this." He took a breath and blurted, "Iloveyou pleasewillyou marryme?"

55

THAT WAS SO not like Joe, not like the man who'd arrived here in a storm and seduced Rowan with his warmth, not like the far-thinking saboteur on Raptor Island, not like the clear-eyed analyst who weighed and calculated every move of the operation. This was more like… Oh.

This was more like Joe the man driven mad with passion… for her.

She turned her head side to side to read the names scribbled on the containers: seaweed and bean curd salad, short ribs in black pepper sauce, pork and shrimp dumplings, BBQ pork buns, spicy chicken wontons, lemongrass beef with noodles, stir-fried vegetables, Beijing roasted duck, stir-fried beef and asparagus, pot stickers, Chongqing spicy noodles, pork fried rice, white rice, brown rice—

Ahhh. Now she understood. Gifts, indeed. A presentation of himself to the woman he loved in a way she could understand with all her senses and all her mind.

See, smell, taste the food. I can feed you.

Wear the shoes. I can clothe you.

Remember your sister. I can give you family.

Look at how I recall what you wear, what you like. I'm thoughtful and I worship you.

Feel me against you. I can pleasure you.

She smoothed his hair again and decided to let the future take care of itself. Right now, right here, this was the most important moment in the world. "I love you, too."

"Really?" He drew back and gaze at her in wide-eyed astonishment. "You do? After all the crap I put you through... I mean, it was necessary, but—"

"You did it for your sister. I did it for Lorenze." She put her finger on his lips. "Now quit while you're ahead." She knelt in front of him, so they were face-to-face, rib-to-rib, heart-to-heart. "I would very much like to marry you and—"

He didn't wait for her to finish. He grabbed her and kissed her, worshipped her, tasted her and encouraged her do the same in return. When they drew apart, they smiled into each others' eyes.

"Do you feel as if you're being watched?" he asked.

Swag leaned against Joe. Lassie leaned on her. They watched Rowan and Joe as if confused.

"I suppose we probably better get used to being stared at," Joe said.

"Probably. They sleep on the bed."

"Oh no. It's a king, right?"

"Queen, and there's not room for a king."

He sighed, but not with any real unhappiness. "I have one last gift."

"The most important gift?" She expected a ring.

"You tell me." He slid a small box out of his jacket pocket and, in a small ceremony that made her wonder, opened it for her inspection.

Wrapped in bubble wrap, there it was—the dragon-knight,

a fierce, toothy green dragon wearing a warrior's helmet and breathing the smallest flick of fire.

Joe lifted it from its protection and placed it in her cupped palms.

"How did you know? How did you guess?"

"I tapped into Torval's video. You were in his library, and you looked at this thing—"

"This very thing?"

"Yes, this is it. And I thought…this means something to her. Something out of place. Something beyond the horror and the torment of that moment. A link to the past that you recognized." He must have really studied her expression to be able to express himself so well. "I rescued it. I hope I didn't screw up at the last minute, because it's either a big wrong or a big right, and I hate to gamble on something so ephemeral and lose. Not now. The stakes are too high."

She sniffed. "The green beans are definitely burning."

Joe leaped to his feet and hustled to the stove. "Shit! Shit! Shit! This isn't the way I'd planned it."

She sat on the floor and laughed. "How much do you think we can eat, anyway?"

He slid pots off burners and put pans on burners. He removed containers from the microwave and added more inside. He plated several dishes and put them on the table. "Lately I haven't had an appetite, and you're looking a little thin."

"I've lost a few pounds." She tried to stand up, but her bad leg was asleep. Putting it in front of her, she worked it, trying to ease the stiffness.

"We'll eat a lot, I hope." He hustled over and picked her up and planted her on her seat. "Planning a wedding takes a lot of calories."

"So does practicing the wedding night." She placed the dragon-knight in the middle of the table, a crown upon the meal and their union, and loaded her plate with all the greed of a kid at a church potluck.

He reminded her, "We're going to be a hundred years old and still going at it like rabbits."

"We probably will." She took his hand. "Can I have a fork? I'm not very good with chopsticks, and I'm really hungry."

He pulled the large serving spoon out of the fried rice and handed it to her. "Eat up. We've got another dozen dishes to go, then rabbits, and then—" he opened his briefcase "—I've got a flowchart for wedding planning."

Flowchart. She mouthed the word. "Let me make one thing clear. After that, it'll be rabbits again."

"Rabbits forever," he promised.

She dug the spoon into her sweet-and-sour soup. "I'd better keep up my strength."

★ ★ ★ ★ ★

acknowledgments

Thank you to my editor, Michele Bidelspach, Executive Editor, Canary Street Press and Graydon House, and Susan Swinwood, Canary Street Press Editorial Director. Thanks to Craig Swinwood, CEO of Harlequin and HarperCollins Canada, and Loriana Sacilotto, Executive Vice President and HTP Publisher: it's a pleasure to be publishing with this talented, dedicated team.

A special thank-you to Jayne Ann Krentz, who, when I asked, gave me her quite decided opinion of Rowan's background and a few other key points that brought the story together.

EVERY SINGLE SECRET READER GUIDE

DEAR READER LETTER

DISCUSSION QUESTIONS

dear reader letter

Dear Lover of Suspense and Romance,

The idea for *Every Single Secret* occurred as I wondered, "What happens when a young woman living an average American teen life has her life shattered by violence? How does she go on? What is the effect on her as she grows into an adult?"

How would you react? How would I? Each of us can in our imagination walk in that young woman's shoes, and make the leap into a fictional life of never making friends, never confiding, never trusting even those people she knows are reliable. For despite his vow to allow Rowan to live, she knows the ruthless crime lord her father offended could never be trusted, and if her companionship led to the pain and death of a friend, how could she forgive herself? Humans are social animals, and for Rowan, surrounded by her beloved clients, yet eternally alone, the temptation to confide must have been almost unbearable. And she does confide in Mr. Bandara, a man she completely trusts…and who is dying. A man for whom, at his request, she hires an assassin.

In the first chapter, her dilemma and her sorrow broke my heart, and influenced the decision she made to trust the wrong man.

One bad decision. She always knew it would take only one bad decision, and her life would be in peril once more. On Raptor Island, she faces enemies on every front, makes an important friend, discovers all the secrets she would rather not know, and when at last her existence comes down to a single judgment, she makes the bravest decision of her life and trusts the very man who blackmailed her.

Every Single Secret is a special tale about a broken life broken in two and made anew through Rowan's intelligent courage in the face of terrible challenges. I hope you enjoyed it, and I encourage you to spend time with the Reader Guide Discussion Questions for a deeper understanding of your own life experiences and how this story changed your perspective of yourself. At the least, it's a reminder that we never know everything that goes on in a person's mind, and to be kind.

Until next time,
Christina Dodd
New York Times Bestselling Author

ChristinaDodd.com

discussion questions

1. When Rowan was fourteen, she was ripped from her normal American teen life by violent events that deprived her of her mother and sister and made it necessary for her and her stepfather to go on the run. In your teen years, did you suffer a loss or trauma that changed you? A move, the loss of a grandparent, your parents' divorce? Do the echoes of those events affect you today?

2. If you hired someone from The Fixer company, what would you have them fix for you?

3. Mr. Bandara has discovered he faces a painful and lonely death. What do you think of his decision to end his life? This is, as far as we know, the only person Rowan feels close to; what do you think of her decision to assist him? If you had the ability to help in these circumstances, would you?

4. Mr. Bandara was obviously a kind, observant teacher who worked to help his pupils when he could. Although Rowan

is not his student, he comments on what he sees in her, and that understanding gives her the courage to tell him her real name. Have you ever had a teacher notice you or your child going through a hard time? How did they try to help?

5. Humans are social creatures, yet after Rowan loses her stepfather, she is always alone, forced into that decision by the knowledge that any relationship leaves her vulnerable as well as the person with whom she would share a closeness. What do you see in her personality that's the result of such an unnatural existence? The first time you lived alone was probably when you moved out of your parents' house. How did you handle that?

6. Rowan lives in a lighthouse. That seems very dramatic and romantic, and she does it for security reasons. At the same time, that increases her isolation. Could you live in a lighthouse? Would you like to? Why or why not?

7. Rowan's experience with Lorenze as her stepfather was positive. Clearly he loves her enough to teach her the skills she needs to survive and, in the end, to sacrifice himself to ensure she has a future. Do you have a stepparent? What was your experience with them?

8. Although for good reason, Rowan is essentially internet-stalking her sister. Have you ever stalked someone? Have you been stalked?

9. Lorenze Winterbourne has become an urban legend, someone no one ever really sees but who is talked about as a kind of superhero who helps the downtrodden and saves those threatened by criminals. How do you think legends like that spring up? Who are the real heroes of the streets today?

10. Rowan makes a terrible mistake when she misidentifies Joe Grantham and sleeps with him. Why did she make such an error of judgment? Does she deserve the consequences?

11. Have you ever clicked with someone the way Rowan and BeBée do? Did it become a long-term friendship?

12. While on Raptor Island, Rowan discovers a relationship that is abhorrent to her. Were you surprised by this revelation? Many people are having DNA testing done. Have you? Do you know anyone who was surprised by DNA results that introduced them to an unexpected relative? Were the results positive or negative?

13. Based on the trials, the deceptions, the intrigues Rowan faces at Gregory Torval's home, do you believe you would be a good spy? Why or why not?

14. At the end of the story, it appears that Rowan is now able to escape her enforced isolation and live a life assimilated into both her sister's family and Joe's. How do you think she will react to the reality of family relationships? How will she deal with the holidays? Will she occasionally long for a return to her isolation? If she has children, how will her experiences influence her as a mother? In other words, what do you see for Rowan beyond the story as told within *Every Single Secret*?